Praise for Melanie Murray's debut novel

Miss Bubbles Steals the Show

"Melanie Murray's story of a cat who hijacks her owner's dreams of stardom had me eyeing my own dramatic pet suspiciously. Miss Bubbles steals more than the show—she steals your heart."
—Megan Crane, author of *Everyone Else's Girl*

"By the end of this entertaining novel, readers see a shallow, hapless Stella grow up into a more serious—but still spunky—young woman."
—*Publishers Weekly*

"*Miss Bubbles Steals the Show* is toasty warm without being sappy, self-deprecatingly hilarious and insanely human in that reassuring way that makes a gal feel comforted, even in the wee hours of a boyless night."
—Elise Abrams, author of *Star Craving Mad*

"With a loveable heroine at the center, Murray's debut is a delightful romp through New York's theater world."
—*Booklist*

Melanie Murray
Good Times, Bad Boys

**RED
DRESS
I N K**
™

GOOD TIMES, BAD BOYS

A Red Dress Ink novel

ISBN-13: 978-0-373-89594-6
ISBN-10:   0-373-89594-1

© 2006 by Melanie Murray.

www.RedDressInk.com

Printed in U.S.A.

ACKNOWLEDGMENTS

Without the following people's time, energy, hand-holding, editorial advice, and good will, there'd be very little to read between this book's covers.

I must thank Lindsay Genshaft, Dan Maceyak, Meg Pryor, and Leila Nelson for being the best friends I could ever wish for; Elise Miller, Savannah Conheady, and Mari Brown for thoughtful first and second and third and twelfth reads; Beth de Guzman, Michele Bidelspach, Kristen Weber, and Devi Pillai for calmly listening to me; Beth & Richard Shepardson and Bill Murray for promoting me from exit 3 on the Mass Pike to exit 7 and beyond; Selina McLemore and Farrin Jacobs for their insightful editorial comments, their willingness to adjust deadlines, and their tremendous poise in the face of my some-time mania; to Tara Mark for her unwavering and wholly appreciated support, and also to Bridget, Colin, Cindy, Bill, MaryJo, Jacob, Emily, and Irene, and the Downing family, Eileen, RuthAnn, and Dennis.

And also, I must say thank you to Chris, for everything.

Good Times, Bad Boys

1

I am on a mission. When I step through the doorway of the Edge Bar, and see the Friday night crowd in full party mode—not unexpected for a New York night out—I'm glad I've brought moral support.

My curly-headed, heartbreaking sister, Thalia, steps up to my left, and my pigtailed waif of a best friend, Alicia, flanks my right. I, unfortunately, am the bland, brown-haired, big-hipped meat in a siren sandwich. But this is still my gig, and for the immediate future, anyway, I'm the boss.

"If I'm not back in fifteen minutes," I coach, tugging my shirt down to cover the strip of skin that pouches out from the top of these pants, "come in and find me."

Thalia rolls her eyes, Alicia nods affirmatively, and I compulsively check the time on my watch before we break. Alicia heads to the bar, and Thalia sashays her way over to the jukebox, oozing femininity and drawing at least one open-mouthed stare as she goes.

Me, I walk determinedly to the back of the bar, passing tourists (identifiable by their pastel-colored sweaters, baseball caps and cameras) and twentysomething concert-goers (betrayed by their Butter Flies T-shirts, their arms slung around each other's shoulders and their loud, off-tune sing-alongs). I push through crowds making toasts to an assortment of accomplishments: to beer, to rock and roll, to Jack Mantis, all the while searching for the entrance to the VIP room, where, if my informant is worth her weight in gold, the crowd's idol should be sitting in front of three shots of Johnny Walker Red, compulsively releasing and rebinding his white-blond hair into a ponytail.

I check my watch again before elbowing past three skater-looking dudes, then pull up the waistband on Thalia's leather pants and adjust the straps of her pink tank top. My borrowed outfit isn't the warmest, especially for a colder-than-usual early September night, and it's certainly not as comfortable as my standard uniform of cargo pants and earth-toned T-shirts. But when one is about to cavort with the hottest rock-and-roll god in the United States, one must look the part, and so I've resorted to raiding my sister's closet.

One of the best-kept secrets in New York is the Edge Bar's hidden room, a secret VIP bar where performers about to play Madison Square Garden can engage in a little pre-concert warm-up. My boyfriend, Matt, also a musician, once asked me to meet him there, but I couldn't for some reason or other. Now I realize I should have asked him for directions, because, as you might expect, a top-secret room isn't exactly easy to spot. I get turned around a couple of times, finding myself back at the jukebox and Thalia's quiz-zical glances twice before finally catching sight of a thick red curtain along the back wall, hidden behind a waitress's station. A big, fat, bald-headed Mr. Clean–looking guy, who slumps on a stool and none-too-casually stares at a blond waitress's assets, is the last tip-off I need. I look at my watch again—I've lost some time here, but I'm good.

"Hi," I say to the bald guard, pulling him from his voyeuristic pastime.

Mr. Clean adjusts his weight and looks me up and down, obviously annoyed that he has to do his job. His silence speaks volumes.

"I'm here for the, uh, room." I point as emphatically as I can at the curtain, to cover for my stumbling speech.

"You on the list?" His eyes have become captivated by my midsection. I swallow the instinct to once again pull down my tank (my father's former housekeeper and current fiancée, Helen, says my hips are good for making babies). This is hardly the time to cater to my body issues. Does Christiane Amanpour think about her waistline when she's about to meet Vladimir Putin? Actually, I don't know the answer to that, but I'm going to go with no.

"I'm on the list." I pray that my voice sounds strong and wholly believable.

Mr. Clean pulls a chart out from under his armpit and I search desperately for a name that hasn't been checked off. Not being the best upside-down reader, my nerves vibrate like a bass guitar. But then, I see my shot—and oh, how delicious it is, too! I plunk my finger onto the name. "There I am."

"Alex Paxton?"

"That's me!" There's a double meaning in the smile that appears on my face. Of course, I want to be charming. But also, when Alex gets here and sees his name crossed off, he's going to be so pissed, and that will be one huge cherry on top of a *very* delicious sundae.

Mr. Clean peels himself off the stool, and pulls the red curtain away from the door. Before I slink inside, I turn back to the main bar, and give an exuberant okay sign to Alicia, who raises a drink and a fist of solidarity in response. Mr. Clean notes my geeky enthusiasm and scowls. Thalia, already surrounded by a gaggle of men and holding court— she's in the middle of her "naked flute player" story; I can tell from her hand motions—doesn't pay me any mind.

The VIP curtain flutters behind me. I find myself in a small, square, black-lit room that's awash in spinning patches of light, courtesy of the dozens of crystal light-catchers and pumpkin-size disco balls hanging from the ceiling. I've read about this room in *Rolling Stone* and *Disc;* heard music insiders speak about it reverently, their voices lowered in awed whispers; dreamt of a time when I'd be a regular visitor to its sacred space. But this is the first I've been here, and I have to say that I'm more than a little proud that I made it in on my own, and not as "the girlfriend."

I scan the layout of the room quickly, keeping an eye open for the reason I'm here. There are three black couches arranged in a triangle just in front of me, populated with several skin-and-bone models sporting severe haircuts and razor-sharp cheekbones, and regular guys in jeans and T-shirts. The guys I recognize. They're all members of the Butter Flies, the hottest band in the western hemisphere, and tonight's main event at Madison Square Garden, just across the street. Their leader is not among them, so I keep looking.

I finally spot him, his back to me, sitting at the bar that stretches along the back wall. I run my fingers through my hair and think that this is just how real reporters get their stories. They maximize their connections. I'm lucky to be so close to Annie Lee, the punk icon herself, and I'm lucky that she's in my corner. She knows Alex Paxton and I are both trying to get to Jack (he's been "choosing" the reporter who will do his first major interview as a superstar for months now, and it's a big deal, because *Disc* is holding their prestigious January cover for him), and though she was honor-bound to let us both know Jack's location tonight, she gave me an hour's jump on good ole' A.P. It's up to me not to blow it.

My watch ticks off the minutes, reminding me that there are other places I have to be tonight, too. I take a deep fortifying breath and make my approach. The expanse of Jack's back is covered in black leather. A ponytail hangs down to his collar and his hands reach up to release his hair. He snaps the rubber band around his wrist as I slip onto the stool next to him. I can barely breathe. For a moment, I can't figure out how to start a conversation, but then the bartender catches my eye and I get an idea.

"Can I have some whiskey?" I imitate the sound of my sister's voice here, molding it into the breathy, throaty, coquettish sound Thalia uses on potential dates. Then I look over to my neighbor, smile and point to the collection of empty shot glasses in front of him. "And another round for him?"

Jack Mantis, lead singer and rhythm guitarist of the Butter Flies, looks over at me with eyes so pale it's as if God forgot to color them in. He looks just the same as he always did. But things have changed since I last saw him play at Annie Lee's two years ago. In the time it's taken me to accumulate enough writing experience to even think about approaching a nationally known musician for a story, Jack and the Butter Flies have enjoyed the kind of meteoric rise that musicians hope for.

Of course, meteoric rises in the world of rock and roll aren't all that unheard of. But for every one Beatle you have ten Hooties and thirty Blowfish (or one of my boyfriend, Matt Hanley), and it's my intention to find out whether or not Jack and the Butter Flies have staying power. Jack's charisma is undeniable. He's kind of a tortured, sad angel, with his pale skin (last week *Star* magazine reported that he was the child of an albino,) his aquamarine eyes, that square jaw that saves his face from looking completely girlish, and his too-skinny physique that's just androgynous enough to be devastatingly sexy. Not to mention that hair. Blond and thick and lush.

He is now binding said hair back into a ponytail. I'm guessing that fame and fortune have only upped the ante on his personal quirks, of which he notoriously has many. I should make a mental note of how many times he rebinds his hair tonight.

"Who are you?"

I smile at him. "Echo," I say and turn to watch the bartender pour our drinks.

"That's a musical name," Jack says, reaching green fingers for one of the three shots of whiskey that have been placed in front of him.

"My dad's doing, I'm afraid. He's a Classics professor. He named me for a nymph who made the Queen of the Goddesses angry and was punished by only ever being able to repeat what was said to her."

"That sucks." His voice sounds just like it does on the Butter Flies' recordings. Gravelly and low-pitched, betraying a hint of world weariness that makes you just want to chuck your life and follow him around, like a Deadhead or a Phish-head.

"Eh, it could be worse. I could be named Medusa."

He looks at me funny. Probably because we've had this conversation before, in Boston, when I was a college student and hanger-on at every club within a twenty-mile radius of my campus, and he was a struggling musician. But Jack's a rock star now. He certainly shouldn't be expected to remember every time a young music fan talked to him after a show.

"Medusa," I repeat. Jack doesn't take his blue-white eyes off me while he sips from one of the shot glasses of whiskey. "She had snakes for hair."

"You're right. That would be worse." He nods and we clink glasses before drinking to my funny name. I check my watch.

"So, it's time to come clean." I turn so that my whole body faces his.

Jack pulls his hair out of his ponytail holder, snaps the band onto his wrist, and then proceeds to run the fingers of his left hand up and down the underside of his right arm. This motion is hypnotic, and I lose my train of thought for a moment before recovering.

"I know *Disc* magazine's talking about doing their big New Year's cover story on you and the Flies."

His eyes go wide, and for a minute I think he might get up and leave me sitting alone at the bar. But he doesn't. He continues running his fingers up and down the milky white underbelly of his arm, and tilts his chin toward the ceiling, which I take as a sign to keep talking.

"I want to write it."

His responding silence crashes over my head like an ocean wave. Maybe it wasn't such a good idea to track him here, and just lay my cards on the table like this. Maybe I should've gone with Thalia's plan: sneak into Jack's downtown apartment, corner him in his bedroom, and throw myself at him, until he was so overcome by my feminine wiles that he gave me what I wanted.

But I'm not so comfortable with Thalia's way, nor could I guarantee that her way would work for me—remember? Bland? Big-hipped? Besides, I do have *some* moral fiber, and if I ever want to work for *Rolling Stone* or *Disc* magazine, I can't possibly expect to get all my stories by seduction.

"And why should I talk to you?" Jack finally asks, a dark look clouding his crystalline eyes.

"Because—" I reach into the bag that hangs on my shoulder "—nobody knows you the way I do."

And I pull out my ace in the hole. Articles on the Butter Flies that go back years, to when they were just a beer band. Reviews of their CDs, even the ones they burned and sold themselves, back when they played small clubs and rooms that only sat thirty or so people. I pull out about a dozen issues of the *Brooklyn Art & Times,* my current employer, and spread them out in front of us.

"I've been following you guys since you started in Boston and then when you started playing all those New York clubs, I just—I paid attention, I guess. I understand the following you have in the Northeast, and actually, you and I met a couple of times—I think you know my boyfriend, Matt Hanley?"

Jack's eyebrows do this funny wriggle. "Matt Hanley?" He starts laughing into his shot glass, and my ire starts to rise. "We played in Germany together. How's his new album coming?"

"Uh, it's coming. They're just finishing it up now," I answer, feeling my jaw clench.

He purses his lips and shakes his head before again smirking into his whiskey glass. He obviously knows how much I'm stretching the truth on that count. Nobody who knows anything about Matt would believe that his album is anywhere close to being finished.

I try to steer the conversation back to the matter at hand. "Anyway, just look at this one. You gave me one of my favorite quotes, let me find it." I dig for the right issue, open to the page, flatten out the story in front of him and run my finger down to the quote, to prove I'm telling the truth. "'The Flies *are* music. And music is life.'"

Jack doesn't move, except for the incessant running of his hand up and down his other arm. It's kind of bugging me out, actually—I wouldn't be surprised if he's programming me to cluck like a chicken or bust out into the Robot at the sound of a whistle. I shake off my paranoia and look at the bartender who stands down at the far end of the bar, surveying his little kingdom of a room. I check my watch again. The room shrinks a bit, the air is still and the music that's playing—instrumental Latin something or other—seems to speed up and get louder.

Jack finally turns his attention to the article in front of him, then lifts his arm and snaps his fingers. Before I know it, Stan Fields, the Butter Flies' manager and the number one reason I've had to track Jack down through underhanded means, is standing next to him, one arm around Jack's shoulders, one arm leaning in front of me, effectively cutting me off from my own paper supply.

"This here is Echo. She wants to write about us for *Disc*. She's Matt Hanley's girlfriend."

Stan Fields turns and gives me a look, a "Give me one reason not to punch you in the face" kind of look. I take no offense. Stan's told me a couple dozen times, through phone messages and e-mail, that Jack's not interested in talking to me. I will say this for Stan Fields: he's an equal-opportunity bastard. Alex Paxton has gotten the cold shoulder, too, hence the need for me and A.P. to resort to this kind of espionage.

I give Stan a no-teeth smile in response to his murderous glance. He's a far cry from the typical band manager. Usually managers are happy to give you a chance to get a quote or comment from their bands, especially if they're trying to make it. But Stan takes pleasure in his self-appointed role as Flies bodyguard. Right now, he's grimacing, and this does nothing for his already troublesome looks. He's about six-and-a-half-feet tall, bedecked in at least five pieces of leather-and-spike jewelry, looks like he just jumped off a treadmill (*just* a bit of a sweat problem shining through), and I'd say there's about twenty piercings in his face and ears. In addition to these classic good looks, Stan has kind of a re-putation around town as being something of an asshole. Bar fights and broken noses are involved in several popular Stan Fields stories. Where Jack is the luminescent angel of the Flies, Stan is the resident bad-ass biker. I swallow hard and wish that Thalia were here to distract him.

My only hope is to get Stan drunk. Because he knows as well as I do that I'm nobody, and that I need Jack.

If I can get Jack to let me write the Butter Flies' story, a story that every magazine across the country has been clam-oring for, then that's it: I'll officially be able to cast off the shackles of my dinky paper. And writing the *Disc* New Year's cover story? Forget it. I'd be able to write for any publication I wanted. *Disc* might even hire me on full-time, and wouldn't that be nice? To have a paycheck that might actually cover my rent? To be able to rely on my own health coverage. I momentarily imagine the look on my father's face when and if I'm able to tell him that he can take his twenty-seven-year-old daughter off his medical insurance.

Also? I don't mean to sound like a big old cliché, but there is a *time* factor involved. I'm not getting any younger; that's a fact. And do you know what famous women have accomplished by my age? No? Well I'll tell you. At twenty-seven Madonna had already released *Like a Virgin*. Janis Joplin was a world-famous rock star—not to mention dead. And don't get me started on Alicia Keys.

Basically, it's time for me to grow up. I'm twenty-seven, and what do I have to show for it? Nothing.

Well, that's not completely true. As the newspapered bar can attest, I've accumulated plenty of clips. But the *Brooklyn Art & Times* isn't exactly a household name. It took me a whole year of working there before record companies finally started sending me review copies of CDs. And I've had to run all over the borough of Brooklyn trying to find bands to cover. Not that I haven't enjoyed having an excuse to hang out in clubs listening to music—it's hands down my favorite pastime. Even so, it's the *Brooklyn Art & Times*. *Brooklyn*. I should be taken to task for the number of Manhattan acts that make it into the *BAT*'s pages. But Walter Gund, my cuddly, apron-wearing boss, doesn't pay too much attention to things like rules or hours or deadlines. And I can't help but think that his lack of "bossiness" is the reason why our paper is so small and disrespected.

Not to say that there aren't good things about working at the *BAT*. It's close to my father's house, and Walter doesn't care if Alicia hangs out there all the time or what time I come in or if I listen to my headphones all day. But it's time I made my move. I can't live this kind of carefree, make-your-own-rules kind of lifestyle forever. And I really need to be making enough money to take care of me and Matt while he gets back on his feet. So sometimes, like my father says, you have to take a mighty leap. Jack Mantis is my mighty leap. And as he and Stan read through my old articles I start to see my leap flopping before I even have a chance to take off.

"Guys. Listen. I *know* you. I saw you at Club Trax in Boston in front of just me and my friend Alicia. At Annie's about a dozen times. I gave your demo CD to Alex Paxton at *Disc* before anyone else had even heard of you guys!" They both look at me—maybe I shouldn't have mentioned that part?

Jack suddenly stands up and walks over to a guy standing by the door, a guy wearing a long black trench coat, like an extra out of *The Matrix*. Stan gathers my papers into a pile and roughly hands them to me. I take them silently, stuff them into my bag. When I look up, pale-faced Jack stands before me, left hand draped across his body and clutching his right forearm, which is extended to me, holding a laminated pass. "Here. Come with us."

Despite my desire to remain rock-and-roll calm, I can't help grinning like a starstruck groupie. "Really? You mean it?" I am such a dork.

Apparently, Jack is moved by my lack of cool. In all the times I've ever seen him perform, he's never once smiled. And if I wasn't here to witness it now, I'd still think he was physically incapable of expressing happiness. Granted, it's a small, slight curve of one side of his upper lip, but the contrast to his usual stark expression is striking. He likes me! "Yeah, come on to the show," he commands softly. "We'll discuss the details after."

And then reality sets in. I stare at the pass then check my watch. Matt's set at Annie's Punk, on the Lower East Side, starts in forty-five minutes. And I promised I'd be there.

"Um—"

"Jack. Let's go. You're late." Stan growls out to him from the doorway, and Jack looks at me expectantly.

"Actually, you know what?" I avoid his gaze and inadvertently wink at him as I'm trying to figure out what to say. "I totally forgot something—somewhere I've got to be. But I can meet you after the show. I'll just, I'll just, um…I'll give you my phone number, so you can tell me where to meet you." I pull a piece of paper from my bag and scribble down my phone number while Stan looks at me smugly, clearly enjoying the fact that I'm about to blow it.

When I attempt to thrust the piece of paper in his hand, Jack has this unreadable look on his face. "Um, so, I'll just take that pass, and meet you after." I reach for the pass and push the piece of paper with my number on it into Jack's empty hand. He takes the number, but extends the hand holding the pass straight above his head. He exhales rather loudly, and looks at Stan.

"Stan?" he asks, clearly unaware of how to respond to somebody not doing exactly what he wants. "What's happening here?"

Okay, this is very bad. Jack Mantis is known for being prickly and very easy to piss off, even before he was famous. Annie once told me that he refused to go onstage at a Joey Ramone tribute concert because the organizer jokingly referred to him as Jackie. And here I am earning his trust enough to get a personal invite to his show, and I am turning him down.

I do a very quick mental pro-and-con list of going with Jack right now. Pro? Pipeline to the entertainment interview of the year. Con? The disappointed look in Matt's eyes when he realizes I didn't make it to his show, and in fact, chose Jack Mantis's concert over his.

That's a dead heat.

But this is ridiculous. I have not come this far to lose my chance at this interview. Why can't I do both? Go to Matt's show *and* keep in Jack's good graces?

"Guys." I take a deep breath and dig deep into the recesses of my soul for a little Thalia-style finesse. "I couldn't be happier about this, really." Oh God. I sound like a prepubescent car salesman. "But why would I expect that a band as important as you would talk to me tonight?"

Jack relaxes a little at the blatant kiss-assiness of my remarks, and this gives me confidence. "I just don't want to blow this, so would it be all right with you if we meet *after* the show? That way I'll have all my materials ready, and we can hammer out the deal of a really great interview. Which is what you deserve, of course."

Neither of them responds right away. Stan shifts his weight and tightens his jaw, but Jack's posture changes. His eyes betray his decision. "Okay, Echo." He hands me the pass, which feels hot when it lands in my hand. "Meet us after the show. We'll talk about it then." He stalks off, around the corner of the bar, and heads out another draped side door, followed by the guy in the trench coat and the rest of the band. The bartender salutes me as I go.

Holy God! It was touch and go for a moment, but it worked! Goodbye, *BAT* and hello, *Disc!* It's all I can do to keep my feet on the ground as I nearly float through the VIP room to the main bar.

My joy is momentarily killed when I step through the curtain. The Mr. Clean guard grabs my arm and barks, "Hey. Alex Paxton?"

I try to yank my arm away, worried for a minute that the bald man's gone cuckoo. But then I remember how I got into the VIP room in the first place.

"What? Oh, yeah. Right. Alex Paxton. That's me. What's up?"

"*That* Alex Paxton wants a word with you." Mr. Clean makes a motion toward the bar, where my number-one enemy, my nemesis, my bizarro self faces me, glowering.

Poor guy. Alex always looks like he's one slice of pizza away from popping all the buttons on his shirt. And his skin. It looks like those grainy pictures of the terrain on Mars. And his eyes are beady little black numbers and he frowns permanently. So, to summarize, not a nice-looking guy. And right now, if we were in cartoonland, steam would be pouring out his ears.

"You are so dead," Alex says when I step right up to him, waving my backstage pass in front of his face.

"You charmer. I beat you fair and square. Want me to buy you a drink?"

"Echo. That is *my* story! What did you do?"

"Gee, Alex, would you look at the time! I'll have to take a rain check on that drink!" I smile at him and spin away, looking for Thalia and Alicia as I go.

"I can't believe you're doing this," my sister, Thalia, says while the three of us sit sardine-style in the back of a cab.

"Don't start, don't start," I mutter while craning my neck

to monitor the driver's progress. We've been idling in traffic for what feels like forever—both "Stairway to Heaven" and "Layla" have come and gone on the classic-rock station and we've barely made it down Third Avenue. I peer at the clock on the driver's panel. The Butter Flies go on at nine thirty-five, and they play for about an hour and forty minutes, plus one ten-minute intermission. That leaves me under two hours to get down to Annie's Punk, listen to Matt's set, and hightail it back up to midtown in time to charm Jack into giving me his interview.

Thalia shakes her head in disapproval and then turns toward the window, making a loud "Pfft" sound. Alicia, who's sitting on my other side, reaches down and squeezes my hand. We give each other a conspiratorial "big sisters are so mean" smile.

Thalia must have radar for this sort of bonding moment, because she whips her head around, and pins me with one of her clear-eyed, pull-no-punches stares. "You may not want to hear this," she spits in that know-it-all tone I've come to know and love, "but you're being a doormat."

"Thalia!" Alicia admonishes.

I, on the other hand, because Thalia and I always play our "big sister, little sister" roles with each other, hit her in the arm and shout like an angry kid, "Shut up!"

Thalia screeches, "OW!" in that dramatic way of hers, puts her other hand to the spot I whacked and cradles it like it's a small child. She looks at me with a wounded, annoyed expression. "What is *wrong* with you?"

"Why don't you just keep your opinions to yourself?" I turn back to my job of gazing out the windshield.

"Oh, come on," Thalia says, still holding on to her arm, as if I had actually hurt her, which I couldn't have, because a)

I'm a weakling, and b) Thalia has *very* thick skin. "We're dropping everything and racing all the way down to Annie's to see Matt perform a bunch of Pearl Jam songs, like every other time he says he's got new material to play. How many times do I have to hear acoustic versions of 'Alive' before you dump this guy?"

Alicia looks to me, waiting for a retort to come out of my mouth, but I've had an entire lifetime to learn that once Thalia starts in, nothing I say is going to shut her up. My only hope is to change the subject.

"How many numbers did you get tonight, anyway?"

Thalia eyes me and returns her stare to the taxicab window.

I'm not merely kissing up to her; I have genuine curiosity on this point. My sister is something of a guy magnet. It's a game of mine to keep track of how many phone numbers and e-mail addresses she can collect in any given amount of time. I believe her record is five numbers in one hour. And all her collected contact info goes into a giant repository, along with the memory of what said person does for a living, to be called upon if she ever needs anything. Of course, she'll only date the ones who have an income larger than the gross national product of a small nation.

This is the delicious incongruity of Thalia's personality. She's never held down a real job. She's never had a lease on an apartment—she joyously travels from sublet to sublet, often inheriting apartments from ex-boyfriends who can't stop thinking about her. Ask her what she does for a living and she'll say, "I breathe." I don't know what this means, but apparently the job description encompasses volunteering at animal shelters, mounting spontaneous street theater productions at parks all over the city, and drawing chalk art on the sidewalks. She's, as they say, a free spirit. Yet, she only is attracted to "Dressers"—her term to describe guys that hold down jobs that require at least two degrees and have some sort of financial association.

"I did fine. But don't change the subject."

Rats.

"Instead of focusing on getting this interview, you're busting your ass to get downtown, for what? So Matt's feelings won't get hurt? That's ridiculous. Does Matt know the roof above his head costs money? If he had half a brain, he'd be *helping* you with this instead of giving you a hard time. He doesn't even know the proper way to freeload." My sister adjusts her batik gypsy top so that you can see her bra straps, and fluffs her fingers through her spongy, honey-colored curls (a bequest from our mother that didn't make it through the gene pool to me).

Alicia chooses this moment to chime in, not realizing that anything she says will only prolong Thalia's rant. "You know, you'd think you'd have a little patience for a fellow artist, Thal."

"Please." Thalia scoffs. "I produce. Creativity pours out of me. Ask Echo how long it's been since Matt wrote a single lyric."

I fold myself over onto my lap and say a silent prayer that when we get to Annie's, Matt will be singing something new. Because Big Sister may not be so good at holding down jobs or relationships or bank accounts, but she's *very* good at analyzing my boyfriend.

"Mark my words, little sister. You're gonna miss the Butter Flies, and you're gonna miss your shot at this interview."

"We're not missing anything," Alicia says flatly before leaning over me and passing the cab driver a twenty-dollar bill. "Let's try to go a little faster, okay?"

Nothing conquers New York City traffic like a little palm-greasing. The cab driver puts the pedal to the metal, and we proceed to whip down Third Avenue, weaving in and out of cars, getting flattened as we zoom at warp speeds to Annie's.

But when we get there, and make our way inside, Matt's nowhere to be found. Annie Lee, owner and operator of Annie's Punk, stands behind the bar, bottle-blond, straight-cut bangs hanging into her eyes, white pirate blouse billowing over her leather-clad legs.

"He never showed, hon. You should have called."

Thalia whispers behind me, "It's time to put this stray dog down."

2

"Sweetheart, what is wrong with that kid?" Annie swats the bar with her dish towel and points a finger toward the back room, which holds one of the most famous concert spaces in all of lower Manhattan. "There are a thousand people back there, ready to riot. Freddy's good, but he's not who they want to see." She refers to her husband Fred, who, thirty years ago, was the original drummer of the Rooftop Six, a punk band that never really made it in the States but was a huge success in Brazil. Nowadays, Freddy and the three surviving members of the Six play at Annie's whenever they feel like it, or as in this case, whenever she needs to be bailed out.

"Can I have a drink?" Alicia's timing is usually better than this. Her question is answered with one of Annie's patented one-eyebrow stares, a look that's been proven to frighten even Thalia into silence.

"Where the hell is Matt, Echo?" Annie demands, her attention back on me.

"I'll—I'll find him. Just give me a minute."

I back away from the bar to avoid any more rancor from Annie, and yank open my bag to get my cell phone. But when I dig around for it, the entire contents of my purse spill out. All my newspaper clips, old lipsticks and jars of lip gloss, a dried mascara tube I've never gotten around to throwing away, three cassette tapes, two homemade CDs and my wallet sail like miniparatroopers only to land in the very unforgiving terrain of Annie's sticky floor.

"Alicia?" I look to her as I grab my phone.

"I got it. Go." She hitches up her cargo pants before crouching down and gathering the fallen pieces of my night. Meanwhile, I make my way toward the front door, hot, frustrated tears springing to my eyes and a hot, frustrating sister on my tail.

"You call Jack Mantis. I'll get you a cab," Thalia commands as I frantically dial my home number, straining to hear the sound of the ring through my sister's orders and the cacophony of a Friday night at Annie's. It's unsurprising that the call goes directly to voice mail. This, unfortunately, doesn't give me any clue as to Matt's whereabouts. He never answers the phone. For all I know, he could be camped out on our sofa this instant, listening to my frantic message over and over again, and hoping against hope that I don't track him down.

I don't even try his cell phone. I don't think he's ever turned it on.

The busy street in front of Annie's welcomes me with nary a glance. All kinds of hipster punks stroll around, ears plugged with iPod headphones, hands full of pizza slices and cigarettes. I am momentarily pleased to be living in a city where the sight of a crying lady barely makes a wave. I turn away from the crowds for a second and stare at a portion of the huge yellow-and-purple mural that covers Annie's exterior—it's a rendering of a giant shadowy skeleton banging away on a drum kit the size of Mount Everest. The sight of the sunken, bruise-colored eyes of the skeletal drummer only reminds me of Matt, of how long he worked on this particular piece of the painting. Exhausted and irritated, I turn back around, lean against Matt's masterpiece, and bend over, putting my head between my legs, brushing the tears off my face and racking my brain as to where Matt could be.

Something was wrong when I left my apartment today; I knew it and I ignored it. Maybe it was the way Matt kept spelling words on the coffee table in Froot Loops or telling me how many riffs Jack Mantis stole from him, or maybe it was the way he kept whining about me not caring about his gigs.

I tried to argue. I reasoned that sometimes I had to see other bands for my *BAT* articles, and I mean, really: no *BAT* articles, no rent. I pleaded with him the way one does with a temperamental child. I said that I always tried my best to make sure my work didn't interfere with his impromptu sets at Annie's. But I'm no magician. I can't predict the schedule of every band that passes through Manhattan and Brooklyn. Sometimes there would be a conflict. Matt just shook his head angrily.

And I, for once, decided to let him be alone in his bad mood, decided to let him get over it on his own. Which he apparently never did.

"Echo! Are you okay?" Thalia sticks her face straight into

mine, which is still by my knees. What a sight we must make. Two upside-down freak shows.

"I'm fine, I'm fine. Just give me a minute to figure out what to do, okay?"

Thalia pulls a piece of hair from my face and tucks it beneath my ear. "Honey, it's Matt's funeral," she counsels, her voice now full of empathy and care. "So forget him. Go up and meet Jack."

I right myself and Thalia follows, moving her hand to my back. I look into the round, all-knowing eyes of my sister. My tears have dried, and my good sense is slowly returning. The night air chills my naked shoulders and I check my watch for the umpteenth time.

"It's okay. I have a little bit of time before I have to go."

Thalia drops her hand from my back and inhales through flared nostrils. Then she doesn't say anything (a small miracle!) and huffs her way into Annie's club.

I watch her go, and think about what she's been saying. I *could* just leave, go up to Madison Square Garden, charm the pants off Jack (figuratively, of course), get my interview, and make it up to Matt tomorrow. After all, I held up my part of the bargain. I said I'd be at his show, and here I am. And here he isn't.

It's hard to believe that just over four years ago, Matt was opening for acts like U2 and enjoying the fruits of both a mildly successful album *and* a Top 100 hit. Now, he's so ramped up full of insecurities, a gig in front of a couple hundred people sends him running for the hills.

I look at my watch. There simply isn't time for me to be having a nervous breakdown, so I push off from the wall and start walking, thinking about where Matt could be.

My search begins in the tattoo parlor across the street.

Matt doesn't actually have any tattoos, but Frank, the owner and operator of this fine establishment, is a regular at Annie's, and he's the closest thing Matt has to a friend.

But the dingy receptionist, who always has a mouthful of gum and a comic book dangling from her tattooed fingers, kindly tells me that Matt hasn't been around tonight.

So I move on. I search through three bars, two delis, a McDonald's, a newspaper shop, and an antique clothing store before finding him cowering in the corner of the $2 falafel place a few blocks from Annie's.

My poor Matt: he's practically curled up in the booth, hunched over a table laden with mostly untouched falafel, and sheets of notebook paper spread out all around. He's wearing the hooded sweatshirt I bought him at a Yankees game two months ago, underneath the corduroy coat I gave him for his birthday last week. Propped up against the wall behind him is the $2500 guitar his parents and I got him last Christmas.

He's a long, tired way from the burgeoning rock star that toured with the world's hottest bands. Now he's this shell of a guy. He sleeps until noon. He'll play unannounced sets around town, and in the three years since he moved in with me, he's been dropped by three managers: two because of his lazy getting-back-to-you skills and one because of an unfortunate incident with a Fender Stratocaster and a pint of homemade guacamole. His current one is hanging on for dear life, hoping to reap the profits from his comeback album—should Matt ever be able to write words for the tracks that have been gathering dust for the past two years.

Did I mention that part? That he has an album all ready to go? I didn't? Wow, and that's the best part, too.

Yup. There's an entire album: tracks laid, mixed, rerecorded, remixed. Matt worked on it steadily for years, bringing musicians in to record flute parts and piano riffs and mandolin accompaniments. We lived like kings off his advance, but it's long since dried up, as has his record company's patience, because these beautifully and lovingly recorded tracks are missing one integral component.

Lyrics.

It's his damn writer's block. All those recorded and mixed songs have the following lyrics: "Hot fudge sauce. Hot fudge sauce." Repeated over and over and over again. "Just place-holder lines," Matt will say, as he sings his songs for Annie or me or his rep at the record company who is ready to pull his hair out.

I pull my shirt down over my pants, check my watch and push open the door to the falafel place. The tinkling of entryway bells echoes as I step inside. The two men behind the counter step to me, and I motion that I'm meeting Matt, who looks up from his mad scribbling and opens his mouth in surprise when he sees it's me.

He pushes all the pages around, forming a pile, and then wipes the booth seat next to him while I approach.

"Hey," I say quietly when I get to him. Matt doesn't even look up. He just shoves a piece of tomato into his mouth and asks, "Want some falafel, honey?" He grabs for a napkin and wipes his fingers.

I slip my bag from my shoulder and throw it onto a chair. I notice that the unpaid check has been pushed to the far edge of the table. I look at it for a beat, pull a five-dollar bill from my wallet, go place it in the hands of the guy behind the counter (who receives it with a smarmy smile), then slide into the booth beside Matt and take a bite of the sandwich I just paid for.

"How'd it go?" He attempts to run his hands through my hair, but I duck, unwilling to let the snide tone in his voice slide.

"Fine. I've got about an hour before I have to be back uptown."

Matt deflates. He sinks into the wall and lets out an audible sigh. Ah. Wonderful. The loaded sigh. My favorite.

It reminds me, in a mangled, beat-up way, of when we were first going out. Well, we never actually went *out* when we were first going out, because he was on tour, so our early courtship was all phone calls and e-mail. But I loved it—I fancied myself a modern-day war bride, waiting impatiently to hear "You've Got Mail" emanate from my computer, frantically dialing my cell phone at all hours of the night, checking to hear if Matt had left me a message, or played a snippet of a song into my voice mail. That became our thing. He'd play me a measure of a song, and I'd call him back to tell him what it was. It was our own, cellular version of "Name That Tune." It's how we fell in love. (On my birthday, Bono left me a message. It began, "Name this song, Echo Brennan." Then he sang "Birthday" by the Beatles. That's when I knew that I was the luckiest girl in the world. I mean, come on, a birthday message from Bono? Tell me that you wouldn't melt into a puddle of goo right there.)

But now the romantic "Name That Tune" has morphed into the more challenging and less sexy "Name That Sigh." The object is to interpret Matt's hidden messages. This is a beginner's round: an outburst of air that arpeggios down a scale of melancholy. It means, "I wish you weren't working tonight. Stay with me instead."

"Honey, I have to go."

"Whatever." He forcefully throws a piece of pita onto the plate.

"How was the rest of your day?" I ask, trying to change the topic and inadvertently bringing up the other challenge of our relationship.

"Don't start."

"Fine." This, of course, answers my question about how the rest of his day was. It was a waste of time. Like all his days have been for the last year.

As couples go, we've fallen into kind of a rut. Here's a rundown of a typical day in the Brennan-Hanley household. I wake up. I eat breakfast, take a shower, make Matt a sandwich so that he'll eat something throughout the day besides cereal. I brew a pot of coffee for him. I watch the morning news. Then, just before I leave for work, I push Matt out of bed. I write down three goals for him on a piece of staff paper and Scotch-tape it to the front of the television, where he's sure to see it. The list:

1. Write one line of lyric.
2. Do the laundry (sometimes the word *laundry* is exchanged for *dishes*)
3. Make the bed.

Then I come home after either a long day at the *BAT* or a night at a club checking out a new singer who is able to write lyrics, and I go over the list with Matt and find that nothing got done.

So I avoid this particular, ongoing, unsolvable fight and jump right on in to the more pressing one.

"So, why did you bail on Annie's?"

"Just didn't feel like playin' is all."

"She was expecting you."

He shrugs his shoulders and mashes a hunk of falafel into a sheet of mush.

"You should play. It's important."

"Nah. I wanted to do my new songs today." He points to the sheets of paper on the table and sighs his "I can't sing 'Hot Fudge Sauce' at Annie's again" sigh. Then he starts chewing on his thumbnail before flipping on the charm switch.

"Honey." Matt lifts a forkful of the falafel mash to my mouth, kisses my forehead, once, twice, three times. "Just blow this thing off, okay? Come home with me instead, and help me write this song, okay?"

I have two choices here, neither of them resulting in a completely 100% happy Echo Brennan.

Choice 1: Enable my boyfriend. Take him home, make the English muffin pizzas he loves so much, rub his feet while he plays his twelve-string guitar and tell him every lyric that he's contemplating is brilliant.

This is the choice I've been making for years now, because I believe in Matt. I've believed in him since that first day I saw him, in Boston. I can still picture it: I was late to a class, and stuck waiting for a train on the T platform, and this guy, this troubadour genius in ripped-up jeans and a battered Dokken T-shirt was holding court, charming the pants off of Boston's commuters. Even underground he had presence. Later that night, when we miraculously ended up at the same party, his pockets were overflowing with bills. I brought him a beer and he tipped me two dollars. It caught my attention.

Later, he played me three songs in a corner: "You've Got to Hide Your Love Away" by the Beatles, "Leavin' on a Jet Plane" by John Denver, and "Every Rose Has Its Thorn" by, you guessed right, Poison. It was the Poison song that did me in. It was so ridiculous, but he sang it so well, his eyes closed, his voice full of passion. He knew the joke and went for it anyway, and I followed him into my dorm room like he was the Pied Piper.

Of course, that was just one night. And years later, when I met Matt backstage after he opened for the Smashing Pumpkins in New Jersey, he didn't even really remember me. He pretended to, but has later copped to the fact that he had no idea who I was.

I guess it's all the history we have that makes it hard for me to just chuck him in his hour (or years) of need. I look at the pathetic shell in front of me, the guy too afraid to strum his guitar in a small New York club, and these previously dormant maternal instincts come out. I know that sounds icky, but it's true. Sometimes he looks at me, from underneath that floppy brownish-blackish hair, with those round muddy eyes of brown, and I'm a goner. I just want to dive in and forget all my goals and play good girlfriend.

But there's always Choice 2. Thalia's choice. *Put the stray dog down.* There's been an incessant drumming inside my head lately, and that drumming sounds a little something like this: "You'll-never-be-the-female-Kurt-Loder-if-you-spend-all-your-twenties-holding-Matt's-hand."

The simple truth is that it's time to grow up a little. Sure, I love nothing more than that butterfly-in-the-stomach feeling I get when the lights go down just before a rock concert, or the rush of adrenaline I get when I rip the plastic off a brand-new band's CD, but I'm almost thirty. I'm not a kid anymore. I need a real job. And it's getting more and more obvious that some things about my life have to change for me to become a bit more, well, adult.

But I suppose I can only solve one problem at a time. I look at Matt. He has a tomato seed on the corner of his mouth and a sleeve lathered in tahini sauce. I sigh deeply, one that has no other meaning other than, "You have tahini on your new coat," grab a napkin, dip it into my water glass and clean him up.

Fifteen minutes later I'm pulling him by his soggy sleeve across Rivington Street. Thalia stands by the door to Annie's, legs crossed at the ankles, arms folded, disappointment on her face.

"Matt," she says by way of greeting. He winks at her, shifts his guitar from his left arm to his right, and enters Annie's.

"What are you doing outside, Thal?" I ask before following him inside.

"Waiting. For Jim Morrison here to get his act together so you and I can motor."

I ignore her comment, push through the door and amble up to the bar. Annie Lee pours Matt a ginger ale and Alicia what looks like a margarita on the rocks. Matt tugs at one of Alicia's blond pigtails, and she puts her arm around his shoulders, stands on her tiptoes and kisses him hello.

"Want one, hon?" Annie asks, reaching for an empty glass.

"No thanks, I've got something to do later."

Annie nods conspiratorially and passes the made drinks across the bar.

Matt reaches for his ginger ale and turns those damn puppy dog eyes on me. "You're not going to stay for my show?" He should *so* not be allowed to look at me that way.

"I thought you didn't want to play anything."

"Well, I will if you stay."

"Emotional blackmail," Thalia whispers in my ear.

Alicia puts her be-ringed hand on Thalia's arm. "Come on, let's you and I go talk to those guys in the corner."

This is why Alicia is the best best friend you could have. Seriously. I happen to know for a fact that the only person in my life who doesn't annoy the crap out of her is my father, and that's because he's legally blind and therefore gets her sympathy vote.

No sooner does Alicia steer Thalia clear of me and Matt, than a vibrating sensation massages my left hip.

I pull out my cell phone—it's so rare that it rings, or vibrates or whatever and I'm suddenly overcome with worry, thinking it's Jack, calling to cancel…oh! My fingers don't fly fast enough over the keys, my heart pounds as I try to get to the text message screen. I check my watch; it's probably just Stan as Jack should still be onstage, but who cares? I, Echo Brennan, am now on a phone-calling basis with the Butter Flies. It almost makes this Matt portion of the evening bearable.

I finally get to the text message screen. I hold my breath as three little words pop up:

U.

O.

Me.

You owe me?

I'm stumped.

What could I possibly owe Jack? I mean, if I write a best-selling cover story on him and have my pick of jobs, then yes, I will owe him. I hit the save number feature, thinking how cool I am to have finagled my way into getting Jack Mantis's number on my speed dial, when I realize that the incoming number looks familiar.

I look up and see Alicia across the bar. I owe *Alicia*. The phone call wasn't from Jack or Stan. It was from Alicia, who at the moment looks bored out of her mind, while Thalia graphically relays the naked flute player story to a group of vest-wearing beer drinkers. Alicia looks up and we make eye contact. She gives me a very fake smile.

I do owe her.

"Let's go," I say, trying to cover the impatience in my tone. Matt hops off his bar stool, grabs his ginger ale, and meanders off through the door behind the bar, which leads to the backstage area. Thankfully Annie understands the artistic temperament. It's not every club owner in the city that would put up with this fickle behavior. (I suspect much of her understanding stems from her appreciation for Matt's rear end, which, considering how much time he spends sitting on it, continues to be quite shapely. Alicia says you could bounce a silver dollar off it, which always makes me angry.)

When we get to the wings, Matt hands his guitar over to one of the Punk's guitar techs. The tech plugs it into an amp and begins to tune it while Matt and I stare out over the crowd. Despite my slight impatience, a thrill sends my heart into frantic beating. That's a *lot* of people. A thousand, Annie said. They mill and murmur and chatter in the half light, and when they hear the first sound of Matt's guitar, they cheer. Matt looks at me and grins, and a little corner of my beating heart turns over.

"I'll be fine, sweetie. Go watch." He kisses my cheek, and hands me his coat. I smile at him, and then make my way through the tunnel that leads directly to Fred's sound booth in the back, that fluttery feeling intently circling my stomach the whole way. It's just, well, it's just that I love live shows, truth be told. It sometimes amazes me that I still, to this day, feel the same excitement as when I was a kid, discovering music for the first time, manically making my way through my mother's record collection. That feeling multiplies a bit when I hear the crowd burst into a vocal roar and thunderous applause, signifying Matt's arrival onstage.

"Hey, Freddy," I say when I get to the sound booth. Annie's husband is perched up on a stool in front of a massive board covered in knobs and lights—he's fiddling with levels, making adjustments as Matt sings his only hit song, "On Top of the World." There's a towel wrapped around Fred's neck to soak up the sweat from his set. "Thanks for covering for him."

Fred nods. Fred's this cool old guy—he and Annie have been together for something like twenty years, and every time I see him he's wearing a different Rush T-shirt. He must own like five hundred of them.

"It's fine. His groupies will be happy. That girl's back." I follow his pointing finger to a girl leaning against the wall. She's got a large camera slung around her shoulder and wears a broad leather belt with Matt's face embossed in it. Her head is tilted upward in dreamy rapture, as she mouths each word to my boyfriend's first song. I've seen her before, too many times. She always comes to Matt's shows, no matter where they are. Alicia and I refer to her as the bead-bug girl, because she makes beaded jewelry in the shape of beetles and ants, dragonflies and caterpillars and passes them out to passersby. She's kind of weird, really.

I look out over the rest of the room as Matt works through his first couple of songs. This room, in line with the décor of the rest of the bar, is completely out of the seventies. It's a punk rocker's dream, with newspaper clippings and beer bottle labels glued to every conceivable surface, and crushed glass lining the tops of the walls. The only light in the room comes from the ten or so lightbulbs hanging from the ceiling, giving the space a spare, stark, kind of creepy vibe. But it's also really kick-ass, in a rock-and-roll kind of way.

"Beach Boys, Beatles, or Stones, tonight, Ec?" Fred asks me. I stare at him blankly, knowing that he's asking what covers Matt's going to play, since half of Matt's sets lately are devoted to someone else's songs. This is an unfortunate consequence of not having lyrics written to most of your music.

"It's just good he's playing, Fred."

"That it is, Ec."

Just then, Matt launches into the beginning strains of "House of the Rising Sun."

"Egads," Fred says, and climbs out of the sound booth just as Thalia ducks in.

"You've got to be kidding me," she shouts over the din of Matt's cover song.

"Shut up."

"What time do you have to go?" she screams.

"I have a few minutes," I scream right back.

"You should make your escape now. While he can't stop you from leaving."

"I'm detecting a theme from you tonight, Thal."

Matt launches into "Blackbird." A moment passes, but then Thalia mumbles, "Hey, you know who does a good version of this song?"

I look at her in the darkness.

"Everyone."

The crowd applauds politely, and I will say that it's a good thing nobody's left. As a matter of fact, just as Matt starts another cover, this one a Radiohead song, the three vest-wearing men Thalia and Alicia were talking to earlier walk in.

"Why don't you go talk to them and leave me alone," I say, nodding in their direction.

Thalia swallows down the rest of her beer and points at my watch. "You've got to go."

She's right. My watch reveals that I have only fifteen minutes to get uptown, weed my way through the labyrinthine underbelly of Madison Square Garden, and find Jack Mantis before he forgets all about me, or worse, before Alex Paxton gets to him. Matt's Radiohead song winds down, and I make my way to the steps, only to hear the smattering of applause and the beginning chords of "Your Body is a Wonderland" by John Mayer. I stop midstep, spin on my heel, and wave at Thalia, who is surrounded by the three suited guys.

Splayed out like a voodoo doll in the back of the cab as it hurtles up Sixth Avenue, I grab desperately for the strap behind the driver-side partition, to keep myself from hurling back and forth against the doors. At least my friendly neighborhood driver recognized the phrase, "Please hurry." Usually it takes Alicia's deep pockets to get drivers to speed in this town.

As he maneuvers around the traffic in starts and fits, I one-handedly dig through my bag, looking for my compact and lip gloss. Even in the dim light of the taxi seat, I can make out the fact that I look rushed. Bland and rushed. But now I'm thankful Thalia put such heavy makeup on me earlier. My eyes still look model-alluring in shades of purple and aqua and my rouged cheekbones cut strong angles across my round face. And my hair remains securely pulled off my face in Alicia's silver barrettes. I coat my lips in shimmery purple gloss, then pull out my little notebook and reread the most pertinent of my Jack facts.

Jack Mantis. Born in St. Louis. Went to boarding school

in California, dropped out when he was sixteen and formed the first incarnation of the Butter Flies. Kicked around Boston and New York for several years before being signed to Magic Records. Married for six weeks to an actress he met on the set of *Clash Vixens,* for which he wrote two songs. Then the Butter Flies broke the music scene wide open, with a string of three hits that captured the hearts of rock fans and teenage girls alike, making all other acts for Magic, Matt Hanley included, barely worth anything.

The cab comes to a screeching halt. I throw a fistful of dollars at this savior of a driver, and hot-foot it out of the car, bags and papers and jacket trailing as I run.

My watch reads eleven thirty-five. They likely have been offstage for at least five minutes. I make a mad dash for the 34th Street side of Madison Square Garden, digging frantically through my bag for the laminated backstage pass that Jack handed me at the Edge Club. Shit! I knew I put it in here somewhere. I dig through pocket after compartment after panel. Nothing. By this time, I'm standing underneath the overhang, next to a large, luxury bus that has purple neon letters saying Butter Flies.

"Hey! Excuse me?" I rush off toward a rather large man, who's milling around the unmarked stage entrance to the Garden. He wears a back brace, which, more than his 360-pound frame and large handlebar mustache, make me think of a circus strong man. "Hey," I pant. "I can't find my pass, but I'm supposed to be meeting Jack Mantis after the show."

Mr. Handlebar Mustache looks at me, shakes his head and disappears into the bowels of Madison Square Garden without so much as a harrumph. "Hey!" I call after him.

I stand there. Bag on my shoulder, blisters on my feet. My toes are freezing, because of these stupid shoes that are far more suited to a casual spring dinner than an early autumn story-hunt. Thalia's leather pants cut into my hips and waist, my bare shoulders are covered in goose bumps. I take a deep breath and try to reconfigure my strategy.

It's okay. I think. Just breathe. I upend my bag right onto the sidewalk, right in front of the band's bus, empty all the folds of fabric, go through my wallet, and my pant and coat pockets. No pass. I lost it. Or left it at Annie's. Or maybe—oh, who cares. All that matters is that I have no pass.

At this moment I hear a loud puff of air as the door to the bus opens. "You all right, miss?"

"Yep, yep. Nothing to see here. Just my dreams dying, that's all."

The door closes. I stand between the empty bus and the door to Madison Square Garden, and look back and forth between them three times before it clicks. All I have to do is wait here for the band to come out and get on the bus! Halle-freakin'-lujah! It's not over yet.

So I pack up all my crap, and lean on the side of the bus. I wait for about twenty minutes and just when I'm about to throw in the towel, a group of men come striding out the stage door of the Madison Square Garden. I hop to attention. It's them. Stan Fields and his brother Michael, who's the lead guitar player, and one man in khaki pants and a pullover sweater I recognize as the drummer Goren Liddell, and then a few other roadie type guys.

"Stan! Hey, Stan! It's me, Echo Brennan, from before? At the Edge Club?"

He looks at me out of the corner of his eye as he steps onto the first step of the bus. "Yeah. What happened?"

I instantly flip into girl mode. "I can't believe it! I totally lost my pass. Space-case, right?" And then I do quite possibly the dumbest thing. I make a shooting gun motion toward my head. I'm such a loser. "Can you guys talk now?"

Stan eyeballs me from the step. "Talk to Jack. This is his deal." And then he disappears into the caverns of the bus.

So I look for Jack, who has yet to come out of the Garden. The rest of the guys shuffle past me, their conversations full of missed quarter notes and faulty mics and gratitude that their whirlwind world tour is finally over—despite, myself, I immediately tune in to what they're saying, because I love these kinds of "insider" conversations. Then, at last, the doors swing open and out comes the luminescent, ethereal specter that is Jack Mantis. My heart speeds up a bit.

Then slams into cardiac arrest.

Because, walking right beside him, jotting things down in his notebook is Alex Paxton.

"Hey!" I shout, forgetting my manners.

Alex and Jack both look up at the same time. The grin that flutters to life on Alex's face can only be described as shit-eating.

"Hey, friend!" Alex points at me and jogs a step ahead of Jack, in order to get to *me* before I get to *him*.

Jack merely stops his stride, and bellows at the top of his gravel-coated lungs, "Stan! Help!"

Both Alex and I turn to him. "Jack, I lost my pass—"

Alex blocks me from running to Jack by planting his foot in my path. We grapple. We're children.

"Jack, don't talk to Echo! This girl likes Matt Hanley for God's sake!"

"Hey!" I turn my wrath on him fully. "You are such a bastard! That CD made almost every top-ten newcomers' list that year!"

"Well, what's he doing now, Yoko?"

Stan Fields chooses this moment to come bounding out of the bus, like a sheriff on speed, a man thrilled to be able to flex a little muscle. Alex and I freeze.

Jack sighs despondently, drops his chin to his chest, then says wearily, "They're fighting over us, Stan."

"Get in the bus."

Jack gratefully does as he's told. But before he steps onto the bus, he puts a sad hand on Stan's shoulder, and announces, "I don't think I'll be ready to interview anytime soon."

Alex and I watch the two of them withdraw into their den of decadence. Then, only moments later, the engine of the bus roars to life and carries Jack away. Alex pushes off me and walks down 34th Street, mumbling the whole time about how I screwed everything up.

3

One of the most reliable of New York City's Murphy's laws is that when you need a cab, you will not find a cab. Actually, I suppose this rule doesn't apply to me this evening, because I did find one. It just so happened that Alex found the same cab at the same time. As you can probably surmise, he beat me to it and refused to share.

After that, all that could go wrong did go wrong. It was disaster-movie bad.

In addition to not being able to find another cab, the trick strap on Thalia's pink tank top snapped. Three guys standing on the corner of 27th and Eighth followed me for three blocks, hooting and hollering and generally making a scene. I finally gave up and got on the subway, which for some reason decided to run express, taking me into Brooklyn. I grew up in Brooklyn. I love Brooklyn. I do not want to go into the heart of Brooklyn by myself after midnight wearing a shirt that is falling off my shoulders every five minutes. Call me crazy.

When I finally get to my apartment, it's well after twelve-thirty. I'm a little tired. I'm a little hungry. I'm a little annoyed. And I look like Jennifer Beal's hippier body double in *Flashdance*.

In short, I'm *not* in a good mood.

I open the door to my home, my sweet home, thinking how I'd like to run a bath, pour a glass of wine, listen to some Nick Drake or maybe Neil Young while Matt rubs my neck the way he does.

But I see, upon stepping inside, that Matt won't be able to rub my neck.

He's busy with other things.

Mr. Matt Hanley—and keep in mind that it's after midnight, after midnight on a day when Matt was home all by himself, doing nothing, not writing songs, not earning any cash to pay the rent—is in overalls and no shirt, holding a paint roller above his head. My living room is covered in the pale blue sheets I bought for myself at Saks Fifth Avenue after getting my first paycheck for writing an article. These sheets are old, but they are my acknowledgment of the first time I was ever published. Now they're covered in drips of red, yellow and royal blue paint. I peer at the ceiling, which is being covered in large, concentric circles.

"Hey, sweetie! Be careful, now!" He shouts over the din of the stereo, blasting Rage Against the Machine, and the television, tuned to the Cartoon Network and turned up loud enough so that *Futurama* can be heard *over* the sound of the music. Matt's oblivious. He greets me cheerfully, as if it is perfectly normal to be painting my ceiling after midnight, only hours after he freaked out and nearly blew off his gig.

I walk over to the stereo and shut it off, then turn down the volume on the TV. I take a deep breath.

"You okay, honey?"

I don't answer. I just stare at him. His pant legs are rolled up to his knees, which makes very little sense as his shins are covered by a pair of red-ringed tube socks (which do not end in shoes).

I take another deep breath, and say very timidly, very quietly, "What are you doing?"

He shakes his head up and down, and runs his hand over his hair, painting it with a lovely streak of royal blue. "Yeah, don't worry, sweetie, it's gonna look way cool."

"Yeah, well, we're not supposed to paint the apartment."

He looks at me and wrinkles his nose. "What'choo talkin' about, Willis?" Of course he's right to question my objection. Over the course of the time we've lived here, Matt's painted every surface in this apartment (and I mean, *every* surface—the closets, the cabinets, the toilet) dozens of times over. It's his special, fun way of procrastinating. I know he's feeling particularly dry in the lyric department when he whips out the paints. The problem, besides the fact that when we move out this place has to be left as white as it was found, is that he's as impatient with his painting as he is with his writing. Invariably, he'll make it halfway through a cloud mural, or a vine-clad picture frame, decide he hates it and then leave it unfinished. Until the next inspiration hits and he starts all over on a different manic creative explosion.

I cover my mouth in an attempt to minimize my fume intake and walk over to the windows, which he left closed. I notice a box of half-eaten pizza thrown casually over the corner armchair.

"You can have some if you want."

"I'm not hungry," I say flatly.

Matt lowers the paint roller to the ground, dotting my sheet in more deep blue, and points at me. "Your shirt's falling down."

I lean against the windowsill.

"That the only way you could get to Jack?"

I throw my bag on the floor angrily, and stomp through the living room into my bedroom, ripping the broken tank top off as I go. There I'm greeted by a sight reminiscent of a tornado's path of destruction. Matt's sneakers lay haphazardly in the doorway, causing me to trip. The bed sheets droop down from the mattress to the floor. The dust in the window that's accumulated in the many days since I last had a chance to clean proclaims "Matt loves Echo." And on top of my bed, molded into an impressive dome, is the pile of dirty laundry that Matt had promised to wash today.

"Matt!" I shout. Loudly. "What is this?" I have no clue why the neglected laundry is what sets me off, when I took the Picasso experiment going on in my living room in such stride.

"What's that, honey?"

I dash out to him, a pair of his dirty underwear in one hand and a stray, yellowed sock in the other, pleased to have found something tangible to yell at him about, something concrete, something not about the fact that he doesn't have to get up for work in the morning and can therefore afford to paint the ceiling at twelve-forty in the morning. Something not about the fact that he made me late to the Butter Flies show, and thereby ruined my shot at covering them for *Disc*.

"Oh, yeah. Sorry about that. But I was in a groove today, working on this song—it was kind of about you, honey, about a girl with a big smile. Anyway, I didn't get around to the laundry. Besides, I didn't have any quarters."

I throw the underwear and socks down. "No quarters! Matt!" His head snaps back in a double-take when he hears my ferocious "You're in such trouble" tone. I storm over to the credenza, punch the TV off, and point to the looming stack of quarters there.

"Matt! What was the last thing I said when I walked out the door this morning?"

"Gee, I don't know, Echo. Was it, 'I pick Jack over you?'" He's into it now. He knows we're going to fight and he's bringing it.

I pick the sock up off the floor, fashion it into a missile, and launch it at Matt's head. I feel a measure of satisfaction when it falls into a bright yellow puddle. "No! It was 'I left you *quarters* to do the *laundry!*'"

Matt bites his lip, dips the paint roller into the paint tray, runs it back and forth once, twice, three times, making me feel light-headed. Finally he says, "Echo! I was still sleepy when you left! I can't process all of your orders when I'm sleepy. I'll do the laundry tomorrow, okay? Jesus."

"Matt! That's not the point!"

"Echo, why are you so bitchy right now?"

There's a crackle of tension between us, like an invisible cord strung from him to me that's fizzing with angry electricity, and I hate it. I hate fighting with him. And I hate feeling like a nagging mother. I pace until I'm standing in the kitchen/living room doorway. Matt throws himself onto the sheet-covered sofa. He drops the paint roller to the floor and I cringe. Then he stares blankly at the turned-off television.

And I snap. I can feel the synapses in my body firing in

a new way, there's a humming sound in my ears, and my hair follicles burn. Then everything, all the energy in my body courses downward to my toes and I become very centered, very focused, completely at peace.

"I don't want this anymore." My voice comes out steady and quiet, and I'm not sure that Matt actually heard me over the tune he's begun to hum. He doesn't even look at me.

"Matt—"

"I can't deal with this now, Echo!" He jumps up and runs into the bathroom, locking the door behind him.

I race over to the sofa, and pick the dripping paint roller up off the ground. "Matthew! You're getting paint everywhere!!!"

"Echo, leave me alone," he shouts through the closed door of the bathroom.

"You're locking yourself in the bathroom? Are you serious? *I'm* the girl, dammit!"

At this, he flings open the door. In his overalls and bare torso, with the band of his underwear showing, his floppy hair and sad brown eyes, I expect to want to hug him. But instead, this steel core of strength fills up my spine. Because Thalia's right. I have to put this stray dog down. Lord, help me.

"Matt," I say calmly. "We can't continue on like this."

"What?" He slams the door shut again, kicks it, and then flings it back open. "What the hell are you talking about?"

"I'm putting my foot down!" I put the roller down into the tray. "There's going to be no more midnight paint jobs, no more guilt trips when I'm making all the money to support you, no more wasted days." I'm resolute, my feet are planted firmly on the ground, my shoulders are back and I'm looking him dead in the eye. "From now on, I expect to hear *one completed line of lyric* every day. Do you understand me?"

The look on Matt's face right now is one of plain fury. His chest rises and falls underneath his overalls, and his eyes are bugging out of his head.

"I can't believe you," he says, looking around him wildly.

"Believe it. You have to get your life together. And you either start living the way I want you to, or you can leave."

"Living the way *you* want me to?"

"That's right," I repeat calmly. "Or else you can get out." I have no idea what the hell I'm trying to prove here, but the more irate he gets, the more this steely feeling fills up my veins; it's like I physically can't recant the things I've said.

And seriously? I'm doing him a favor. He's got to shape up. And this is the only way. Being the nice, supportive, girlfriend hasn't worked at all.

"Listen, Matt, you are in a dark place right now. You're not writing—"

"I am, too!"

"Nothing whole! You haven't finished one song in—"

"Who cares how long it's been?"

"I care!"

I sit on the arm of the couch and watch as Matt gently walks to me. He kisses my head. "Honey, I'm sorry about the paint, okay? I'm sorry about the laundry, okay? I'll do it in the morning. I promise."

I look into his eyes, those eyes I've loved since I was eighteen years old and saw him on that stupid T platform. He kisses my forehead again.

"Honey, come on."

I can't help it. He coaxes a smile from me, just a little, itty-bitty smile. He's almost got me. His hand drops to my shoulder, to the exact spot that is wound up in a knot.

He kneads my shoulder until I can't think about anything other than how good it feels. "Better?"

"Yeah, much."

He kisses my forehead for a third time, and continues working his magic on my knots. He looks at the ceiling. "How cool is that gonna look, anyway?"

I hear the faint triumph in his voice and, just like that, the spell's broken. I jump out from under his massaging hand. "Matt," I say, lowly and intensely. "I want you to move out. We're done."

4

My father's house, my childhood home, smells like baklava. You might say to yourself, "Now that'd be one delicious-smelling house," but it's surprisingly unpleasant. It smells sweet and overly romantic, and these are two sensations I am increasingly uncomfortable associating with my father, who, until very recently, was not what you would call an emotive guy.

We live in Carroll Gardens, a section of Brooklyn that was neighborhoody until about 1989, when it became tremendously trendy and full of yuppies. My father didn't seem to notice—he was too busy reading old texts, or grading his students' papers, or listening to recordings of classic plays while nursing a glass of Glenlivet to pay attention to the cosmetic changes taking place on our block. And then, of course, when his eyesight started going, it mattered little to him that our local butcher was bought out by a Starbucks.

Anyhow, my father is getting married. To Helen, our

Greek housekeeper. Thalia's excited about participating in the wedding events, because she loves the idea of dressing up and this is likely the only time she'll ever be wearing traditional wedding clothes. She says she looks forward to using the word *stepmother* in everyday conversation. She's also thinking of keeping a blog of her favorite wedding moments. When I remind her that she's not a writer, that not only has she never kept a diary but in fact used to read *my* diary pages aloud to the kids on our block for kicks, she merely shakes her head at me and repeats that the wedding is going to be "an experience."

I have a far less anthropological view of the whole thing. On the one hand, I'm really happy for my dad, who has been more or less alone since my mother left, with nobody to keep him company except one daughter who collected potential suitors like bracelet charms and another daughter who skipped the playing-with-dolls stage and jumped headlong into obsessions with Ziggy Stardust, Mick Jagger, and the Clash. So I'm happy for him. It's nice to see him smile about something other than Greek translations and ancient texts.

On the other hand, well, I'm not sure what the other hand is. I know that I should be much less selfish about it, but I liked being the good daughter, the one to take care of him, the one to drive him to his doctor appointments. And now he doesn't need me for that. He has Helen. It's an entirely childish take on his happiness, which I'm more than aware of.

"Hello?" I have a new habit of announcing my arrival when I come over here, because no matter how old you are, you don't want to see either of your parents engaged in sexual activity. Helen has really brought out the lustiness in my dad. And he's legally blind, so there's a *lot* of touching. It's just terrible.

"Hello?" I yell again and throw my keys down onto the antique end table by the door.

"Ah! Echo's in time for dinner!" Helen shouts from the kitchen.

Helen refers to lunch as dinner, and dinner as supper, and every Saturday, as I arrive on time for our standing mid-morning meal, she announces, "Echo's in time for dinner," which somehow always makes me feel like a *guest*.

Helen comes bustling out of the kitchen, her figure wrapped in a yellowing apron that reads *Kiss the Cook,* but stops in her path as soon as she sees me. "What happened?" She clutches her heart and says something in Greek.

Okay. I know I don't look my best. I tried to force cheer by wearing green army pants and my hot-pink "Brooklyn Girls Have More Fun" T-shirt. The neon color, apparently, draws attention to the bags under my eyes and the pasty complexion earned from my late night.

After my ultimatum to Matt, we spent an hour making our own version of a Lifetime movie of the week. I'll give us this—we really milked our New York breakup for all its dramatic worth. There was fifteen minutes of top-of-the-lungs screaming, followed by ten minutes of the classic breakup shuffle (fighting in the hallway of your apartment building, running through the halls, slamming and opening and reslamming your apartment door); and then there was the back-and-forth drama in the downstairs doorway. We were yelled at by our neighbors no less than five times and told to shut up by at least six passersby (that's impressive, huh?). Then Matt disappeared into the night. I followed, visiting every place I could think to find him, diners and clubs and movie theaters. I called Alicia and Annie and Matt's manager. I even took the subway to the Silver

Records studios, thinking maybe he had taken shelter there, seeking a place that actually would make him feel worse, being, as it is, the site of his life's most blatant failure.

But I couldn't find him anywhere.

"Nothing happened," I say, while Helen tilts her head and narrows her eyes.

She purses her lips, hangs up my coat and walks into the kitchen—a lovely, bright square of a room, covered in the same yellow and white curtains I picked out just before I went off to college. "You have long night of fun?" Her eyes are still narrow, her intuition urging her that there's something I'm not saying.

I say nothing to answer her question. I make myself busy by grabbing a box of cereal.

"Echo," she admonishes. "You need meat. Look at you." She picks up a frying pan covered in sizzling meats and holds it dangerously close to my head.

"It's okay, Helen. I'm going to the office later. I don't want to work on a full stomach."

"You work too hard." She shakes her head, commiserating with the bacon over my day's plans.

"Good morning, Dad." I make my way over to where my father sits in a wing-back chair, a large overstuffed leather number that is completely out of place in Helen's utilitarian kitchen. He has dark glasses on over his eyes, because the morning light that streams through the windows bothers him. I take his hand and hold it, then touch his cheek and kiss his forehead. My dad, even in early morning light, and before his coffee, is handsome. He's always dressed like you'd expect a college professor would be, and today's no different. He's in brown corduroy pants and a maroon sweater.

"Ah, Echo, I was just regaling our good chef here with tales of Medea."

"She killed her kids, right?"

"In the name of revenge. To get back at their father."

"Lovely breakfast conversation."

Just then the door slams and the thick plunk of Thalia's footsteps battle it out with the sound of the sizzling bacon. She appears in the kitchen doorway a vision of soft fabric, large dangly earrings and dozens of matching copper bracelets—like my mother redux. Sometimes I wonder whether it's a blessing that my father can't see so well.

"Good morning, Miss Thalia," Helen calls out as Thalia steps up to her sizzling pan, chooses a piece of bacon, starts chomping away, then marches to the table, grabs the chair nearest me, flips it and sits with her arms draped over the backrest, facing me.

"Did you close it?" She pops the last bite of bacon in her mouth. "Please tell me you didn't screw it up."

I throw my hands up in the air, in a clear, "I don't want to talk about this now" signal.

"Close what? Close what?" Helen calls from the stove. The presence of a woman in my father's life has really cut down on what Thalia and I can get away with. "What happened?"

"Nothing, Helen, nothing. I'm just trying to get an interview, that's all."

"What interview?" My father folds his hands in his lap, and tilts his face toward mine. He's long registered his displeasure at how I spend my time, thinking a writer such as myself would be better served at a college somewhere, researching *other* writers and not spending my days listening to garage bands. This is the one characteristic of my mother's that I inherited. I love music, and can't quite think of a way to spend my life that doesn't involve it. Unfortunately, neither of my parents had any musical ability to pass down to me, other than my dad's resonant speaking voice.

"An interview that would catapult her out of the side streets of Brooklyn and into the offices of an actual establishment," my sister answers.

I grab a seat and say nothing.

"Echo——" My father intercedes. "Please answer the question posited earlier. Did you 'close' it?"

I chase a wheat flake around my cereal bowl. "Almost. It's just a matter of time, really."

Thalia catches my eye, and I know that she knows I'm keeping something back, but she also knows that I'm not going to spill it now. It's far too early in the morning for a lecture from my father about taking my career more seriously. I'm fairly sure Thalia understands this, because she asks, "Helen, could I please have some juice?"

Helen immediately runs to the fridge.

"Dad, did you set the date for the wedding?" Thalia continues to shift the conversation, which is nice of her, since it didn't need shifting until she opened her big mouth. "I need to know so that I can figure out who to bring."

"The Saturday after New Year's," my father answers as Helen places Thalia's juice on the table and stands over him with the bacon pan. She proceeds to serve strips of meat onto his plate, where it lands next to a pile of sausage and a stack of pancakes.

Thalia reaches for a piece of bacon from Dad's plate. Helen slaps her hand away.

"And you'll be bringing Matthew, of course?" my father asks me.

A flake gets caught in my throat, causing me to cough uncontrollably. Thalia hands me her juice. "Um. I don't know. It's a long ways off."

Thalia breezily chimes in with: "Right. Matt might be busy then, learning the three chords to 'Blowin' in the Wind' or 'Row, Row, Row your Boat.'"

Before I can find something to throw at her, Helen freezes us all with a bloodcurdling, piercing shriek.

"Are you okay?" my sister asks, like Helen's a crazy person and she doesn't want to set her off.

Helen merely shrieks again, but this time using words. "I knew it!" She throws the scalding hot frying pan onto a pot-holder on the table, and gestures wildly in the air. "You break up! Look at you! Ah, Jamie, she's single!"

"You didn't!" Thalia is so shocked that she absentmind-edly puts her hand on the bacon pan. "Shit!" she shouts before scrambling over to the sink and immersing her fingers in a stream of running water.

"Language, Thalia," my father intones, removing his sun-glasses. "Echo? Five hundred words, please."

I exhale a bit and fold my hands in front of me. "Well, we're—we're just probably gonna, um, take a break. I think."

They stare at me. I spend a moment trying to meet all of their gazes, but give up and inspect the contents of my cereal bowl instead. Finally, I lift my head, avoid three ex-pectant faces and continue on. "I asked him to move out."

"No, you didn't," Thalia spits as if I just confessed to marrying the Pope and dancing naked in Central Park all in one night.

"Thalia, let her finish," my father commands.

Usually Dad's teacher voice is enough to stop Thalia from giving me a hard time, but no luck this time. There's too much juice to be had in the fruitful gossip I'm giving her. "He made you miss Jack, didn't he?" The smirk on my sister's face could not possibly be smugger.

I ignore her question, and try to spin the story in a way that won't make my father and sister able to mutter the phrase, "I told you so." "It just wasn't working out. I wasn't happy, Matt wasn't hap—"

"Are you kidding? Matt had it made in the shade with you."

My father, I notice, says nothing to shush Thalia. Or disagree with her.

"Listen, I'm fine. Matt's fine. He's moving out today."

I look from Helen to my father to Thalia, all of whom stare back at me in silence.

"Daddy?" I finally ask. "Can you say something, please?"

He takes a big breath, sips his coffee and eats a big bite of pancake.

Helen's the first to speak. "Jamie, what about that boy you talk about? The one in your class?"

My father taps his fork against the side of his plate. "Ah, the one writing the thesis on the chorus works of Aeschylus? That's an idea, I suppose."

"No, no, no." I nearly choke on my coffee. "Let's not all try to matchmake me into happiness. I need to sort things out with Matt before I can move on, and anyway right now all I want is to focus on my career, okay?"

My father mutters something about what I do for money not being a career, and I ignore it. "You'd be better off marrying a nice college student, who can take care of you." This, he says loud enough for me to hear. I merely exhale.

Thalia says to my father, "You know what I'd like to see, Daddy? I'd like to see her with a banker."

"That *would* be lovely," he agrees, taking a healthy drink of coffee. "Or perhaps a man of the law."

While they debate what kind of man I should date next, Helen dishes a few pieces of bacon onto my plate (I push them as far to the edge as I can) and pats my hand. "Echo, I'm sorry. Matt was a nice boy."

I watch her walk to the stove, and try to tune out the conversation my father and sister are having about six-figure salaries. I pour another pile of cereal into my bowl, and think about how Helen's right, that Matt is a nice boy.

The rest of the breakfast is carried on with barely a mention of Matt or Jack, and I'm grateful when Thalia asks Helen about her latest favorite topic of conversation—her wedding dress.

Her face lights up at the mention of it—she's been working on the design of the dress for weeks, months. She keeps saying how nice it will be for me and Thalia to work on it with her, and that someday we'll be able to wear it. I don't know how she'll feel about this plan when she discovers my lack of sewing talent. But for now she's content and continues to chatter on and on about fabric and lace and needles. My father eats; Thalia asks about dress patterns; I slurp my cereal.

And so the time passes peacefully, until the sound of my ringing cell phone filters in from the hallway. I run to get it, thinking maybe it's Alicia, who I've called six times since Matt left, or Walter, my boss at the *BAT,* or by some miracle, Jack Mantis, who, in my two-second fantasy, would have realized the error of his ways after a long night of tossing and turning and is calling to apologize and to beg me to conduct his interview.

But my caller ID displays my own home phone number. "Matt?"

"Hey." His voice is scratchy, and sad, and tired-sounding. My heart slips into my shoes.

"Who is that?" Thalia appears behind me, hands on hips, fumes in her eyes.

I swat at her and mouth the words, "Go back inside." She doesn't budge from her spot.

"Are you there?"

I grip the staircase banister, and kick my shoe into the wall, my heart feeling as heavy as a bowling ball. "Yeah. Are you okay? Where'd you go last night?"

"That's not your problem," Thalia says.

"Is that your sister?"

"Matt, I—"

Thalia lunges at me and shouts into the receiver, "You have thirty seconds before I grab the phone and hang it up!"

I push her away from me. "Matt?"

"Yeah, listen, I just wanted to apologize."

"Really?"

"Yeah, for everything, and for being—well, just for last night. I'm sorry."

"I'm sorry, too."

Then Thalia makes another run at me. This time I'm completely unprepared to defend myself. She snatches the phone out of my grasp and bellows, "You are broken up. Any of your things I find there will be thrown out. No hard feelings, sweetheart." Then she hangs up the phone, and disconnects the battery before slipping it into her back jeans pocket.

I stare at her openmouthed. "You don't have to be so mean!" I storm back into the kitchen, only to find Helen on my father's lap, kissing him. "UGH!" I hold my hand up over my eyes. "The kitchen, you guys?" I turn on my heel, and rush past Thalia up the stairs.

The *plop, plop, plop* sound of Thalia's following footsteps chases me all the way into my childhood bedroom. "You should be proud of yourself! It's the best thing you've ever done! Don't be upset!" She doesn't stop shouting at me the entire trip up to my room.

I don't even bother trying to close the door. Thalia never lets a closed door stand in the way of giving unwanted advice.

"Can you go away?" I beg, flopping onto my bed, which is still covered in the Sesame Street blanket I got for my third birthday.

"No, I cannot. I want the whole story."

I bury my head underneath a pillow that's covered in smiling, dancing Elmos and hold my peace, until Thalia begins impatiently jabbing my side. I grit my teeth for a moment before giving in to the fact that I'm going to have to come clean sometime. "I got to the Garden late, and Alex Paxton was there, and we kind of had words, and it scared Jack off. Then it took me forever to get home and your hooker clothes weren't helping. I was just pissed. Then I get home, and Matt's half-naked, my apartment's covered in primary colors, and he acts like everything's cool. So I let him have it, and he fought back, and I kind of kicked him out."

Thalia lifts the corner of the pillow that covers my eyes and waits a beat before speaking. "I have to say I'm shocked."

"I know. I don't know what happened to me. It's like you took over my body."

She sits down on the bed. "I think you're better off."

I grunt my response.

"Echo, your relationship wasn't going anywhere. And now, you'll be able to get things done." Thalia takes my hand in hers and starts giving me one of her patented hand rubs.

I peek out from underneath my pillow. "Like what?" Part of me is so grateful for this moment, to have her here to keep me on the right path, to keep me from flying to Matt and begging him to stay, to keep me focused on what I want for my life.

"Well, for starters, no more missing deadlines because Matt's feeling blue."

I sit up. The dancing Elmos fall to my lap as I ponder this. "I guess that'll be good."

Thalia adjusts herself so that we're lying side by side on my bed, the way we did when we were little girls, and continues pummeling my hand. "No more going straight home after concerts—you'll be able to hang out, meet more people now."

"That's true, huh?" I rest my head on her shoulder, ignoring the growing pit in my stomach and focusing on the image of me mingling with rock stars and record executives.

Thalia nods and takes my other hand, which she immediately kneads and pokes into submission. "It's true."

I watch her work her masseuse magic on my fingers for a minute. "I don't know if I'll like being single."

At this comment, she squeezes my hand and drops her head on top of mine. "You won't like it. You'll *love* it. You'll *love* dating money-men, men who actually pay for stuff. It'll change your life."

We fall into a companionable silence. Then, as I'm slipping into a peaceful zone of complete hand-relaxation, this rock-hard nugget of ambition solidifies in my chest.

"Thalia?"

"Yes?"

"I want that Jack Mantis interview."

Thalia drops my hand and looks at me with the same look on her face she had when we were in middle school and she planted a stink bomb in Sherry Howard's locker.

"Then go out and get it."

5

I leave my dad's a new woman. With my belly full of cereal, my heart full of filial advice, and my head full of ambition, all mental pictures of Matt leaving his half of our matching "Best Friends Forever" key chains on the kitchen counter have been eradicated.

The weather that greets me on the front stoop of my father's brownstone helps my mood, too. It's clear, bright, and a bit brisk, but nice enough for a few brave birds to be chirping and hardy children to be riding their bicycles up and down the street. I bound down the stairs, and make the six-block walk to the *BAT* in record time.

Work. Even on a normal day, I love coming to the office. Some girls I know would rather spend their days off at the manicurist or Macy's or mostly anywhere other than their jobs, but not me. Writing, music: these are the drumbeats supporting my life, and there's nothing I enjoy more than sitting with a good song blasting through my earphones and a blank word document humming on the computer monitor in front of me. Today, I am going to brainstorm story ideas. So what if my Jack Mantis leap ended in a gigantic belly flop? He's not the only rock star in town. There's a way to get a better job. I just have to find it.

But, when I step through the green *BAT* door, I realize that coming up with a game plan might be more difficult than I want it to be.

"Honeybee!" Walter Gund, my portly teddy bear of a boss stands in the doorway of the *BAT*'s kitchen, his round belly covered in a yellow-and-blue polka-dot apron, his features hidden beneath the puffy result of too many afternoons spent eating sweets. A smile sitting sadly on his face, he clutches a roll of cookie dough in one hand, and delicately twirls a champagne flute full of OJ in the other.

"Walter." I throw my stuff down on the floor and take a deep breath, fortifying myself. "I just, uh, I thought I'd come in and finish that review—"

"Rubbish!" He moves toward me with arms extended, his hug as inevitable as my empty apartment. As he crushes my body into his pudgy one, he says, "You poor, poor dumpling. Thalia just called. Men."

I'd be annoyed with Thalia for spilling the beans if I weren't so relieved not to have to be the one to break the news to Big W. He doesn't handle change well.

Releasing me from his sticky embrace, he takes a disturbingly large bite from the log of cookie dough and walks toward the plush, overstuffed, Play-Doh-yellow couch that is crammed against the far wall of the office. He takes a seat, patting the cushion next to him in a signal for me to follow. "Don't think about working today. We're going to cry it out."

"Walter," I say, making no movement to join him, "*I* broke up with *him*. There's nothing to cry about."

"There's always something to cry about, cookie." Walter shakes his head from side to side. "There's no need to be brave. I can handle it."

I slump down into the cushions and exhale, telling myself that I'll have plenty of time to fashion my get-a-new-job game plan later. Then I look around at this Romper Room of an office. *BAT*'s headquarters would be an ideal site for a kindergarten class, with its bright orange walls (courtesy of Matt) and large, fuzzy purple-and-red wall hangings. "Art you can touch" Walter calls it. There are two busted-up beanbag chairs in the corner, and two desks, only one of which has a computer. Nevertheless, Walter has a dedicated IT guy on staff, though I know the only reason Jason's stayed on is because he loves music more than he loves computers.

Anyway, it's good for me to have Jason here: while I write, he sits on a beanbag chair, eating cookies and talking to Walter. This is the only way for me to get anything done. If it weren't for Jason keeping him occupied, Walter would spend all his time harassing me.

Alicia has long since decided that Walter must come from money. She says she recognizes the mark of the lazy rich, as she is among the lazy rich herself. I think she's on to something. He's certainly not supporting himself with the *BAT*. It barely makes enough money every month to pay my salary.

"And Echo, it's Saturday." He's pleading with me now. "You shouldn't be working on a *Saturday*."

"Walter, you know listening to music isn't work for me." I point to the desk, where a stack of shiny new CDs awaits.

"But Echo, are you sure you don't want to cry? I can brew some tea. I'll even put on some of that wailing girl music you love. It'll be fun!"

Despite the fact that I should stay wholly focused on fashioning a strategy for my new life, Walter's sweet pleading tugs at my heart a little, and honestly, sitting around eating cookie dough and listening to tunes does sound like a good way to pass an afternoon. I take a small piece from the cookie log.

"There's my girl." Walter gets up and heads off to the kitchen, presumably to brew the promised tea.

I take another bite of dough, and look around the orange room once more. All of a sudden, an image of my father pops into my head, sitting in his study, working on a paper. Then I think of my sister, collecting her Dresser phone numbers, counting the clothes in her closet. Suddenly my stomach doesn't feel so good. I toss the cookie dough down, and sit up.

There's only one surefire way to get Walter off my tail. While he's in the kitchen, I make a break for it, and put the first demo CD I can find—from some Minnesota cousins who look like they worship the Allman Brothers—into the stereo system. Walter appears with a mug of tea, looking completely disappointed in the direction his afternoon is taking. I feel bad for a minute, then remind myself that I'm too old to be playing tea party with my boss.

After a few minutes of listening to the screeching sounds of these wannabe rock stars, Walter takes the cookie dough log and waddles off into the kitchen.

Feeling a little guilty for chasing Walter off, I make my way to the typing desk. I'm noticing that my stomach is still feeling a bit nauseous, and I wonder if this has to do with the cookie dough or if some meat particles made it from Helen's bacon pan into my cereal bowl. I dismiss this notion with a strong sip of tea, boot up my computer, pull over the latest copy of *Disc,* and start thumbing through it.

After about an hour of listening to music and compiling a list of possible story ideas to pitch to Dick Scott, the editor-in-chief at *Disc,* my stomachache starts getting to me. The pain is spreading into a vast, dull ache—the kind of ache that could just as easily come from falling asleep in the wrong position, like if you could situate your body in a way that your lungs were crushed for eight hours. I curse my aversion to bacon, and pack my gear to head for home.

As I'm picking and choosing which CDs to bring with me, the phone rings and Walter comes tottering in with his cordless.

"Hello?" I say into the receiver while Walter leans against the desk, preferring to do his eavesdropping right out in the open.

"You go home now?" I take the phone from my ear and stare at it before answering. Helen's psychic awareness of my day freaks me out.

"Um, yeah. I'm just packing up. Do you guys need anything before I go? Is Dad okay?"

"Jamie's fine. I go with you."

"Go with me?"

"Come pick me up. I go with you—be your backup, eh?"

I zip up my bag and hoist it over my shoulder. "Helen, that's really nice of you, but I'm okay."

"Stiff upper lips are no good."

"Helen, really, I'm okay— I'll call Thalia if I need help, okay?"

She *tsk-tsks* as I get off the phone, but I'm not in the clear yet. As I hand the phone to Walter, he says, "I'll get my coat."

He's off to the hall closet before I can protest.

"No, Walter—"

"It's okay. You don't need to be tough. Helen's not your mother, I understand, but *I* can be there for you."

"You're not my mother, either."

Walter cocks his head and smiles a grim little grin. "Echo, I want to help you."

I hug him and he wraps those flabby arms around my middle and squeezes. "You're really sweet, Walter, but this is something I have to do on my own."

He completely buys my faked bravado, and backs off only once I agree to take a tin of comfort cookies with me. Also, he makes me promise to call him as soon as I feel like crying.

Helen and Walter must have slipped something into my subconscious, because as I'm walking down the street to the subway, I start to feel odd and like I should've taken one of them up on their offers to accompany me into the city. It's more than a stomachache. My body feels achy, and weighted down, and my head's a bit fuzzy. I walk into a biker, get tangled in a dog leash, and trip over an empty Snapple bottle before putting it together that I probably just need some coffee.

Fortunately, there's a Starbucks perfectly situated between my subway stop and the *BAT.* I probably make about three visits here a day—I'm a whore for Starbucks coffee, though I know how *un*-rock and roll that is. But who can resist the Starbucks service? They know me, they know what I like. The minute I walk through their door, they scramble to make my drink. I can't help but enjoy that.

"Echo! Your Saturday visit! Just a coffee today?" The perky manager, a guy I'm betting is gay, and who Alicia and I have actually contemplated introducing to Walter, smiles at me like I'm his best friend. This hospitality alone makes me feel better, more awake. But while he makes my coffee, the sound of the opening bars of "On Top of the World," Matt's one and only Top 40 hit, filters through the radio.

My stomach gurgles, and a wave of nausea cascades through my middle. I can barely muster the energy to smile back at Randy when he hands me my giant paper cup. Even the whipped cream doesn't cheer me, doesn't help me to forget what that song symbolizes: Matt's only achievement in life, the last set of lyrics he ever wrote.

This trip only succeeded in making me feel worse, and at the end of the block I toss the coffee into a trash can, the muddy mess of brown liquid and whipped cream trickling after me as I walk down into the subway station.

The New York subway system is a very bad place to be when you don't feel good. There's very little air down there, and even though it's Saturday, the car is packed with people and I'm forced to stand the whole trip into Manhattan. The stopping-and-starting motion does nothing to settle my stomach, and watching the stations tick by like a minute hand, seeing people milling around on the platform reminds me of Matt strumming his guitar down in the T all those years ago. My stomachache shifts; something heavy presses down on my chest, something electric and furry and hard to carry around. Like the feeling you get when you've just sprinted around the block in thirty-degree weather.

So I switch trains and head for Alicia's stop on 14th Street. See, I've got this vague notion that my stomachache is all in my head. And if the mere sound of one of Matt's songs can make me feel so awful, imagine what it's going to do to me to walk into my red, yellow and blue-ceilinged apartment. I won't last the hour. I'll dissolve into a puddle of regret. I'll rip up my list of story ideas and chuck it in the garbage. I'll throw all my issues of *Disc* and *Rolling Stone* out the window. There's only one course of action here.

Alicia's palatial Chelsea apartment happens to be across the street from a Home Depot. When I go in, I walk past the rows of colored paint swatches, past the yellows and greens and reds and pinks and oranges that would catch the eye of a certain musician I know. I stop in front of a shelf full of white: pearl, off-white, lace, eggshell. After carefully mulling over which shade of white is the most mature, I select a warm, shiny, slightly yellowish color called Antique Lampshade.

Four bought gallons later, I trudge across the street and say hello to the doorman in the lobby of Alicia's building. He lets me up to her apartment without even calling her first. I visit a lot.

Alicia's apartment is a thing of beauty, a professionally decorated marvel that could easily grace the pages of *inStyle* or *Better Homes and Gardens*. The kitchen (yes, a real kitchen!) is outfitted in hanging copper pots and an assortment of gadgets neither of us know how to use. The living room is full of furniture handcrafted by some genius who works out of a yurt in the mountains of Washington State. The bedrooms (more than one!) are each a shabby chic photo op. The kicker, though, is that the living room Alicia lives in is always kind of a mess, chockfull of clutter: magazines, CDs, books, DVDs and more computers than at the *BAT* (one desktop and one laptop).

But no matter how polished her living situation, Alicia always looks like a high-class punk rock kid living in her grandparents' place. When she opens the door, she's wearing men's boxers that her nonexistent hips can barely hold up, and a ripped white T-shirt that's held together by a baby's pink diaper pin. Her pigtails are uneven, lopsided, and falling out of their holders. But somehow she still looks adorable, her skin glowing, her blue eyes clear as a sky on a spring day.

I hold up a can of paint and beam a huge smile at her. "What are you doing this afternoon?" Then I waggle my eyebrows.

A look of confusion makes its way to the middle of Alicia's cute, heart-shaped face. "What's going on?"

I push past her and drop all the cans just inside her door. Their combined weight makes the floor shake.

"A project! Do you have any plain white sheets? I forgot to get a drop cloth."

"What's going on out here?" I turn around to see Jason, the computer tech guy from the *BAT,* standing in the doorway that separates the living room from this art-covered entryway. I whip around to face Alicia. She doesn't meet my eyes. First she fiddles with the doorknob, then bends down to inspect the cans of paint.

I look back at Jason, who waves at me.

"What's with the white?" Alicia asks nonchalantly, as if I haven't just caught her red-handed. I try to catch her eye, but she pretends to be absorbed in the paint can label.

See, Alicia knows that I disapprove of her relationship with Jason. And here's the thing: I would wholeheartedly *approve* of a relationship between them, if Alicia could just admit that she *likes* him, and treat him a little better.

Poor Jason. He's a sweet, puppy-dog type who I'm betting has been in "true love" at least three times in his life. His bedraggled, tattooed, skinny-as-Iggy-Popp exterior does little to disguise the fact that this guy is a drippy bundle of loyal affections, and Alicia's the unhappy recipient of most of them. He does whatever she wants: shows up at three in the morning when she's lonely (which is what I'm betting happened last night), stands in as her date at family functions, answers her phone when she's screening calls. But she barely gives him a second thought most of the time, and I don't understand why. He's really cute, with spiky, dirty-blond hair, and a really attractive wardrobe—he's partial to this kind of navy, velour track suit that wouldn't work on paper but in real life—wow!

In short, they're an adorable-looking couple. But for whatever reason, she just can't commit to him. And she continues to take advantage of his feelings for her, even though she doesn't realize that she's doing it. All she knows is that I get annoyed when I catch scenes like this.

But, considering that I'm in the middle of a major transition point in my life, now is hardly the time to pick a fight with my best friend. I'd be out a support system in only two days. Not a good track record.

"Um—" I stutter "—w-well, did you get my messages?"

Alicia stands up. "No, what's up?"

Jason walks toward us and puts his hand on my arm. "Is everything okay?"

Standing there, in the middle of a *very* dysfunctional relationship, I blurt, "I broke up with Matt."

Both Jason and Alicia freeze.

Then, after just a moment, the two of them start speaking all at once.

"Shut up!" Alicia shouts.

"Oh, honey!" Jason gasps and starts rubbing a hole in my back.

"Jason, leave her alone!"

He drops his hand from my back immediately, and Alicia replaces his hand with her own. "Come on then," she says, pushing me into the gray-and-silver decorated living room toward the monstrosity of a couch that sits in front of a window looking out over the Meatpacking District.

I sit, uncomfortably, with the two of them on either side of me. Despite myself, I start sinking into the cushions. Before I know it, my hips have been gobbled and sucked away into folds of the softest material you've ever felt. It's so soft and shiny, that I can't get the traction to pull myself out. I'm going to die this way—a meal for a $5000 couch.

Alicia senses my disappearing act. She yanks me loose, while dialing her cell phone with her free hand. "I can't believe I missed this! What time did you call?" She presses her phone to her ear.

"You don't have to listen to those. I'll just tell you now."

Comprehension cracks open on her face as she listens to my messages. "You broke up with him!" She collapses the phone and throws it to the ground. Pulling up the waistband of her boxer shorts, she snaps at Jason, "You made me miss her calls!"

I open my mouth to protest, but Jason's way too used to apologizing. He beats me to speaking. "I'm sorry, Lic, and I'm sorry to you, too, Echo." Then he pats my shoulder, gets up and says, "Don't start yet. I want to hear everything." He disappears for thirty seconds only to return with three spoons and a tub of Cherry Garcia Ben & Jerry's ice cream.

"Where'd I get that?" Alicia questions, while I take the spoon Jason offers me.

"I brought it last night, remember?"

Alicia looks at Jason like she has no clue what he's talking about, but digs in anyway.

"I have cookies in my bag!" I say through a mouthful of ice cream.

Jason leaves again and returns with my bag. I pull out Walter's cookies and then the three of us abandon our real utensils in favor of cookie spoons.

"This is good. This is good!" I swallow a bite of cherry-slathered cookie. "You're supposed to eat ice cream when you break up. Everyone knows that. Then we'll go and paint my apartment, and I'll be completely ready to move on. This is much easier than I thought it was going to be."

"*We'll* go?" Alicia holds her cookieful of ice cream in midair.

"Oh. Yeah. I need you to come home with me." I look at Jason. "You, too. We'll paint faster with three of us."

That's all Jason needs to hear. He's up and putting on his Pumas faster than you can say, "Supportive boyfriend."

I wrap up the remaining cookies, and pack them in my bag. Alicia leans back on the couch, though, skeptical. "What happened? Why don't we start there and then see if we need to go paint your whole apartment?"

I stand up and sling my bag over my shoulder. "Put some pants on. I'll spill the whole story on the way over."

During the walk to my apartment, Jason does a very nice impression of a frisky puppy. It's making me antsy, because his frenetic pace is putting Alicia on edge. Get him in a room alone, he's cool as an ice cube. But when Alicia's near, he always overplays his hand and now's no different. He's hovering over me like a soup-bearing grandma. He slings his arm around my shoulder and Alicia rolls her eyes at him the whole time and keeps stopping at the sidewalk tables, the ones selling jewelry and fake pashmina scarves and $2 shoes. The comforting thing about Alicia is that in times of stress, shopping remains her constant. Matt and I had been together as long as she's known me, and yet she's still able to keep her mind clear enough to judge the value of home-made necklaces and knockoff bags.

By the time we've wandered east to 6th Street and 1st Avenue and are standing in front of my door, Alicia's too worried about me to be cold to Jason. She holds my hand and steps into me. Jason does the same.

I have a vague sense of how dramatic they're being, clutching my hands tightly, breathing audibly as we stare at my yellow door. But as I take in the blue swirly effects Matt painted on it in the throes of procrastination a few years ago, the strong steely feeling I had last night when I told him I wanted him to move out returns. All I can think of is how psyched I'm going to be to paint over this, and what a relief it'll be to not have to worry about the super telling my landlord about my zany door.

But I'm so caught up in this fantasy of the landlord coming over and complimenting me for how nice I keep my apartment, that I lose track of how long we stand out in the hall. Alicia breaks me from my spell. "Are we going in?"

I hand her my "be fri for" key chain. "You go first. Prepare me for the mess."

She does as she's told, raising her eyebrows just before turning the knob, pushing the door inward, and stepping into my apartment. Jason blows some air out of his mouth and pats the top of my hand.

I stare at the blue swirls and await the verdict. "Well?" I scream like a child when Alicia doesn't return right away.

Finally she pokes her pig-tailed head out. "It's clear. The apartment is clear of the evil boyfriend spirits."

I let out my breath, and release Jason's hand, and slowly push open the door. I stand at the threshold. Jason is right on my heels.

I realize that I half expected to find Matt still here, strumming his guitar. Surrounded by his slacky, arty filth. And stacks of hastily labeled boxes.

But he's not.

Over Alicia's shoulder, my apartment appears free of boxes, free of piles of sheet music, free of used paper plates and empty pizza boxes.

"What do we do now?" Jason whispers, like a blundering uncle.

I can't answer. Alicia turns her head to follow my line of vision. I push past her and walk to the middle of my living room, where I stand stone still and look around me.

The walls—yesterday covered in varying shades of pink stripes—are *white*. The wood floor is covered in a veneer of shiny polish. The decorative pillows I bought at Target a year ago are fluffed and situated decoratively atop my sofa. The books I never read are neatly stacked in the credenza according to height.

I take a deep, shaky breath, raise my head and peer at the ceiling.

It's white.

He painted over the circles.

I take another breath and notice the absence of paint fumes, the presence of lemony freshness.

Alicia and Jason are frozen in place, staring at me expectantly, waiting for my cue on how they should behave here.

I walk to the window, calmly, and close it.

"Jase—" My voice emerges like an unearthly chime. "Please check the bedroom. Tell me what you see."

He tentatively walks toward my bedroom, pats at the door causing it to swing open, and walks slowly through.

Alicia finally speaks. "Do you have any beer? I think you need a beer."

"Alicia, don't do that," Jason calls from inside my bedroom, before sticking his face back through the doorway.

"What?"

"Don't try to make this a party! Look at her! She's not moving! She's devastated!"

It's this comment that shakes me from my stasis. "Wait! This isn't right." I run to the open front door, push it half-closed so that I can see the outer side. There it is: the three-inch high metallic 4F, confirming that this is indeed my apartment.

But I haven't seen it look like this in years. No. Never. I have *never* seen my apartment look like this. Not only has Matt packed up and moved out all of his stuff, but the place sparkles. That son of a bitch *cleaned*.

"That bastard!" I wail before dashing into the bedroom.

Painted. The gauzy white clouds and blue sky I've been sleeping under for two years have been painted white. Also gone are the posters of Van Halen and Metallica and the Beastie Boys and Burt Bacharach that have lived here for so long. And the bed! It's a brass four-poster my father brought back for me when he taught a summer at Duke University. Normally, it is covered in piles of mussed sheets and dirty, stained underwear and guitar picks and a copy of Bob Dylan's biography. But atop this (made) bed are stacks of crisp folded shirts and creased pants, laundered and pressed and waiting for me. I drop onto the bed, stare at the ground, and try to steady my breathing. But it isn't working. The deeper I breathe, the more pissed off I seem to get.

The whistle of a sailor precedes Alicia into the room. She swigs a bottle of beer.

"Alicia?"

"Yeah?"

"Would you or would you not say that this floor has been mopped recently?"

"It smells nice in here, that's true."

"I'm gonna kill him!" I catapult myself up and almost knock Jason over as I boomerang into the kitchen.

The kitchen's as clean as the rest of the apartment. I can freakin' see my reflection in the damned toaster. When Alicia approaches, I grab the bottle of beer she's holding and chug the whole thing down.

"I'm not getting the problem here."

"I'm good, I'm good."

"You're *not* good." She points at me. "You're freaking."

What I do next is perform the clean test Helen taught me. I fling open cupboards, checking the plates and cups and cutlery. They're all spotlessly washed and in their proper places. The Brita's been filled. Clean dish towels hang from the handle of the oven. My mail waits patiently for me on the counter. When I run my finger along the edges of the television in the living room and hold it up, expecting the thick layer of dust that has veiled our shelves for days now, I find nothing. Just my spanking-clean, dustless finger.

And then, standing in the middle of my sanitary apartment, I start to cry.

6

The next morning, when I drift into wakeful consciousness, I have the vague notion that I'm in a strange bed, and that time has stopped. My throat feels constricted and thick. I open my eyes quickly and shut them faster, the sight of blank white walls confusing and tricking me into thinking that maybe I'm in a hotel. Maybe I'm on tour with Matt.

Finally I open my eyes for good and stare at the walls. I'm in *my* room, spread eagle in *my* queen-sized bed. Alone. All the memories of the previous day and night come flooding back. I pull the covers over my head, then, and swallow three times, trying to open my throat. My eyes feel puffy, too, and my head throbs.

This is what a nighttime full of crying gets you.

Alicia. Alicia and Jason stayed at my place until 3:00 a.m., and thinking of how I blubbered on both their shoulders makes me yank the covers tighter round my head. I vaguely remember drinking a bottle of wine, and making Jason check my fire escape, to make sure that it could support Matt's weight should he be moved to climb up there and win me back with an apologetic serenade. I remember going on a rant, calling Matt a freeloading jackass who wouldn't survive two days without me. I remember cursing the shade of white Matt used to paint the ceiling, cursing out the haphazard Windex streaks he left in the mirrors and windows and toaster.

I pull the sheet flat across my face, making it difficult to breathe, and press myself into the mattress, willing away the shame. Wondering what kind of a show I would've put on if *he* had broken up with *me*.

I stay there until the phone rings. After sighing once, deeply, I scramble Scooby-Doo-like over to the side table and grab the cordless.

"Hello?" I croak out, sounding like I'm a sixty-five-year-old, chain-smoking truck driver. My head hits the pillow. The impact rattles around the inside of my brain while I stare at the ceiling. Holding the receiver to my ear is monumentally difficult.

"Hey, I'm calling to check in," Alicia says, calmly. "You okay?"

"Yeah. Yeah, I'm better. Thanks."

"You don't sound better. Did you just wake up?"

I look over to the clock and am shocked to see that it's 12:04 p.m. "No, I've been up for a while."

"You're lying."

I sigh and rub my eyes. "Yeah. I'm lying. I just woke up."

Alicia laughs, and then says gently into the phone, "It's okay for you to sleep in once in a lifetime."

I sit up and pull my knees up to my chest. "Maybe I'm coming down with something."

"You're just sad. It's okay to be sad."

"Nah. I'm not sad. I broke up with him. I'm fine. I just must be getting sick or something. I didn't feel well yesterday, either."

"Okay, Echo. Do you want me to come over?"

I do. My instinct is to say, "Yes, bring pancakes and sad movies. Bring Helen and Walter and two tubs of ice cream." But I realize how silly and self-indulgent this is, when I've actually gotten everything I wanted: Matt out of my apartment so that I can concentrate on my career. So I lie again and tell her that I'm doing fine and don't need any company. Alicia knows enough to let me get away with this, and hangs up after I promise to call if I change my mind.

I lie there for a few more minutes before forcing myself to look at the clock. "Get up!" I scold out loud, then launch myself from the bed.

It's cold in here. And quiet. I pad into the living room, which looks like the inside of a psychiatric hospital. It's just so *plain*—Antique Lampshade wouldn't have been nearly this creepy—and the smell of the paint hasn't entirely dissipated yet. But I refuse to give in to whatever it is that's making me want to crawl back into bed. I turn on the television, disappointed to see that I've missed the morning news programs. At twelve on a Sunday, all that's on are preachers and cartoons and sports shows. So I turn on VH1, which has on some kind of a "One-Hit Wonders" retrospective, and go put on a pot of coffee.

While I'm in the kitchen, I walk around in circles, looking for something to do with my hands. I search the cupboards for a cereal I feel like eating, and run my thumb over three boxes of fiber-filled, whole-wheat choices before slamming the door in frustration. Of course, the day after

Matt leaves is the day I get a craving for Froot Loops. I sigh, lean against the sink, stare at my reflection in the shiny toaster, watch the coffeemaker drip its contents into the pot. I made eight cups. Enough for two people.

Once the coffee's done, I grab the last three issues of *Disc* from the kitchen table, and haul my load out to the sofa, telling myself how great it's going to be to spend a Sunday morning in a clean apartment, watching what I want on the television without having to crank the volume high enough to out-drone the sound of songs being written on a twelve-string guitar. I snuggle into my couch, raise the volume on the segment about Lita Ford, and rock my head along to the chorus of "Kiss Me Deadly" while stuffing my face full of soggy whole-wheat flakes.

Maybe it's the fact that I'm imbibing twice my normal amount of coffee, but once they've run through "Groove is in the Heart," "Funkytown," and "Just a Friend" by Biz Markie, I'm starting to feel pretty pleased with my afternoon. I've got some good tunes on the tube and issues of my favorite mag here to inspire my responsible, creative self. What more do I need?

I look around my home for an answer. And then focus again on the issue of *Disc* with Jack White on the cover, to avoid the rolling emptiness of my still apartment.

Well, at least I know I'll never, ever break up with *Disc*. Man, does this magazine make me happy. The ink doesn't rub off on your fingers when you riffle through the pages, the photos are colorful, and there aren't spelling errors in the articles. True, half the bands they cover in the "New Tunes about Town" section are ones Jason and I and Matt discovered over a year ago, but what can you do? That's why *Disc* needs me. I turn up the volume on the Dexy's Midnight

Runners video and grab for a notepad. I jot down ten or twelve bands that I can pitch for this section, and then get so excited by my output that I end up on the couch, jumping around shouting, "Come on, Eileen."

But as I'm midair in a split, Dexy's Midnight Runners fade out and in fades Matt Hanley. The opening chords to "On Top of the World" pounce at me. I miss my landing, and topple down so that half my body's on the couch and the other half is on the floor. My leg is seized in an ache, and I assume a bruise the size of Atlanta is taking up residence there.

"You should shut this off."

"Ahh!" I shout, terrified at the sound of a human voice in my apartment. I peer up over the sofa to see my sister, gorgeous in a peasant skirt and top, standing in my doorway, hands holding four candles. "You scared me!" I pull myself up and watch her march over to where I am, grab the remote and shut off the television.

"You shouldn't be watching this." She arranges the candles in a line, and pushes my *Disc* copies into a neat, folded pile. Then she carries my coffee to the kitchen.

"I was drinking that."

"Get dressed!" she barks. "We've got somewhere to be."

Per my sister's instructions, I am sitting in a manicurist's chair in a Korean spa down on the East Side of Manhattan, on a street that straddles the border between Nolita, a neighborhood where models frolic and pay out the nose for coffee and clothes, and Chinatown, where, for five dollars, you could conceivably walk away with two pairs of designer knockoff jeans, four pairs of Chinese slippers, and thirty pounds of fish.

Currently, my hands are being kneaded into relaxed madness by a friendly, round-faced lady whose name tag reads Grace. In between watching her press my wrist back and forth, I peer over my shoulder to Thalia, who has been sitting in the waiting area for as long as I've been getting this $4 manicure. I raise my eyebrows at her in frustration for what must be the twelfth time. And for the twelfth time, she ignores me and continues to read her magazine, not bothering, again, to tell me what I'm doing here.

I exhale and smile at Grace, who nods, drops my left hand, and expectantly peers at me for about ten seconds before I start madly brushing at my face, trying to get off whatever bit of food she's staring at. She guffaws, and looks toward Thalia, who screams loud enough for all ten people in the shop to hear, "It's time to pay her!"

I sneer at Thalia the way only a little sister can, and reach for my purse, still trying to figure out why I let her talk me into this. I don't like getting manicures, which, incidentally, is Thalia's fault. When I was ten, she thought it would be cute if we had matching fingernail polish, but of course, my sister always thought big, even as a tween. She went to the hardware store on the corner of Union and Smith in Brooklyn, bought a can of forest-green spray paint, and spray-painted my hands. The color didn't wash off for weeks, earning me the charming fifth-grade nickname, Fungus Fingers.

But as I watch Grace coat my nails with "ballet slipper" pink, the lightest shade I could find, I think about how grown-up my fingers look. They look like my mother's hands, except pretty and polished. I imagine Christiane Amanpour's hands looking similarly fancy, and smile at Grace to let her know how pleased I am with the results. She responds by standing up and gesturing for me to follow her into a back room.

I catch Thalia's eye as I go. She gives me a thumbs-up sign.

Grace leads me into a mint-green room, and sits me in front of a bank of nail-drying stations. She puts my hands inside what looks like a nuclear Easy-Bake oven, presses a button and walks out.

"Wait!" I call. "Can I get a magazine or something?" It's too late. She's long gone.

I twist around in my seat, hoping to catch someone's eye, but nobody else is in here. I just have to wait it out, something I've never been good at. Ants in my pants, baby. That's what I've got, sitting back here, without even a radio to keep my mind occupied. Soon enough I'm humming aloud— "Just a Friend" still—and reading the wall. It's covered in printed-out pictures of cartoon girls spouting platitudes like, "Be kind," "Love is the best-saved thing for a rainy day," and "The early bird gets the worm."

I hang my head until my forehead is nearly zapped by the ultraviolet rays of the nail-nuker.

"It's too quiet in here," I moan into the oven, not caring that I'm probably going to get brain cancer. Or a third eye.

"You can say that again."

With my head down on the microwave as it is, I hadn't realized that anyone had sat down next to me. I jerk my head up to see who has witnessed my shame, and nearly swallow my gum. Actually, scratch that. You can't swallow your gum if your mouth is so wide open that the gum falls *out* of it. Which is what it does.

Right in front of Jack Mantis.

"Oh, my God!" I reach to pick up the offending piece of Bubble Yum from the ground.

"I wouldn't—"

But Jack's too late. My zeal to rescue my gum has resulted in three smudged nails. Ballet Slipper is smeared all over the tips of my fingers.

"I don't believe this."

"You shouldn't remove your hands from the beds until the polish is dry."

"Um, yes, I see that." I look at Jack, Jack Mantis, the main attraction of my career aspirations. His hair is pinned up in a bun—black bobby pins stand out in stark contrast to the near-translucent white shade of his hair—and he's wearing a baseball type T-shirt, the kind with the bright blue three-quarter length sleeves. He's kind of got an Axl Rose thing going on. "November Rain" Axl. Not "Welcome to the Jungle" Axl.

"Let me get Grace in here. She'll fix it." Jack calls out only to be answered by three bustling, pink-jacketed ladies. "This lady's nails need fixing."

Grace looks at me, unmistakably grits her teeth in frustration at my klutziness, and rushes out of the room, only to return to my side with an open bottle of Ballet Slipper at the ready. She fixes me up in no time, and hustles back out of the drying area, but not before issuing a stern, "Don't move your hands!"

Jack and I sit in silence for a few moments. As near as I can tell from my peripheral glances, he's staring at the mint-green wall.

"The early bird gets the worm," I try.

He doesn't say anything.

But of course, I can't shut up, because I'm a Grade A dork. "The early bird gets the worm, I said."

He jumps at the sound of my voice.

"I'm sorry. I didn't mean to startle you."

He merely cocks his head and purses his lips and raises his eyes in a gesture that I decide to interpret, "Please continue."

"How'd the show go the other night?"

No answer.

"Listen, I'm really sorry about what happened. Me and Alex are just both so into yo—"

Jack exhales dramatically and turns his head from me, as if he's ashamed. "Why can't you guys leave me alone? I can only give so many pounds of flesh to the media. Soon I'll disappear into nothingness."

Hmm. A flair for the dramatic. He could be my sibling. "Jack, I'm so sorry you have to go through this."

"Nobody understands."

I chew my lip. "Maybe what you need is a chance to let out all that you're feeling."

Jack merely raises a perfectly arched brow at me. I swear, if I wasn't fighting for my life here, I'd be rendered speechless at what a beautiful specimen he is. He looks how I imagine the love child of David Bowie and Princess Diana would, if that love child were raised in complete darkness and fed only vegetable juice his or her whole life.

"You were saying?"

"Oh, right." I shake the thought of David Bowie and Princess Diana having sex out of my head. I'm losing my mind. "I was saying, that I understand that feeling, that feeling of being torn in two."

"And you are?"

I can't believe this. This guy is genetically engineered to never remember me. "Jack. I'm *Echo*. Echo Brennan. I met you the other night, remember? I showed you all the articles I'd written on you?"

His face is a vanilla confection of nothingness.

"At the Edge Club? Remember?"

"Echo. That's a musical name."

I exhale in utter frustration. "Yes, yes, it is."

"You covered us in Boston?"

"Yes! Yes! I did!" Now we're getting somewhere.

But just when he looks at me and says, "Huh," the buzzer on his drying contraption dings and he pulls out his perfectly baked, bright orange fingers.

I check the timer on my own microwave, disappointed to see that I have another five minutes to go. I'm weighing whether it's worth having Grace cut off my hands (which is surely what she'll do if I pull my fingers out too soon) in order to catch Jack as he walks out the door. But he evidently sees what I'm doing and makes a "tsk, tsk, tsk" sound. "I wouldn't do that."

As soon as I'm out of his line of sight, I yank my fingers from the drying beds, and check them quickly for dryness. Then I whisk my bag from the floor and trip over the chair on my way through the doorway.

Turns out I didn't need to rush. Because Jack Mantis hasn't left the building. Oh, no. He's lingering by the front door, practically coiled around my sister.

"What the—"

"Echo!" Thalia hollers brightly and sharply, and I do my best to paste a nonchalant look on my face. But this scene looks a bit cozy, and come to think of it, how the hell did she know to bring me here anyway? "Come here," she commands.

I don't move. And, apparently, my mere presence is all it takes to break Thalia's spell over Jack. He looks from me to my sister to me again, shakes his head, and walks out of the manicurist's. The clattering sound of the bell hanging from the top of the door snaps me from my immobility, and I rush Thalia.

"What—how did you—"

She lurches up before I can finish my sentence, shouts, "We've got to move!!" tugs me out of the shop by the hand and then propels me down the street.

"Ouch! Let go!" I shrug and try to pull my arm out of her death grip. She pays me no mind.

"Keep up! I don't want to lose him!" She's weaving and bobbing through the crowd like a boxer. We pass fish stands after purse stalls after sticky-bun-eating families, and only stop when a double-decker tour bus nearly flattens us on the corner of Hester Street.

"You're hurting me!" I yell at her. "Let go of my arm!"

She ignores me. "Do you see him?" We both look out across East Broadway. Thank God for Jack's towering iridescence. It's no harder to spot him in the throngs of Chinatown than it would be to find an alien in a crowd of cats.

"There he goes!" I point with my available hand.

The light turns green and Thalia once again jerks my arm, pulling me in her wake, like a water-skier who's got no choice but to brave the choppy wake of an out-of-control speedboat. We cross another street and I finally catch up—mentally, I mean. I start walking faster and faster, the wind whipping through my hair, my fingers spread out in front of me so that I don't smudge Grace's handiwork. I only stop when I accidentally trip over a single sneaker lying in the middle of the walkway.

"Echo! Watch where you step! You'll break your neck!" Thalia speaks in one of those stage whispers that is as loud as regular talking.

At this I stop in my tracks, but thankfully, Thalia won't have any of my childish tantrums. She pushes onward and gestures for me to follow. "This way. Move at my pace. We don't want him thinking we're on his tail."

I grit my teeth and keep just behind Thalia as we come to the entryway of what is supposed to be a park, but in reality is a plot of land covered over in cement, with a rickety set of swings, a rusty merry-go-round upon which two senior citizens are being spun by a young kid, and a gaggle of those springy animal rides. We stop here and peer out across Canal Street. Jack's nowhere to be found.

"Where to?"

"There!" she shouts, like she just discovered gold.

We take off across the street, and Thalia continues to lead me through Chinatown as if she were a local. She's dragging me all over, through side streets, across alleys, through intersections, until finally we find ourselves standing in front of what must be one of the best-kept secrets in the city of New York.

It's a club, but the façade is covered in black glass, so that you can't see in. A burly man who looks like he could bench-press me and Thalia at the same time stands at the ready, looking thrilled to be able to turn girls like us away. It never ceases to amaze me how bouncers in New York City are in such great shape. Somebody should let them know that there are other vocations awaiting them. Professional wrestling. Olympic weightlifting.

Thalia leads me down the block a ways so that The Rock can't overhear us. "Fortune. This has to be it." She wipes her brow with the back of her hand, and cups her curls. "Am I buoyant?"

"Oh, you're buoyant, all right." I look at the façade of

Fortune, and immediately feel my courage dissipating in the wind. "So what do we do? Go in?"

Thalia looks to the sky and says a prayer out loud. "You're seriously adopted. Yes. In. You. Vamoose."

The two of us take about three steps toward Fortune when I reach out and stop her. "Wait. How do I look?"

She checks me out. "You'd look great if we were going grocery shopping." I check myself out. She's right. My dark green Bauhaus T-shirt and brown corduroys are fabulous manicure clothes, but I am sure they'll stand out at Fortune.

"Just give me something to fix it," I bark. Thalia proceeds to pull out a tube of lipstick and we fight over it for five seconds before I throw my hands up and allow her to affix it to my lips.

"You're such a control freak," I say as I blot on the Kleenex she offers.

"It's too bad about your hair. You'd have more luck with men if you had mine." I bat Thalia's hands away from my head and punch her in the arm for good measure.

We step toward the Rock. He looks us up and down and this way and that, and narrows his eyes at Thalia.

"I don't know. Who are you?"

While Thalia starts a ridiculously flirtatious conversation and wholly preposterous story about me being her second cousin twice-removed who's in from Iowa and wants to see a real New York City club, I consider how much of my happiness is held within the grasp of Manhattan bouncers. They wield infinite power, keeping me from rock stars and comfy, low-lit meeting grounds. If I were more like Thalia, this man would be no problem, as is being demonstrated right now. She's reading his palm, and coquettishly smiling, and then says to me, "Go on in, Echo. I'm just going to hang out here. Help solve Theo here's girl problem."

Theo blushes to his roots, and pulls open the door.

And I walk into a cavernous room. The ceilings are so low I could probably touch them without even straightening my arms. The walls are slate gray and glass brick, and brass candelabras support hundreds of lit candles. A brass railing runs the length of the room; I imagine it's to help you walk in the darkness. My eyes aren't adjusting quickly enough. I continue to stand here, conscious of my flat head of hair, my neon purple lips, my womanly hips covered in brown corduroy. It's probably a good thing that nobody will be able to make out my outfit.

Just then a black-shrouded wraith brushes past me, a girl so thin you could break her in two just by breathing. Her ponytail swats me in the face as she rushes by, and when she opens the door, a bit of light slips in and illuminates the room long enough for me to spot Jack. He's sitting with his back to me, his orange-tinted nails visible as they wrap around a small glass full of whiskey.

I pull the T-shirt down around my hips, remind myself that second chances are easily blown, like bubbles or breaths, and walk toward him, moving through the air like a stealthy huntress. This place pulses with energy, the sounds of clinking ice cubes, whispered conversations, techno beats.

I single-handedly disrupt the vibe by crashing into something. A strangled caterwaul cracks the atmosphere in two: "Yeee-ouch!" I am instantly drenched in something wet. Or somethings wet. I've collided with a tray full of drinks. Lemons and swizzle straws and ice cubes adorn my Bauhaus T-shirt and I am again glad that I cannot see, because the weight of the glare of the woman I collided into is enough to make me want to run away.

"Clod! Watch where you're going!" she screeches, her voice thick with an eastern-European accent and hatred.

"Um, sorry," I mumble, furiously brushing the debris off my shirt. The girl huffs another judgmental huff, spins on her heel and leaves me there, wet, embarrassed, persecuted by all the club-goers who didn't want to be interrupted by a fool in a concert T-shirt.

Someone, thankfully, thrusts a towel under my nose. "Here."

It's the gravelly, whiskey-coated voice of my dreams.

I tilt my head up, and declare, "If I could see you, I'd kiss you."

Not my best line.

Then a firm hand grips onto my elbow, and before I can pick up the lemon slices and plastic straws, I'm being maneuvered toward the back. It's seriously dark in here. I trip over what I think is a bench and step on a few feet before Jack sits me down on a stool.

"So—" He moves three white candles in between us, and suddenly my environment is awash in a soft, heavenly glow. "Are you a deranged stalker?"

He stares at me with an expression of honest curiosity. And he asked the question with complete sincerity.

It's unnerving. I hadn't thought about how my cropping up everywhere he goes could be construed. "Well, yes, I guess I am."

It must be the light. But I swear, he does that quarter-lift smile again. It stays on his face even while he orders a round of drinks.

"Where's your friend?"

"Huh?" It takes me a minute to realize who he's referring to. "Oh, she's either outside talking to the bouncer, or long gone. I don't know." I can't get to that drink fast enough.

"Oh," he says dejectedly, and his voice sounds the way it does on the Flies hit, "Neverland Girl." I tamp down the urge to ask who he really wrote that song about, and watch as he deflates, pulled downward by gravity. It's the funniest thing, but he seems *tired* somehow.

I tap my newly prettified fingers against the top of the bar, suddenly distracted by an overwhelming sense of déjà vu. I swallow hard to return my focus to the matter at hand. "Jack, I'm sorry that I followed you."

"And tracked me to my nail appointment?"

"Yeah. That, too. I'm sorry."

He looks at me sadly, and I realize that this feeling of familiarity is coming from *him*. It's the something in his drawn mouth and crinkled eyes—the same kind of slightly depressed, resigned forlornness that Matt's been carrying around for so long. I feel my hopes and dreams crashing down into a pit of concern. And I recognize that I can go two ways here. I can either treat him like a human being or like a story.

"Your nails look nice though." I smile at him shyly, trying to buy time while deciding how best to handle this moment. "I like the orange."

Jack spreads his hands out in front of him and contemplates them. "My therapist says that I should surround myself in happy colors." Then he passes both orange-fingered hands over his face, as if he's trying to wipe away his own shame.

I rap my fingers against the bar again, louder. *Therapist.* God, this interview would *rock.* I feel slightly sick at what I'm about do here, but I go for it anyway. "What else does your therapist say?"

Jack drops his chin to his chest, wiggles the ice around in his whiskey glass, and flashes one of his phantom grins at me. "I'm not telling."

"I'm just trying to help," I try.

"Um-hmm." He tilts the glass back and empties it. "That's what that other guy said."

"What other guy?"

"The round short guy. From the other night."

I bite the inside of my lip to keep myself from exclaiming in a great hoot of laughter at Jack's assessment of Alex Paxton. "Well, Jack, can you blame us? You're, well, you're the hottest rock star in America! Everybody wants to talk to you."

He looks at me for a beat, and continues to shrink into himself. The longer he looks at me like that, without even attempting to hide the sadness in his eyes, the more uncomfortable I feel. It's like sitting with a pale-enough-to-see-through, long-haired version of Matt. It's making it really hard to remember what I'm trying to accomplish here.

"I just didn't bargain for all this," Jack grumbles. "I can't even meet a pretty girl in a nail salon without her being bait for some reporter." Then he sighs, an up-and-down chromatic scale of dejectedness.

And that's it. The *sigh*. What is it with the loaded musical sigh? It's like my Kryptonite. It tickles my spine like fingers on a piano, and I know *exactly* what it means. Before I can help myself, before I can think of a way to manipulate this situation for my own benefit, before I can trick him into giving me at least a quick quote for the *BAT* (think of what the folks at *Disc* would do if I printed something from Jack this week!), before I can put my career first, I slide forward and clutch his arm, and say, "Jack, Jack, do you want to go out with Thalia? I can give you her number. She won't tell me a thing, I promise."

Jack's eyebrows knit themselves into one long, clear tapestry of confusion. "Really?"

"Really." Even as I'm answering him, I'm cursing myself out for being so vulnerable to sad musicians.

And I experience a full moment of "my sister's going to kill me" panic before suddenly realizing that, despite myself, I've just come up with the *greatest plan ever.*

This is what comes of breaking up with Matt! Now even my involuntary actions will be for my betterment. Because Thalia loves nothing more than meddling in other people's lives, and it seems like Jack could use some attention from someone who's not interested in his rock god status. This could only lead to him giving me a gratitude interview.

I slap the top of the bar in emphasis at my own genius and exclaim, "Oh, my God!"

Jack jumps and momentarily teeters on the back two legs of his stool.

"No—oh!" I grab for him, and yank him by the arms until his stool is flat on all four legs. "Sorry."

"You're kind of an accident waiting to happen."

"Oh, yeah. I know. Give me your phone," I command and Jack does as he's told. He thrusts his phone into my hands, and I nimbly enter both my number and Thalia's. "See?" I hold the screen up so that he can see it. "Thalia Brennan. This is her number. Now, I'm going to tell her to call you, but if she doesn't in, say, a day or two, you call her."

Jack's brow relaxes, but only a little. "You're sure?"

"Of course!" My voice is teeming with confidence, and I press the phone back into Jack's cold hands. "Seriously, Jack, you should be able to go out on a date with somebody who's only interested in *you,* not the rock star. And believe me, Thalia could care less about fame. It's a great match!"

He takes the phone in his hand, and looks at me, I assume

trying to size me up. And, again, I feel my desires at war. I swallow hard.

"Thanks," he says finally, standing up.

"You're welcome." I peer up into his aqua eyes, and think I see a spark there.

And as he's walking away, I grab his arm, and say, "Oh, remember to money-drop. Mention how much you make. It might not seem like a good idea, but, just trust me."

He squints.

"Oh, and wear a suit. Don't forget."

Before he goes, he brushes my arm. "Echo, this is—this is kind of you."

I feel awful, but remember that nobody makes it to the top without stepping on a *few* people. "Of course. I just want to help."

And he disappears into the darkness. I sit there for a minute, rubbing my thumb around the rim of the whiskey glass.

I'm fairly sure this will work. Thalia will whip him into shape, and everyone who's ever dated her has fallen head-over-heels in love with her. That'll make him happy, right?

Now the trick is getting her to go out with him. All I can picture is Jack's blond bobby-pinned hair and his baseball T-shirt. Actually, if I can convince her of Jack's worthiness as a life-coaching test subject, it shouldn't be too hard. Maybe I'll lump in his poor dressing skills with all the other things he needs her help with.

Yep. I'm on the right track. Thalia won't be able to refuse the chance to play God with somebody, and Jack will be so grateful to me for everything, he'll let me write his story for *Disc.* Then I'll quit the *BAT,* I'll date a Dresser or two of my own and *presto-chango,* my life will really begin.

The bartender interrupts my musings.

"It'll be twenty-one dollars," he says.

I look at the two empty glasses and curse my rotten luck. Jack's a millionaire rock star and he didn't think to pay the tab? God, if he does something like that with Thalia, she'll sell his life story to *Star* magazine without a second thought.

"Hold on, I'll get you right now," I say to the bartender while digging around in my purse. But when I pull my wallet from its depths, a moving pair of shadows in the corner catches my eye and stills me, midmotion.

"Ma'am?" The bartender prompts, but I don't pay him any attention.

A couple of things: one, it's dark. Two, it's highly unlikely that Matt, the man who two days ago would only leave our apartment after weathering serious onslaughts of emotional blackmail and, as of yesterday, is in need of a place to live and a job, would be sitting in one of the corner booths of Fortune, in the late afternoon, with that curly-haired hippie jewelry-maker from Annie's club.

So I blink. Shake my head. Squint a little.

And yet, I still seem to be seeing the same image.

"Hey." I turn on the bartender and scare the bejesus out of him, reaching across the bar and clutching his sleeve. "Are you a music fan?"

"Yeah."

"You know Matt Hanley?"

He nods. "Yeah! I like that song of his. 'On Top of the World.'"

"Yeah, that was a good one. Is that him?" I point to the specters giggling in the corner.

"Holy shit!" the bartender shouts. "I thought that guy was dead!"

Yesterday, I would have met a comment like that with a frosty reassurance that no, Matt Hanley was not dead. But it's no longer my job to defend him anymore, so I mutter, "No, it's his career that's dead."

But no parting shot, no matter how venomous, will make me feel better right now, because at that moment, my one-day-old ex-boyfriend stands up, and with his hand clearly (as clear as I can make it out in this dim light) on the small of the girl's back, makes his way out of the club. But not before catching my eye.

"Hey!" I shout, to the annoyance of all the other shadows occupying space in Fortune.

Matt stops for a moment. He looks pale and like he hasn't slept in thirty-six hours. He purses his mouth and spits out, "How's Jack?" Then he scrunches his face up in an angry contortion and stomps out of the club with the curly haired girl in tow.

7

I never used to be this dramatic.

But seeing that girl on Matt's arm has brought out all my worst qualities. Some I didn't know I had.

Like the proclivity for not showering, and wandering my apartment while randomly ranting at the walls.

I shock Walter (and myself) by calling in sick three days in a row. And then Walter shocks me by announcing a company-wide Matt Hanley ban. He's forbidden all the *BAT* employees from ever again mentioning Matt or the fact that we were a couple. Walter's really taking this breakup hard. We haven't had a company ban since the Aniston–Pitt debacle of '05.

I spend the days off padding around my stark apartment in a ratty pink bathrobe that previously saw time just after what has come to be known as the CB (that's college breakup). The CB marks the second half of my junior year, a time when I fell from my boyfriend/TA's graces, and he took up with a classmate that had a chest as big as her daddy's wallet. I was crushed. I spent January until May wearing this bathrobe, crying and listening to a soundtrack for the brokenhearted: Tracy Chapman, Indigo Girls, Joni Mitchell. For the MB (that's Matt breakup) my mix is more self-righteous anger, less crushed dreams: Bob Dylan's "Idiot Wind," "Rip Her to Shreds" by Blondie.

I try to go the sad movie route—I watch the first thirty minutes each of *Field of Dreams, Out of Africa* and *Ghost*. My aim here is to find something—anything—to help me shed some tears, in the hopes that crying again might lead to me feeling good enough to actually, oh, I don't know, write, go listen to a band or two. You know, do something that might be considered career-oriented. But nothing seems to shake me into productivity, or crying.

The closest I come to sadness is seeing the scene in *Say Anything,* when John Cusack holds the boombox over his head and blasts Peter Gabriel. Everyone knows this scene. Everyone loves this scene. Everyone wants to be Ione Skye just one time in their lives. But of course, I realize that I'll never be Ione Skye, because Matt Hanley, from now on, will be playing the role of John Cusack in some other girl's movie. From here on out all his serenades will probably go to the bead-bug girl. Not to mention that if he tried to blast music like that on our block, he'd be shot at.

Now I'm wading through a Liz Phair-athon, and the most energy I've expended all day was this morning, when I spent about an hour writing my name a hundred different times in a hundred different colors, imagining how "by Echo Brennan" would look underneath a photo of Jack Mantis. But now all the juice is gone. I'm now contorted so that my nose is smashed against my left knee. This position allows for maximum exposure to the musty odor of the sofa (it smells like a mix of Matt and Bud Light). The soft tuck of my pink bathrobe caresses my cheek, and Matt's half of our key chains must be leaving an imprint in my hand from how hard I'm squeezing it.

This is how Thalia and Alicia find me.

"This doesn't bode well for your mental health."

I lift my head up, find two concerned pairs of eyes, then drop my gaze back to the floor.

"I hate to agree with Thalia, but I agree with Thalia."

I reach out and tug at Alicia's shoelaces in response.

"Come on. I brought donuts." Alicia shakes the Krispy Kreme bag like a maraca.

This is enough to propel me into an upright sitting position. "Did you bring any for yourself?" I ask after ripping the bag from Alicia's hands and eating one of six glazed donuts faster than you can say "pathetic."

Alicia smiles. "Tea?"

I nod, my mouthful of donut preventing me from using words.

Thalia watches her go, then sits down next to me, sinking into the couch and leaning back, putting her feet up on the coffee table. "You should decorate this place."

I glare at her.

"You realize of course that now *you* have to start dating."

"Yeah. I know," I grumble into the donut bag.

"How do you think he got into Fortune anyway? You have to have money or be somebody to get in there."

I swallow down some donut. "Well, I got in, and I'm nobody."

"That's true," Thalia agrees. "But you had me helping you. You don't think that hippie girl *is* somebody, do you?"

I get up, walk to the computer and shuffle my Liz Phair playlist. It's all the same songs. Just in a different order. I hit Play and walk into the kitchen.

Thalia follows me. "Because that'd be really crappy, if Matt had some quasi-famous groupie waiting in the wings this whole time."

"I thought we agreed that we weren't going to say anything obnoxious while we were here," Alicia admonishes as she pours three cups of tea.

Thalia just rolls her eyes.

I stand with my back against the refrigerator door and watch Thalia supervise Alicia's tea-preparing, realizing, for the first time since seeing Matt and his bead-bug date that I told Jack Mantis Thalia'd go out with him.

But seeing as Thalia's here and speaking to me, I can safely assume that Jack has done as he was told and waited to call.

My hands ball into fists, and I add to the top of the "Reasons I hate Matt" list the fact that he made me completely forget about setting Thalia up.

"Echo," Alicia interrupts my ruminations, "sit down."

I do, and because Thalia has caught on to my staring, and is now staring back with buggy, questioning eyes, I change the topic. "Have you talked to Walter?"

"Yeah. And you can thank me. He wanted to come over with us."

Thalia's still staring at me, and her eyes have narrowed into thin slits. "What's going on with you?"

I shrug my shoulders innocently. "Nothing. I'm depressed." But my voice doesn't sound depressed. It sounds defensive.

Thalia's eyes retain their narrow, speculative shape. "*What* is going on?" she asks again.

Thankfully Alicia interrupts her interrogation by placing the three mugs onto the table. "After our tea," she says, "I thought I'd take you out. We can go to the Cocktail and listen to bluegrass."

And now my spirits plunge into my slippers again.

The Kentucky Cocktail is our place—me and Matt's. It's this awesome bar on the Lower East Side that, ironically enough, was opened by a kid from Tennessee who wanted a club in the city where his bluegrass band could play. So he and his band mates plunked down some cash and opened the Kentucky Cocktail, where one can get a jigger of whiskey for $2 and bottles of beer only. Matt and I discovered it one night a few years ago, just before it became intensely popular. But because Matt liked to sit in and play sets with the owner's band, we would always get in and drink for free. We were kind of Kentucky Cocktail VIPs, and now I'm wondering who I'll go there with, which is crazy on all kinds of levels, seeing as Alicia just volunteered to take me there. Nevertheless, this leads me to think about all the other places Matt and I like to go together: the pizza place on the corner of 7th Street, the Irish pub around the corner from my apartment, the falafel place near Annie's. I've lost my "place partner."

Then an even more awful thought takes hold. What if Matt starts going to *our* places with the bead maker?

This, for some reason, is unacceptable. I slam my fist against the kitchen table and watch as Alicia and Thalia both jump. "Seriously!" I shout, in a desperate wail that betrays my lack of hold on any sanity. "Matt and I make fun of that girl on a regular basis. She wears *flowers* in her hair! Do you know that for six months she followed him around? When he was on tour, opening for Sting? He said that she would wear his concert T-shirt, and sit by the stage-door entrance every night. And she wouldn't say anything to him. Just hand him a bunch of daisies wrapped in a beaded spider holder and then walk away."

"Creepy," Alicia says as she opens and closes drawer after drawer in my kitchen. "Where are the spoons again?"

"Well, maybe that's her name," Thalia says.

"Huh?"

"Daisy. Maybe it's her name."

I look from my sister to my balled fists, then shake my head and keep ranting. "And now he's dating her? Isn't there supposed to be a mourning period or something like that?"

Thalia takes the seat next to me. "I think his entire relationship with you was his mourning period. He was mourning the mediocrity of his own creative output."

Alicia apparently found a spoon, because one goes sailing past my eyes and thwacks Thalia squarely on the side of the face. "Ooouuuwww!"

"Well, what would you say something like that for?" Alicia screeches.

"Listen, I speak the truth and you both know it! Did you ever witness one productive moment in their relationship? Where Matt did anything self-starting at all?"

Alicia just looks at me. I start chewing on the end of the bathrobe belt. Because I know the answer, too.

"Of course you didn't. And isn't it odd? That a man whose life is so focused that he's touring with U2 by the time he's twenty-three devolves into a puddle of inactivity after three months of exposure to my sister's love and devotion?"

And my head's on the table.

"You're not helping," Alicia says through clenched teeth.

"I'm not trying to help yet!"

Alicia walks over to me and runs her hand up and down my back. I shift position to maximize the comforting effect. "What she needs is a date."

"Oh, have no fear. Dating is on the horizon, but I certainly can't leave it up to her. She'll be saddled with another two-bit musician in no time."

And here, despite my despair, is where I see an opening, a chess move to be made in the quest of getting Thalia to go out with Jack. And this, more than anything, makes me feel better. Makes me feel like I'm able to see what's important in my life.

I shyly (calculatedly, really) ask, "What's the next step, then?"

Thalia is never as happy as when she's in charge and deferred to. So the shift in her countenance is visible. "Dad and I talked about this yesterday."

It takes all I have in me to not yell at her about talking to my father about my love life. Just knowing that there are discussions of my shortcomings in this area makes my shoulders feel weighted down by forty tons of bricks.

"I want you to go on a three-button dating regimen," Thalia continues. "Oh—hold on. I have visual aids."

She goes bouncing off toward my hall closet, talking all the way. "Alicia, you may want to listen in. What I'm about to say can help you get Jason in hand."

"I don't *want* Jason in hand!"

Thalia returns to the kitchen, large cloth bag extended in one hand and a condescending expression on her face.

I get up and pour what seems like gallons of honey into my tea, and top it off with a nip of Jack Daniel's, which Matt always kept in the freezer and apparently forgot to take with him. I pass the bottle to Alicia, and she also fills her tea to the brim with whiskey.

Meanwhile Thalia has placed two ripped-out magazine pages on the table. One—an ad for Men's Wearhouse, featuring a twentysomething model, with dark hair and perfectly gleaming white teeth—and one an article from *Rolling Stone,* with a picture of Billie Joe Armstrong in the middle of a performance, sweat visibly dripping off his head, eyes bulging, fist wrapped around a mic, and a throng of fans clamoring for his sweat to fall on them. His hair is spiky and his eyes are lined in black. He wears three shirts layered one on top of the other; identifiable only because of the different-colored sleeves lying atop his tattooed arm.

The Men's Wearhouse guy, on the other hand, carries a briefcase, and walks down an office hallway, where three well-dressed women and one mailman ogle him. His hair is perfectly parted, his shoes shine, and even his briefcase looks like a million bucks.

Alicia and I look at each other. She nods her head one time, as if in complete understanding that our job here is to patronize my sister.

"Now, Echo, here's what you've been dating." She puts the Billie Joe Armstrong picture in front of my face. "I know your first reaction to this is one of fiery loins—ow!"

I punched her. So much for being patient.

"—but we're retraining you. Look closely. He's dirty. Angry. Trying to find his self-worth in a crowd of people who, by all accounts, look like they're unemployed—"

"You're unemployed," Alicia says flatly.

"I'm employed in something right now, thank you very much. Right. Now look at this one." Mr. Perfect looks up at me. "The key is the buttons."

I realize that convincing my sister to go out with Jack Mantis is going to be a miracle on par with the turning of loaves into fish, water to wine, raising Lazarus from the dead.

"You want men who take the time to button buttons in the morning. Men who pull T-shirts over their heads and then call themselves ready for the day are Neanderthals. Dogs. Only evolved men, men with the motor skills and opposable thumbs to actually manipulate shirt buttons, are beings who are evolved enough to handle an adult relationship."

Alicia's mouth hangs low. I have nothing to say. There is nothing to say to this.

"I propose that you girls should always aspire to a three-button minimum. It's an inclusive theory. We accept men who wear henleys or polo shirts—they have three buttons. But T-shirt-wearing men, zipper-lovers, these guys should not be included in your dating pool."

"I see your point, actually."

I turn on Alicia; now *my* mouth is hanging down.

"What? I'm not wholeheartedly agreeing, but in the case of some people I know, this theory applies, that's all I'm saying."

I push myself into straight posture, choosing to ignore Alicia's complete insanity when it comes to Jason until I've secured the deal I want to secure. Seriously, I can only deal with one crazy girl at a time. "Thalia, this all sounds great. Really. But I'd have no idea how to meet a three-button man."

At the intimation, the slightest hint that I'm actually subscribing to this theory, that I'm actually asking for help, my sister's face lights up like a large Christmas tree. "Well, I could set you up with one or two nice guys!"

I ignore Alicia's puzzled expression and say, "Really? Do you think I'm ready?"

"You're ready when you say you're ready, Echo. If Matt can move on, I think you should, too."

I thumb the two pictures, the Men's Wearhouse boy and

the Billie Joe Armstrong. It's true, the suited man does nothing for me. But I bet he'd be able to pay for a nice dinner. An actual *date.* In a restaurant. With menus.

Thalia senses that she's winning me over. She places a hand over mine, and says, "I can have a date for you by the weekend."

I look at her, look back to the picture, think it's probably a good idea for me to experience real live dating with a real live adult. But when I raise my eyes back to hers, I pretend that I'm not thinking this.

"I don't know."

"Oh! Come on! What could be bad about just going out on a date?"

"Well, maybe I'd do it. But, Thalia, here's the deal. I'll go out with a banker or a lawyer or a whatever, if you do something for me."

Thalia's features gather at the center of her face, her gaze a study in confusion. "I'd do anything for you, Ec. Just name it."

Well, that's all I need to hear. I sit back in my chair, smile grandly, and announce, "You have to go out with Jack Mantis."

Despite the fact that I have near-successfully manipulated my sister into dating Jack Mantis, therefore securing his beneficent feelings toward me, I still can't wholeheartedly enjoy my afternoon with Alicia. I think she had hoped for a girly-moment-filled time of shopping and frappucino-buying and, if necessary, bluegrass-listening. The kind of outing you see on a teen show or a Cameron Diaz movie.

But I can't get into the mood. Something still isn't sitting right in my heart, and the worst part of having seen proof with my own eyes that Matt was likely using my goodwill, my money and my time the past couple of years, is that now I know that all I can do is sit tight until these sad feelings pass.

At least I've abandoned the pink bathrobe. And if Alicia has her way, I'll end this day with a brand-new wardrobe.

Usually, I'm not one for primping. Mostly because when I was growing up it never mattered what I did in the beautifying-Echo department. The boys in school always saw Thalia first, and at a restaurant or shop with my mother *and* my sister? Next to the two of them I look like a sideshow discard. So I cultivated my other talents instead: hard work, diligence, good spelling. I'm a real find at a party.

It's, I'm sure, psychologically in character that Alicia, my best friend, is a first-rate primper. Despite her casual use of canvas clothing and barrettes, bobby pins and pigtail holders, she's a born shopper. A born beautifier. Go through her cell phone and you'll see numbers for personal shoppers, boutiques, masseuses, beauticians, manicurists. This, she tells me, is the by-product of growing up on the Upper East Side and going to high school with classmates straight out of *Mean Girls.*

I hate to tell her that watching her spend her mother's money does nothing for me—it's the dirty little secret of our friendship. But one good thing about accompanying her on these massive spending trips is that she always makes sure I'm good and pacified with drinks from Starbucks and gelato from Ciao Bella. And today's no different, though when I remembered that Matt once told me Daisy was a nonsugar, nondairy vegan, I tossed my caramel frappuccino in the trash.

I spend the afternoon trying clothes on like I'm Alicia's doll, and asking her about Jason. It's kind of funny, actually. To avoid trying on shirts and pants that make me look like I'm wearing an inner tube around my middle, I ask about

Alicia's relationship. And to avoid talking about this, she drags me into a succession of different boutiques, makeup stores and salons. We end at a draw. She answers no questions, and I walk out with $300 worth of lipsticks and moisturizers and blush, and two pairs of pants that I'll only be able to wear in public if I starve myself for three weeks first.

Finally, Alicia tires of me dragging three paces behind her, and we decide to go to the *BAT*. But when we get there, Walter's waiting for us in the doorway. His apron is wrinkled, and his face is covered in red splotches. Alicia and I stand at the head of the stairs, and I can feel her take two steps backwards.

Walt's crying.

"Echo?"

"Hey, Walter." I give him a hug. He buries his face in my shoulder and blubbers a bit. If I wasn't on red alert, I'd muse over how heavy his head is, and how the sensation of it digging into my shoulder blade feels remarkably like jagged glass.

"Is it true?" He picks up his mountain-head and leans back, peering into my eyes with a morose, pleading look. "Hey, you look really pretty. I like that color lipstick, Alicia." He looks over his shoulder at her, knowing instantly that I would never spend this much money on makeup.

"It's M.A.C.," she replies.

He looks as if he's going to respond to her, but instead asks, "Do you have a tissue, Twig?" He calls her Twiggy, because, well, for the obvious reasons. Though I suspect that the real Twiggy has about a foot and a half on Alicia.

"Walter, why are you so upset?" I intercede. "Let's talk about it in the office, okay?"

He nods twice, and lifts his apron up to his nose. After a long, lusty wipe, he allows me to herd him into the *BAT*.

Alicia scoots in after us, shuts the door, and runs—*runs!*—into the kitchen.

I lead Walter over to the shaggy sofa, ask Jason for some tea and sit next to him.

"Did Thalia call you? Because Matt and that Daisy aren't worth your tears, okay?"

Apparently, this wasn't about Matt and Daisy, because even the mention of a girl's name in the same breath as Matt's brings on a fresh onslaught of Walter-size tears.

"No, no, Walter. He's not worth it. Really."

Jason comes in with a steaming cup of hot chamomile, hands it to our blubbering boss, then sinks down next to him. "He's been like this all morning. There's no cheering him. Even when I offered to take him to the park."

Walter swallows his sip of tea, then puts his chubby paw atop mine. "Echo. If you're quitting, tell me now."

I look from Jason, who shrugs his blue-veloured shoulders and then to Walter. "Walter, we've gone over this. Someday I will be quitting this job."

"Is that day today?"

"Why do you think it is?"

"Because Jack Mantis called for you."

"Right on!" Jason goes to high-five me, but as his hand is suspended over Walt's blubbering head, I decline the celebratory display.

"He did? He called me here?"

"I thought you said you were in a *holding pattern*. Echo! This isn't a holding pattern if he's calling you here! And now look at you, all made up like a doll. You were with him this morning, weren't you? Admit it! You were with him!"

It's like he's accusing me of cheating on him. "Walter, why would he have called here if I had been with him?"

Walter just looks at me, his eyes wide circles and his nose red like a Christmas elf's.

Jason puts his arm around Walter's shoulders, and says very gently, "Why don't we let Echo call Jack back. Then once we know what's going on, we'll freak out. Okay, Walt?"

Walter turns big, puppy-dog eyes on him, and nods his head in a wobbly way. "Okay. But, Echo, nobody will ever love you the way I love you."

Jason raises an eyebrow of horror before ushering him into the kitchen.

When I dial the number written in Walter's loopy script, it rings and rings—I don't know what it is about rock stars and their inability to utilize their cell phones—before a voice finally answers. "Is this the voice of my favorite stalker?"

The sound of Jack's voice sends a little spasm of anticipation through my body. And I can't help but notice that he sounds, well, *friendly.* "It's me. But I'm hanging up my stalking shoes."

He laughs. It's not a bad sound.

"So, what's up?"

"Well, I just wanted to thank you, that's all."

"Thank me? Really?"

"Your sister called. We're going out."

I quickly clutch the phone to my chest, and give a sign of victory to Alicia, who I can see in the kitchen. She claps excitedly, and Jason looks terrified when Walter collapses onto his shoulder in a fresh burst of wailing tears.

I recover my composure, though, and speak softly into the phone. "Well, that's great news! I think you guys will hit it off."

"I do, too. Our phone call was, well, *rad.*" Then an odd sound comes over the line. "Oh, Echo. I've gotta go—my call waiting. But I'll be in touch very soon."

8

I seriously overestimate my own genius.

Because here it is, two weeks since Jack called me, and there's been not so much as an e-mail from Dick Scott at *Disc,* or a call from Stan Fields. After Thalia agreed to date Jack, I'll admit I indulged in some Grade-A fantasies: me hanging with the Butter Flies, playing tambourine on one of their new tracks, Jack's mother and I whispering over lemonade, sugar cookies and his baby pictures, Dick Scott throwing open a door onto my new *Disc* office.

None of those things have happened. Instead, I've been filling my days compulsively going through demos, scouring the Internet for new bands, sending Dick Scott story ideas like it's my job, assuring Walter that my heart's in one piece, and waiting for Thalia to call with Dresser blind dates.

My nights have been an orgy of forgetful music and quality future-stepmother time. I've accumulated plenty of

Mediterranean dinners, stabbed pointer fingers and ruined hemlines these past weeks.

At least I'm not obsessing over Matt Hanley. In fact, I think I'm getting over the whole thing, which doesn't say much for my heart muscle—that it can be exercised in one activity for three years and recuperate from that in only three weeks. But there you go.

Everything would be great if I could get a new job.

Speaking of needing a new job, I'm going to pull my hair out if Dick doesn't get back to me. Even a "no" would be better than silence. It drives me mad. To punctuate this restless feeling, I kick my shoes off underneath the writing desk at the *BAT* before crossing my legs on top of the chair, so that my feet aren't touching the floor. I turn the volume button on my computer speaker and Mick Jagger screeches that he will not be my beast of burden. I concur, and open my e-mail.

It's Friday afternoon at the *BAT,* traditionally a mellow time. Today, Jason sits behind me, Mork-style, on the yellow couch, strapped into a large, old-school-style set of headphones while I manically reread every story idea that I have sent Dick Scott over the past week and count the e-mails I've sent Stan Fields asking if they've chosen their interviewer yet.

"How's it going back there?" I inquire over my shoulder. I've charged Jason with the very important task of finding three bands for us to see this weekend, bands that I can write up for the "New Tunes about Town" section in *Disc* magazine, should Dick ever read one of my pitches and hire me.

Jason sits right-side up, pulls a headphone can from one of his ears and screeches, "Wha??"

I twist around in my seat. "Have you found anybody good?"

He smirks, and picks up the notebook I gave him, a

makeshift log where he can write down every new band he knows of. He waves it in the air. "We're booked for the weekend!" He tosses it back onto the coffee table in front of him where it lands with a plunk in the middle of piles of demo CDs and papers open to the concert sections and flyers advertising gigs at local bars.

"Good work, young Baker. You make Momma proud." I twist back into my seat, and continue the self-flagellating task of the afternoon.

I suspect Thalia is involved in this Echo-blackout that's going on, though I know it's just paranoia.

Nevertheless, as I pick up the phone and dial her number, I remind myself to be nice and accommodating when she answers, to promise to date anyone she tells me to, and to cover for her when she bails on the weekend brunch with the fam for the third weekend in a row.

But all my promises are wasted, because after two rings, Thalia's prerecorded voice greets me with, "If you have nothing nice to say, don't leave a message." Beep.

"Thalia Joy Brennan. Call your sister. I need dating advice."

I hang up only to find Alicia's horrified face looking down at me. "Dating advice? What?"

I wheel the chair over to give Alicia room to lean on the edge of the desk. "No. I'm just trying to get her to call me back. It's been weeks."

Alicia clasps her hands and bends her fingers backwards, cracking every one of her knuckles.

I blanch.

She ignores the disapproving sound I make. "Maybe she and Jack Mantis fell madly in love, and they're too busy plucking the petals off of flowers to call you."

"I'd buy it, but Jack has *people. Disc* has people. The phone calls wouldn't be coming from him at this point."

"Hmmm." Alicia reaches for my wrist and twists it so that she can read my watch, despite the fact that her own diamond-laden watch stares me in the face. "It's four o'clock. Friday. Let's motor."

I shut down the computer, grab my bag from the floor and walk over to Jason, who is lying down. His eyes are closed but his foot taps along to an unheard beat.

"Looks like he found something he likes," I say quietly to Alicia, who stands next to me and watches Jason, too.

"Yeah. Wait—what are we doing tonight, anyway?"

"He's the man with the plan," I say, and nudge Jason lightly with my knee.

He jumps. Apparently he was so into whatever he's listening to that he didn't even realize Alicia and I were watching over him like a newborn babe.

"Jeesh! You two could kill a guy!" He tears the headphones off his head and tosses them onto the table, and the angsty croon of a sad-souled girl can be heard filling the empty space around it.

"What is that?" I ask, picking up the phones, cradling them to my right ear.

Jason pulls the cord from the CD player before I can really hear anything. "Maggie Brown. She's the next Jewel."

"Just what the world needs," Alicia cracks. "Okay. I'm going home. Are you coming with me?"

It isn't clear which of us she's asking, so I answer, "Nah. I'm going to stop in at Dad's."

Alicia looks at me accusingly. "Don't you go home anymore?"

I ignore her, and slip a handful of CDs into my bag. "So

I'll just meet you two at the bar, okay? Where are we going, Jase?"

When he says to meet him at the Kentucky Cocktail at ten-thirty, I hold my breath a moment longer than I should.

A few hours later, after Helen's fed me as if I were embarking on a three-month fast, after Dad's read aloud to me from a text older than Brooklyn, and after Helen's poor wedding dress has been made to suffer from my sewing skills, I'm leaning against the worn, wooden Kentucky Cocktail bar, anxiously keeping an eye on the crowd.

Though it's Friday night in Manhattan, the interior of the KC is made to transport its patrons south of the Mason–Dixon line, with the wood chips on the floor, the non-functioning mechanical bull in the corner, and the chicken wire guarding the pictures of Dolly Parton, the Carters, Loretta Lynn and Johnny Cash. But there's no mistaking the fact that the pretty girls and perky boys here are strictly of the northern, New York variety. Most of the kids probably weren't even here for the show (which, incidentally, wasn't bad but wasn't *Disc*-worthy, either). Anyhow, right now every single person in here looks suspiciously like Matt and Daisy.

Case in point: the medium-sized guy in the corner, leaning over the jukebox.

"Hey—" I tug Alicia's sleeve "—is that him?" I point past her to the person in question.

Alicia follows the trajectory of my finger and asks, quizzically, "Who? The guy with the dreads?"

"No! Him! In the leather jacket. With the pink rose symbol on it."

Alicia stands on her tiptoes. "That guy? Echo! That guy's blond!"

I lean forward and squint. She's right. Rose Jacket is blond. "Oh. Yeah. The build looks like him, though, right?"

She spins around to face me, and shouts over the twang of Tammy Wynette, "Echo! I love you, but I'm two minutes from instituting a cap on how many times you're allowed to mention Matt. He's not here. Daisy's not here. Chill."

I make an actual harrumph sound and sink back into the bar, disappearing into the woodwork and balancing my elbows on the flat surface. Alicia's just looking out for me, I know, trying to make sure that I don't have Matt on the brain. Even though it is perfectly normal and natural for me to be thinking about him. In fact, thinking about him makes me feel less heartless.

"Thalia's right. Maybe I do need to go on a date."

Alicia looks at me, and sips her drink. "Why don't you try to meet someone tonight?"

I drink this idea in, while actually drinking in my drink. I've never been any good at picking guys up in bars. First of all, I usually have to do the approaching, and in the past only the guys who have either just performed or are clearly going to be performing sometime in the near future have caught my eye. And then, I've never been good at giving the potential girlfriend/good-date-material vibe. First of all, if I'm with Thalia, I have no chance. But, more importantly, I get too keyed up about the music (no pun intended) and the gentlemen in question automatically think of me as a "friend." But now I'm sworn to only date men who can pay for my dinner, and I don't think any of the gents I see here fit the bill.

Not to mention the fact that in the back of my mind lurks the possibility that Matt *will* show up. In the back of my mind, and only in the back of it, mind you, my fantasy goes a little something like this: I'll catch the eye of a cute adult gentleman of the non-painting variety, we'll look at each other across the room, he'll approach, we'll flirt and exchange coy witticisms, and just as we cozy up on the dance floor, I'll hear the opening strums of "On Top of the World." I'll look up to the stage, and find myself smack-dab in the middle of my big Lloyd Dobler moment. Matt will have bribed Ted K. (the KC's owner) into letting him appear with the House Band (Ted K.'s band), whereupon he'll serenade me with a banjo-ridden version of "And I Love Her" by the Beatles.

But, like Alicia said, Matt's not here. Matt won't be here. And he's not singing songs for me anymore. Not that I want him to.

"So—" I return to the present "—which heart should I break?"

I love putting it this way, as if I'm a siren with a trail of broken, beaten-down boys behind me.

"You don't want to start with Rose Jacket, do you?" Alicia scrunches her face adorably and looks at me nervously.

"Nah. There's gotta be better choices."

"Right on."

Alicia and I survey the scene as if we're window shopping, and Jason finds us, bringing three fresh drinks from the other side of the bar where he was chatting with a waitress. Alicia barely looks at the bottle as he passes it to her, and puts it on the bar behind her like it's a hot potato. Jason catches my eye and I nervously look away. "Here's to the weekend producing better bands than tonight did." Jason clinks his beer bottle neck to mine and then drinks.

After I take a drink, I let him in on the night's new plan.

"We have a new goal for the night. Boys. And, so you know, my bar is set high."

Alicia, I notice, can't keep her eyes focused on me and Jason, nor is she scanning the crowd for my new boyfriend.

Jason notices, too, and to cover the gaping hole of awkward asks me, "Well, do you see anybody you want me to scope out for you?"

"Echo, let's just get out of here, okay? There's nobody good here. The band's a bust. Let's call it a night."

Okay, now she's just being rude and it's not cool. I look to Jason, whose face is turning from bubble-gum pink to fire-truck red.

Then, he smashes his bottle down so hard I'm surprised when it doesn't shatter into a zillion little pieces. He storms off through the crowds, en route to the back of the huge room where at this moment, dueling guitars are engaged in a melodic fight to the death.

"What was that about?" I ask, shocked to see any kind of "masculine" display come out of the sugar puss that is Jason.

Alicia, to her credit, looks genuinely bothered. She's kicking her foot into the ground and furiously peeling the Bud Light label from her bottle. "Oh, we had a fight today."

"Really? When? At the *BAT*?" I am incredulous, because this implies that Jason had to express discontent with Alicia, or raise his voice. And in the year that they've been together, he's never so much as uttered a peep of dissension with anything Alicia has said, even when he was well within his rights to tell her off. Not when she brought another guy to her parents' anniversary party. Not when she told him that while she reserved the right to see other people, he wasn't allowed to. Not for the entire month of May, when she decided she would only see him on Friday afternoons.

"It's Thalia! She's ruining my life!" My little friend looks ready to burst into tears.

"What did she do?"

"It's the buttons! The damn buttons! Why can't that kid wear a shirt with buttons! It's in my brain, just eating away at me. The other day I went through his closet, and he doesn't own a single item of clothing that has buttons!"

Before I can catch up to what we're talking about, I stupidly ask, "What about his jeans? All zip flies?"

"That isn't the point!" She runs her hands over her face and stops them so that they're resting atop her head. She looks like someone about to be thrown against a car, searched and handcuffed. "I have to end it."

My stomach literally drops into my feet. "You can't!"

This outburst surprises her as much as it does me. "But you hate us together!"

"No! It's you who I hate in this!" As soon as the comment slips from my mouth, the color seeps from Alicia's face. She looks like I slapped her. "I'm sorry. Hey, I'm sorry. I don't hate you. I love you."

She looks away and recovers slightly, and I have to just stand here and feel like, well, the opposite of a million bucks. Negative bucks.

Finally, Alicia takes a breath and faces me. "Echo, we have both known that I wasn't dealing well with this."

I exhale, and it sounds like the strangled sob of a sick rooster. "Lic, I'm so sorry."

"No, it's cool. You're right. There's a reason that I've never wanted to commit to him—"

"The shirts?" I interrupt.

"—and it's time I owned up to it. I'm just not that into him."

"Two more, please!" I shout to the passing bartender. This is awful. Poor Jason. Right now he's blowing off steam in the back, listening to a crappy band, thinking that Alicia just needs time to cool down. Little does he know that he's about to get canned. For real. For good. "This isn't right. We're here to *find* love, not destroy it."

Alicia breathes deeply, and accepts the beer from the bartender who, I notice, leers a little flirtatiously at her. I'm outraged. She's been single for what, two seconds? I've been leaning against this bar all single like for *hours* and not so much as a *look*. Alicia catches me staring after the bartender intently, and tilts her head up. "What, you like the bartender?"

"No."

"He's wearing a button-down," she says forlornly, watching after him.

If I wasn't so worried about Jason, I'd take the moment to be furious that Alicia is excelling so easily at something that I find completely challenging—meeting men. It seems to come easy to all the women in my life.

And now it's like we have nothing to say to each other. I don't know when Jason inched up the "important to Echo list" but there he is, hovering near the top of my concern meter, when I should be worried about Alicia and only Alicia.

She finishes her beer. "You know what? I'm gonna go. I'll call you tomorrow, okay?" She leans in to hug me, and I can barely lift my arms to reciprocate. "Don't hate me, Echo."

I feel like three thousand pounds of shit as she walks out the door. I mean, no matter how angry I am at her for treating Jase like the dirt at the bottom of her shoe, I can't just tell people I *hate* them.

To prevent myself from living that exchange in my head

over and over again, I put my beer bottle on the bar, and go to find Jason.

He's where I thought he would be, clinging to the shadows near the stage. Wow. He so wanted to be away from Alicia that he's enduring this debacle: two Nelson look-alikes wailing away in an attempt to harmonize.

Jason sees me and places his hand on my shoulder while chugging his beer. "Did she leave?"

"Jason, I'm so, so sorry. I don't know what to say." I stack myself next to him, my back meeting the cool surface of the wall like a lover, the cold sending my body into a shiver. "She's— I just don't get her."

"I wish I was a country songwriter right now. I could make some serious cash." Jason places the empty bottle by our feet, and runs a hand through his hair.

"I just—"

"You want to get out of here?"

I look from him to the stage to the crowd. "I can't take all this change anymore," I say to the ceiling, to myself, to Jason.

"We can stay. I know you want to catch a man tonight."

"No. Absolutely not. From this moment on, the night's about nursing our ills."

So we leave. We take a cab to the *BAT,* and find, refreshingly, that nobody else is there. Jason flips the lights on, and opens the music closet, a closet that holds all the CDs mailed to us from labels both major and minor, and by folks who are hoping to get a write-up of their basement-made inaugural CDs. I often look into this closet and wonder what next McCartney or Stevie Wonder awaits our ears. Tonight I'd settle for a mid-career Stevie Nicks, post Lindsay Buckingham, mid-breakup hell.

"Ah. Let's find our mood maker." By this time, I'm a little tipsy, and a weird sensation of grief, panic at the impending upheaval of my friends' breakup is already rendering me as ineffective at taking care of myself as a college coed.

"What's yer poison, madam?" Jason asks, twisting the top off a 40-ounce bottle of malt liquor we picked up in a deli along the way. It's times like these when you really see the seams of a guy.

"Fiona Apple, girl with painful childhood, piano ballad style. Or maybe I want Elton," I say, reaching for a tower of unopened CDs. My clumsy movement sends three whole stacks sprawling to the floor. Jason laughs and we dive, grabbing for the scattered CDs like maidens picking flower blossoms in a field.

I'm giggling. "Look! It's a metaphor!" I can explain no further than this, however, my tipsiness dulling my powers of speech into inactivity.

Jason giggles, too, and then sits with his back against the wall, his feet sole-to-sole with mine, the two of us like sad mirror images. "Single and loving it. That'd be the caption under this picture."

My face hurts from trying to smile. "I don't get why I'm so sad. You're totally better off without her."

Jason's face looks ruefully melancholy. He sips from the bottle of liquor, and says evenly, "I'm not the one you're sad for."

9

As you probably predicted, my first solo venture at the Kentucky Cocktail ended unceremoniously, with me puking into the *BAT*'s toilets and Jason spouting "breakup haikus" from atop the *BAT*'s couch.

The next day I woke up to Walter rubbing my tummy and nearly suffocating me with a scalding hot towel. You don't know shame until you wake up hungover at your *office,* and find your boss thrilled to be able to nurse you back to good health.

I staggered home, and slept the entire Saturday. For the first time since they've been a couple, I didn't make it to Helen's and Dad's brunch. This set off a chain of events that will apparently lead to the end of the world. We're talking phone calls, wailing worry, concern that I'm dying. I did my best to explain to Helen that I was in perfect health while keeping to myself the fact that I was a drunken slob.

My week didn't turn out to be worth much, either. After

seven more days of receiving exactly zero job offers, I got to thinking about Sisyphus and how he never makes it to the top of the mountain. The first time my father told me this story, well, let's just say that most Greek myths aren't made for four-year-olds. Thalia had to sleep in my bed with me for a week, because the idea that somebody could be crushed by a giant rock over and over for all eternity was more than my young brain could comprehend.

But now, I see the wisdom of the story. Let's face it. *Disc* is my boulder. I'm so fixated on getting a job there, I'm not even trying to get work elsewhere. I've placed my entire future in Dick Scott's hands. If he doesn't feel like giving me a little help getting to the top of the music journalism hill, I'll never get there.

So I've decided to focus my efforts into dating. It's a bold move, seeing as my number-one potential match-maker has gone MIA.

Thalia's still not returning my calls. She's not answering her door (I've stopped by her apartment about a dozen times in the past month). She's either gone the way of the dinosaurs and my mother, or is in the middle of one of her famous "sabbaticals." She's been known to disappear, just vanish for weeks at a time. Once she didn't call me or my father for three months. I was worried, my father wasn't, and one day she showed up in our Brooklyn kitchen armed with a brand-new tattoo and homemade quivers and arrows from Guatemala as presents for us. In short, I'm not entirely sure whether her lack of response to my calls has anything to do with me or with the fact that I set her up with Jack Mantis.

And I can't wait for her. I need to do this on my own. Not only because my career efforts are resulting in a big fat zero, but because I'm tired of being that *girl*. The "girl who just broke up with her boyfriend" girl.

Fortunately, I've recruited Alicia to help me get started with the dating part of my adult life. Our words at the Kentucky Cocktail have been long forgotten. Well, forgiven, at least. I don't know how she could forget that I said I hated her. But we've known each other since our first semester at Emerson, when we were two confused New Yorkers lost in Boston. It'd take a lot more than a little spat for us to stay mad at each other. And it's a good thing, because I'd be lost without her.

"Hey, how do I look?"

I sit up, and watch as Alicia parades in front of me like a runway model. She's wearing a gray one-piece mod-style dress she picked up today at a sample sale.

The occasion?

Our first annual "On the Market" party.

"Foxy. Hot," I drawl, and then whistle. She stops mid-strut, and throws a balled-up stocking at me. I collapse back onto her bed and stare at her ceiling some more.

"You've got to get dressed," she commands as she goes into her closet (which is bigger than my bedroom—I'm not kidding).

"What's wrong—"

She pokes her head out and interrupts before I can finish my sentence. "You can't wear that."

I look down at my brown "Rock Me to Heaven" T-shirt, and green cords. I've got a long-sleeve purple shirt on underneath the shirt and three plastic bracelets in varying colors on each wrist. I guess I don't look very "On the Market."

Alicia can read my mind. "You could dress that way for

Matt. He loved you for you. You've got to polish up if you want to meet people." She throws a black thing at my head. "I bought that for you. And there are some shoes in here somewhere."

I stare at the ceiling some more, hoping that this party is a good idea, and that there will be somebody good for me to meet, somebody with a disposable income and maybe a car and a nice record collection.

I get up and join her in the closet, where there's more than enough room for us both to change. She finds the shoe box, and of course, the shoes and the dress fit perfectly. She knows my sizes better than I do.

After I'm zipped and fitted and stockinged, I stare into the mirror while she puts the finishing touches on my face.

"Not too round?" I ask, gesturing with my eyeballs toward my midregion.

"You're on crack. You're not too *round*." She pinches my chin, and I don't say another thing, until she's painted a face on me that could stop traffic.

Two hours later, our "On the Market" party is in full swing. Alicia's apartment, which, as mentioned before, is big by any city's standards let alone New York's, is packed. We were fair-minded in coming up with the guest list—anyone could come as long as they brought at least one single friend, male or female. I think it was nice of us, to facilitate other on-the-market people possibly finding love. Oh, and all the men had to wear buttons (this was Alicia's idea, but I allowed it since she not only offered to hostess this event but paid for all the food and drink, too).

My personal goal is to meet at least ten new men. I know—who do I think I am? J-Lo? But I figure that doing it this way will be faster than signing up with a dating service. Plus immediate meetings have the added bonus of quick judgment and input from Alicia.

We tried to invite a variety of types. I'm trolling Thalia-style for Dressers and moneymen, and Alicia's always been a sucker for the arty boys. I don't know if this is because she really *likes* arty boys or because she likes how much her mother *hates* them.

At any rate, coming up with the guest list was no easy feat. First of all, I'm out my three best pipelines to single men: Matt, Jason and Thalia. Obviously we wouldn't have been able to ask Jason to invite his friends to this party, even if either of us has seen him, which we haven't. He's called in "heartbroken" to Walter every day since the Kentucky Cocktail night, which isn't doing him any favors. Alicia's made a conscious effort not to visit since their breakup.

So that left us scrounging. We ended up inviting everyone in each of our buildings, all of Alicia's brothers (the one who now lives in Colorado sent three of his best buds in his stead, all of whom happen to be in finance—yay!), Annie's husband, Fred, told a bunch of random musicians and bartenders to come. I left Thalia an unanswered message, detailing what we were up to; she apparently got it, because there's been a steady stream of guys in suit jackets showing up that neither Alicia nor myself can place. Helen got wind of our party and insisted on sending her butcher's son; Walter invited the guy who waters the *BAT*'s plants; I randomly started inviting people I saw at shows around town. Alicia got her mother's younger coworkers in on the action, plus a lot of her high school friends (who all look like Gwyneth Paltrow and Selma Blair), and Walter's here, of course.

I immediately target Alicia's brothers' friends, specifically the one who looks least like Matt. Daniel is medium-height and blond, stocky and brash. As soon as his two friends head into the kitchen to get another round of drinks, I ask Daniel what he does for a living.

"My buddies and I work downtown at Fitch." His teeth should be photographed for dental brochures, they are so bright. His smile blinds me.

"Oh!" I hold my drink up and cross my arms. Daniel doesn't say anything. "What is that?"

Daniel looks at me like I'm a dumb girl. I *hate* that look. I wonder if I should quiz him about Sophocles and Euripides just to show off how dumb I'm not. "It's an asset-backed securities firm."

I stare at him blankly before mumbling, "Oh." I have no idea what that is. Again, there's silence. How does Thalia talk to these people? After three more seconds of bone-gnawing silence, I ask, "Do you like music?"

Daniel nods. "Yeah. I'd say I'm a music guy."

"Oh! Good! Who's your favorite?"

"I'm from Jersey, so you know, Bon Jovi."

That's it. I don't care how much money he makes. Bon Jovi's a deal breaker. I excuse myself politely, and head to my home base—Walter.

"Hi, sweet potato!" He air kisses my cheek and appraises my outfit. "Lovely!"

I put my arm through his crooked elbow. "Okay, Walter, this is going to be tougher than I'd hoped. Find me someone else to talk to. How about that guy?" I point to a tall, skinny, string bean of a man in the corner, who is talking to Helen's butcher's son, which tells me he's good at making conversation, because, seriously, what could he possibly have in common with a butcher's son?

Walter exhales dramatically. "I don't like him. You've already met your soul mate, anyway."

"Walter, don't start. You knew what this party was for."

He sinks onto his hip and says nothing. I only have to count to two before he can't control himself with the nagging, "But you and you-know-who are perfect for each other."

I close my eyes. Walter may not want to name him, but he hasn't stopped wanting Matt around. "Okay, I'm going in. Wish me luck." I leave Walter muttering to himself about how I'm not going to find anybody tonight.

After a few more hours of chatting with every single man sent by Thalia and finding something wrong with all of them (Creed is your favorite band? Carrot Top makes you laugh?) I'm in the corner with Alicia, standing in front of her stadium-size television.

"What do you think?"

"I think we don't know our own power," she exclaims. "Babies might get made tonight." She points to her couch, where two separate couples are necking.

She's right. Alicia and I have brought love to the masses. Everywhere, people are macking. It's like an open house for lonely people. Seriously, somewhere along the way the lights were dimmed, there's some Caetano Veloso on the stereo, candles are burning. Couples stand in corners, talking, cuddling in some cases, laughing and exchanging numbers.

And I'm with Alicia.

She puts an arm around my shoulder. "I guess you can't force some things."

"Dating can't be a boulder, too."

It's like I just spoke in another language. "Huh?"

"Nothing. I just can't believe there wasn't one guy here I liked."

"Well, Ec, you weren't talking to the right people. I bet you'd hit it off with some of Freddy's friends."

"Nah. I'm done with musicians."

She widens her eyes. "Okay, Echo. Good luck with that." And with that she's off to introduce herself to the *BAT* flower-waterer, who's talking to Walter over by the bookshelf.

I decide it's time for another drink. I stumble over a stray handbag on my way to Alicia's kitchen.

And when I get there, my night gets worse.

"What are you doing here?"

Alex Paxton raises his glass in the air in a mock toast. "I was invited."

"You weren't."

"Oh, Echo, you're a peach. No wonder Matt dumped you." He drinks. I cross my arms and watch him ruefully.

"*I* broke up with *him*."

"Well, it was the best thing that ever happened to him, huh?"

"Oh, shut up," I spit. He has the decency to look, well, I guess it's shamed. His face loses a bit of color, and he immediately finishes his drink.

"I could use another round," he says. "Want one?"

I walk toward him, but keep my arms crossed. "Fine."

He grabs a bottle of vodka and one of tonic and begins pouring. I reach for the ice tongs and drop cubes into our cups, extra for me.

I take my drink, sip and look at him. I wait a moment, then ask the question I'm dying to. "What's going on with the Jack Mantis story?"

Alex looks right back at me, suspiciously. "We know who's *not* writing it, Echo."

"Nice."

He raises his eyebrows once, and peers into his drink, shakes the cubes around the cup and gulps some down.

I lean against the table with the booze on it. "Alex."

"Yeah?" He looks up.

"Why won't Dick let me write for *Disc?*"

Now he chugs his drink. We're talking bottoms up. "You'd have to ask him."

"I would, if he'd ever get back to me."

"He's a busy man, Echo. And you're not the only person who wants to work there. I'll give it to you, chasing Jack was the right idea. You need something to make you stand out from all the other wannabes."

I consider this, and decide that taking advice from Alex is definitely the signal to end my night.

Unfortunately, it's not the end of my night. Because after I've had two more drinks, I forget my no-musician edict.

He's one of Freddy's friends. I don't know if Alicia told him to come introduce himself to me, but he corners me in the bedroom. One look at his Pixies T-shirt, messy brown hair and nice eyes, and my brains fly out the window. We stand in the corner and talk about Neil Young until Alicia kicks us out and closes the door on her and the plant-waterer.

So we move our conversation into the living room, where the party's virtually at an end. Walter and Alex are gone, as are most of the others. Before I know what's happening, I find myself draped across the sofa on this guy's lap.

He holds my hand in his, tracing circles in my palm and talking about playing guitar for a Cheap Trick tribute band and how Rick Nielsen is his idol. But for some reason, I can't concentrate on what he's saying. All that's in my head is Matt—the memory of the first night we met in Boston, in that dorm room when I was just a kid who should've known better than to fool around with a perfect stranger.

I come to just as this guy is leaning in for a kiss.

And the thought of Matt drives me up from his lap. I stagger on my feet before steadying myself, and apologize to Freddy's friend—God, I don't even know his name. I grab my bag, and leave him there, with the half-dozen other hangers on.

When I get home that night, well after 4:00 a.m. (the only time I ever come home now), I walk into the kitchen and drink two glasses of water. I feel a bit shaky, so I place my hand on the counter to steady myself, and think about how I have to remember that I *shouldn't* be dating kids anymore. I have to learn to like the men who work for asset-based securities firms and don't get so wasted at parties that they'll kiss any girl they happen to find in their laps. I bet that kid didn't have a steady job. Or a 401K. He definitely couldn't bring me to a nice restaurant.

And if I wanted that in a date, I'd still be with Matt.

I put the glass in the sink, and teeter into the bedroom, where I take my new dress off. I place it into the closet, next to the dark purple, satiny tea-length dress I bought for my father's wedding. Four in the morning seems as good a time as any to try the dress on. But when I take it out of the closet, a shiny, small piece of purple fabric floats to the floor and falls in a heap at my feet. It's the matching bow tie I bought for Matt. It had been a joke; I was going to insist he wear it just to get under his skin. I throw it into the small garbage can in my bathroom, shed two tears, brush my teeth and blast the Ramones as loud as I can without summoning the hateful complaints of my neighbors, until I fall asleep on the couch.

10

When I was young, my sister used to walk me down Sackett Street to the bakery on the corner. The bakery was owned and operated by a strict Italian woman named Phillie (I think it was short for Philomena), who had a very hairy wart on her cheek and the thickest eyebrows I have ever seen. She would call out to Thalia and me, "Don't touch nuthin'. Stand against the wall!" Phillie hated kids. It was known in the neighborhood not to go in there, especially without your parents, and there were all kinds of tales about missing kids who were last seen going into Phillie's shop, as well as a few well-worn myths about where Phillie got the ingredients for her cookies.

But Thalia, even at ten years old, could work some serious mojo on people. She would whisper in my ear, "Stay still, Echo. I'm going for a whole boxful." And she would. She'd trot around the counter and hug Phillie around the middle, and a smile would crack open on

Phillie's fat hairy face like an egg, and soon Thalia and I would be covered in powdered sugar, chocolate sprinkles and multicolored cakes. And she'd never share a drop with any of the neighborhood kids.

I'm reminded of this ability of Thalia's two weeks after Alicia's and my party, when Thalia summons me to meet her at Annie's and I arrive to find her there with Jack Mantis.

I slide into the booth, my heart beating a bit faster than usual, and my palms suddenly sweaty. "Um. Hi."

Thalia stands and leans over the table, giving me a light kiss on the cheek. "Hi, honey."

I surreptitiously catch Annie's eye. She stands behind the bar and shoots me a "What the hell's going on there" look. If I weren't so confused, I'd be laughing. Instead, to calm my nerves, I attempt to not only signal that I have no idea, but that I'd like a drink. She reads my messages loud and clear, and soon, there's a tall, icy vodka tonic in front of me.

"You shouldn't be drinking so early, Echo," my sister admonishes. Jack has yet to speak. I notice that his hair's been cut since the last time I saw him, and he's wearing a black button-down shirt over dark canvas pants.

"Helen's worried sick about you. Have you called them?" I hold my glass, but don't drink. I have a feeling that I'll need to keep my head clear for this meeting.

"Of course, Dad was the first to hear the news!" Thalia picks Jack's hand up in hers, and holds it in the air. "We're in love." She says this matter-of-factly, like she's talking about the weather.

My mouth drops open. I'm desperate to not say the wrong thing. That's all I can think.

"And it's thanks to you," Jack gushes, and reaches his free hand forward to clutch mine.

I take a quick sip of my drink before surrendering my hand, and try to recover my powers of speech. I shake my head. "Okay. Let's hear it."

Thalia beams at me, and spends the next hour regaling me with the greatest love story ever told.

The upshot of which is that they're officially dating.

Now, when I say the word *dating* I am not referring to dinner, movies, long walks up Madison Avenue where Thalia gets to point to desired items behind cased glass, or evenings of my sister being girly and Jack being gentlemanly. Nope.

Apparently, it didn't take more than a phone call for Jack to figure out that Thalia wasn't to be wooed with the normal activities, so their first date was at Jack's therapist's Wellness Center in the Bronx. They met there and underwent a three-hour couple's therapy session. Over the course of a "sharing exercise" (I don't know what this entails), they—confirmed by each of them—fell in love.

"You didn't tell Dad this, did you?"

Thalia looks stumped by my concern here, and plunges onward. "Oh, Echo," she exclaims, flinging an arm around Jack's shoulder. "We've had the best time."

And then they start talking over each other, like a couple that's been married for fifty years:

"He took me to Costa Rica for a two-week getaway—"

"Your sister rocks in a bikini! We snorkeled—"

"And then we spent a weekend sky-diving—"

"The sensory deprivation tank! Changed my life!"

"It was inspiring!"

"And Thalia has made the most charming chalk drawings. I'm using one for the cover of the next Flies album."

And this is where I sit up at attention, because Jack's eyes gather a very special-looking twinkle in them. I lean forward.

He reaches forward and clasps my hands. "You've introduced me to the most wonderful woman in the world."

Thalia's nodding her head in assent as he leans toward me. "I'd be honored if you conducted my interview for *Disc*."

My kitchen looks like a paper factory exploded. The day Jack offered me the interview, Dick Scott called to confirm. From that moment on, I've been a woman obsessed. My apartment is no longer stark; it again has life, purpose, activity.

Clips and pictures and magazines cover every surface (the table, the counter, the front of the fridge). There's also a healthy representation of staplers, glue sticks, pencils, pens, tape dispensers. I've tacked a picture of each member of the Butter Flies to the wall (the super's going to charge me an arm and a leg if I ever move out of this joint) and Alicia and I rigged up a cotton-thread system linking people to each other. I have two lists of people (one interviewed, one to be interviewed). On these lists, in addition to the band and Stan, are Jack's childhood friends, family members, the first promoters they worked with in Boston and New York. I think I can probably even get a quote from Annie.

I've been living my life, for the past two weeks, the way I always imagined I would, flying from meeting to meeting, getting admitted to secret clubs like Bungalow 8. Running from the *Disc* photographer's to Stan Fields's offices, to Michael Fields's—the lead guitarist—palatial Jersey mansion, where I interviewed the bass player, too. And I've loved every minute of it. Fleeing the doldrums of the *BAT* is amazing, especially since Jason no longer shows up and my days have become exceedingly lonely and boring. And Walter's guilt trips are things of beauty, too. It's like the man can't keep a dry eye when I'm there.

But other than those small annoyances, nothing can get me down. My dream is on the verge of coming true. And not just this interview. Once Jack agreed to use me as the writer, it was like the seal on the dam of my usefulness to *Disc* was ripped open. Dick, all of a sudden, was in receipt of every e-mail I ever sent him. I've now contributed to my first "New Tunes about Town" section, and have two more articles pending.

When I showed my father a copy of *Disc,* and said that I'd be writing the January cover story for it, he looked prouder of me than he ever has.

Today, I'm heading over to the Henry Hudson Parkway and one of the most prestigious mixing houses in the entire world—Silver Records studios. There I'll be questioning the Flies' drummer, Goren Liddell, about what it's like to work with Jack, about how fame has affected the band and changed their music.

It'll be good to walk through Silver Records's heavy oak doors with my head held high. The last few times I was there, it was as Matt's crutch, keeping him upright while his label execs and his manager yelled at him.

The first time I got to come here with Matt, I was like a kid at Christmas: butterflies in the stomach, nerve headache, chewed-off fingernails, the whole bit. It was my Taj Mahal, my Mount Rushmore, the site of the recording of more of the world's greatest records than you could even imagine. It's where Yoko Ono and John Lennon staged their famous "Dozen Window Display," an installation of twelve naked girls who stood in the windows for twelve days. This place has churned out more gold and platinum albums, more creative masterpieces than anywhere in the country, and a little old journalist like me would never have gotten in without the help of a real musician.

On that first trip, Matt was as eager as I was to digest the history of the place, to quiz all the sound engineers and mixers about different albums they'd worked on, to ask questions of the receptionists about the personalities of his favorite musicians.

Of course, then he became *persona non grata* here. Because we'd go, he'd lay down guitar tracks, then make me call him on his cell phone in a fake emergency to get him out of singing lyrics. This happened six or eight times, before his record company and his manager pressed the pause button on the whole shebang, and it was decreed that until he laid down a set of lyrics, he wasn't allowed to fiddle with the recorded music.

Now, I'm coming to the studio as a professional, not merely an ornament on the arm of some musician. I'll admit that this feels pretty good, and my confidence level is pretty high. I pull the collar of my coat up around my ears and run my fingers through my hair, the early winter Manhattan air turning seriously chilly. My breath lands on the glass panel just beside the oak door. I reflexively draw my initials into the condensation, realize what I'm doing and then rub my hand over the whole thing, leaving nothing but a streaky marker of my presence.

I then reach out, press the button, and wait for the receptionist to buzz me in. I can see her through the glass panels in the doors—being able to see in, to see the records mounted on the wall, but not being able to get inside unless they let you always struck me as a slap in the face. But I suppose if any place has the right to keep the nondesirables out, it's Silver Records.

The receptionist takes her time. She raises her eyes above the top of her magazine and goes back to reading. She must be new, as I've never seen her before. Silver Records runs through receptionists like water. I think what happens is that girls move to the city, think they'll get a job where they can meet producers, they think they'll slip them their demo and—*bam!*—their career will be born. In all the time I visited this place, I can categorically say that not one Silver Records employee "made" it.

The girl behind the desk finishes her sentence or whatever is more important than taking care of me, and looks up again, clearly sizing me up. I look as professional as I possibly can, and suppress the urge to wave at her, as I don't think that conveys "cool." I borrowed Thalia's long black trench coat for the occasion (I took it from Dad's, where she left it), as well as a Pucci scarf of Alicia's that cost as much as my weekly allotment for food. I'm even wearing sunglasses (also from Alicia) and am carrying a leather-bound notebook, which was a gift from my father. He bought it for me when I told him I wanted to be a journalist. When I told him, a week later, that I wanted to be a *rock* journalist, he asked for it back.

Finally, the girl buzzes me in. I apparently pass muster.

The interior of Silver Records is, as one might expect, silver, even in the lobby. I know from past visits that the silver theme is carried throughout the building: silver couches, silver walls, silver light fixtures. The only nonsilver decorations are the mounted albums on the wall (from the old days) and photos of newer rock stars: Jack among them.

The girl, whose neck is wrapped in a blue scarf and

whose ears are accentuated with globular golden hoops that kiss the top of the scarf's head, looks up as I walk to her.

"No demos, no walk-ins, no groupies," she says, and then casually flips over a page of the magazine she's reading. It's *Disc*.

I take particular pleasure in being able to say, "No, I'm here for Goren Liddell. He's expecting me."

"No groupies."

"I'm not a groupie."

She punches a couple of buttons on her phone. "A girl's here. For Goren." She casts her glance my way and says, "Uh-huh." Then she hangs up, and asks, "Echo?" I nod and she slides a sign-in book my way.

I smile at her. Even though she hasn't earned it. "I like your scarf. The blue really catches the light in your eyes."

She eyes me. "I have a boyfriend."

"No! I did—"

"Just sign in. I'm not giving you any scoop."

I take the pen and sign in, bristling on the inside. I'm writing my name, and my floor number, and who I'm going to be seeing, then I check my watch for the time. And as I do that, my eye latches on to something, like a fish getting a scent of bait.

I scan the page, the list of people who have been at Silver Records in the past couple of days. There it is, three names from the top:

MATT HANLEY.

And below that?

DAISY DORFMAN.

The pen bounces from the front desk to the floor, where it clatters against the silvery metal flooring and rolls away.

The Blue Scarf Girl goes all bug-eyed on me, and truthfully, if I could see myself, I'd go all bug-eyed on me, too.

And then I go a little bit crazier.

"I'm sorry," I say, and start scratching behind my ear, like a dog, because all of a sudden I'm itchy all over. "But was Matt Hanley here today?"

"No groupies."

"Believe me, I'm not a groupie. I'm an ex. Was he here? With a girl? Frizzy hair and done up like a Christmas tree in beads?"

I've spoken some sort of secret code to this receptionist, because her countenance softens. Her shoulders round, her head tilts, her lips scrunch up in what I can only assume is sympathy.

"Yeah, wait, you said your name's Echo?"

"Yeah." When I say this, it comes out sounding like a question.

"Dude. I'd be wrecked. That guy's really cute. I don't care what they say about him." When the girl says that last part, she hooks her thumb toward the elevator, intimating that the honchos behind the walls don't speak so kindly of Mr. Hanley, which doesn't surprise me in the least.

I drink in the silver walls like a thirsty desert dweller, breathing in deeply. So what? Do I care? That he's still squiring that girl around? I shouldn't care. And, if I'm honest with myself, aren't I a tad thrilled that Daisy's the one dealing with Matt's neuroses now?

That answer would be yes.

But still, I don't want to run into them. Or maybe I *do*. There is a little, mean-spirited, awful side of me that hopes Matt finds out that I'm doing this interview. I check the log. "They're gone now?"

"Yeah, they left. Listen—" the girl grabs my hand, and for a split second I think maybe I should tell her *I'm* straight

"—there are better guys for you, guys who appreciate you for what you are and don't give a crap about the size of your hips. We're girls. We *should* have curves."

I'm horrified. And completely blindsided. I wrap my arms around my waist, bring my big bag around to block the girl's view of my body. "Um, just, I'm…I'm gonna go. Thanks."

Then I run to the silver elevators, humiliated that I've been counseled by a complete stranger to love my body.

When I'm safely tucked away inside the silver cocoon, the superimposed images of Led Zeppelin smiling down at me, I wrack my brain trying to figure out what I did to get that girl to say something like that. By the time the elevator doors open onto the proper floor, I've decided that not even Thalia would be so honest with a complete stranger.

Goren Liddell stands in front of the elevator doors, waiting for me. Man, is he a sight. If I hadn't just been cut down to size, I might throw my hat in the ring for him. He's much taller than I remember. He's thin, and a study in black-and-white. Eyes dark as coal, with hair to match, blanketing skin that's pale without looking lifeless like Jack's does. And he's dressed like an FBI agent on his day off: black jeans, white T-shirt, black-and-white sneakers. The only hint of rebel in him is his earring, a diamond-crusted cross.

I stop in my tracks, and realize, only after he extends his hand and quizzically asks, "Echo?" that I've been staring.

"Oh! My God!" I shuffle my bag over to the other shoulder and grab for his hand. "Hi, it's—it's nice to meet you."

His hand feels, in a word, *phenomenal*. "Hey," he says, and continues to hold on to my hand.

"Yeah, hi."

"Hi, so—"

"Oh, right, um, so, where do you want to, uh—"

"Oh, back here's good. Let me take that for you." He takes my bag from me, and steps aside so that I can pass in front of him. Then he guides me down the wood-paneled hallway until we're in front of a doorway. He opens the door for me and says, "It's comfy in here. There are pillows in here."

He isn't lying. We enter into a blue-silver room with large pillows that adorn the floor, pillows the size of mattresses. They line three of the walls, and the fourth is made of floor-to-ceiling windows that look out onto the river. It's breathtaking in here, sunny and warm and friendly.

Goren hands me my bag, and says in a goofy, endearing way, "Pick your pillow, I guess." He towers over me, and when we sit we're positioned so that we're looking at each other dead-on.

I pull a voice recorder from my bag, and he chuckles bashfully when I turn it on.

"Are you ready?"

"I'm ready, Echo. Are you?"

Annie's Punk is heaven. That's what I'm thinking as she carries over a pitcher and plunks down a heaping pile of peanuts on top of the sticky table I've designated as my happy zone for the night.

"Is it light?"

"You don't need light beer, Echo." Annie pops a fistful of nuts into her mouth.

The foam on my beer threatens to spill over onto the table, so I slurp it up like a kindergartner. "Annie, I was told by a stranger today that it's okay that I'm round. It's light beer from here on in." I look her in the eye.

She grimaces at me. "You've got serious problems."

I smile at her and raise my eyebrows, trying to decide how much to confide in her. I decide to go whole hog. "I think I'm ready to start dating, for real."

She looks at me skeptically and then throws a handful of peanut shells onto the floor. "You're not ready to be dating," she sings to the tune of Neil Young's "Are You Ready for the Country?"

I sneer at her.

She smiles, and says, "I thought you tried this already, with your little party."

I swallow a peanut. "Yeah, but I was going about it all wrong. Seriously, I can't date guys who like Bon Jovi and Creed. But I think Goren might be a nice midpoint between who I was with and who I thought I *should* be with."

Annie smacks her lips. "Goren? Goren Liddell?"

"What do you know about him?" I ask just before taking a heaping swig of my nonlight beer.

Annie gives me the eyebrow and giggles, that whiskey-soaked laugh wrapping around me like a blanket. "A drummer. It's not a bad choice." She pulls her chair forward, conspiratorially. "I've had them all, kiddo. And drummers have *rhythm*." She stares at me. I have no idea what she's getting at.

"Of course they do."

Annie laughs and looks around for a beat before looking me dead in the eye. "Echo. They have *rhythm*. Dig what I'm saying."

"Oh! Annie!" I shriek and pull my chair away from her. "Stop it!"

She shrieks right back, but it's a merry sound, her pleasure at embarrassing me sending her into guffawing convulsions. "You're so easy."

"I am not." I drink.

"But it's true. Matt couldn't have been very good in bed. He's too much of a sad sack."

"I feel like I'm talking about sex with my parents." I put a hand on my stomach, to contain that queasy feeling.

"Aw, toughen up, kid." Annie gets up, walks to the bar, and comes back with a refilled bowl of nuts.

"So you agree."

"Agree with what?"

"That I should ask Goren out."

"Kid, of course. Get back on the bike. You'll love his drumroll."

11

My apartment's alive with the sound of music.

Janis Joplin. Sleater-Kinney.

Empowering, girl music.

And I'm bopping along as if I was a teenager.

The occasion?

A real live date.

"Should I be nervous?" I ask Alicia, who's planted on the lip of my bathtub, rubbing different color rouges and lipsticks into her hand while I stand in front of the mirror and give myself a first-date makeup job.

"Why? Why would you be nervous?" she asks with a confused look on her face.

I'm reminded that all the women in my life are the pretty, popular girls you wanted to punch in high school. "I have butterflies. I haven't had this feeling in forever."

"Don't tell him that. You'll never get to second base."

"Huh?"

"*Butterflies?* Butter Flies? It'll make you look lame. Here, try this." Alicia walks ups to me, clamps her fingers around my chin, and begins to rub pink lipstick into my cheeks. It tickles.

"I'm giggly," I say into the mirror, watching as her fingers work magic and turn me into a pretty girl.

"Well, it's exciting. Your first date in four years. That's something."

"Yeah."

"You're going to take his breath away." Alicia pulls my hair up, clipping it into perfection.

"Do you think if I'd had the nerve to break up with Matt when I should have, that by now I'd be married, with kids and a job?"

"No. Something else would've come up. It's not Matt's fault that you've sat at the *BAT* for four years. It's not."

My mind goes to my father, to Helen, to the weather-worn pages of the books in my father's library, pages I've turned every night for years, spending my evenings reading instead of writing, caring for my dad instead of for myself.

Alicia finishes beautifying me, rubs a thin line of Vaseline on my lashes for effect, and spins me around. "You look hot. I'd do you."

"You're such a lady." And I laugh.

Goren Liddell takes me on a great first date, a first date they put in the middle of romantic comedies. He takes me to King Street Tavern, a four-star restaurant in Greenwich Village, and orders appetizers *and* wine. It's the nicest meal I've ever had that wasn't cooked by Helen. And then, because our dinner conversation is easy, and comfortable and not overly animated in that fake way you do when you're biding time until you can be alone, we dispense with the movie in favor of a walk along the Hudson River Park. We get there by taxi, and when we walk by the pier near Houston Street, he clutches my hand and puts it in his jacket pocket.

His hands are calloused. It makes sense for a drummer. The pads of his fingers are rough and the skin is thick. Matt's fingers were soft and long and kind of feminine, all qualities I never put into words until Goren's man hand grabbed mine. Until I had a pair of hands to compare to Matt's.

I look out over the river. The air is clear and the skyline pulses with light; even an early winter night looks good when you're near the waterfront. The other strollers are bundled in hats and gloves and scarves. I should be chilled in my thin plaid button-down coat, a hand-me-down from Thalia that was probably the pinnacle of fashion when she first got it, and is now hip in how out of fashion it is. But I'm only marginally on the cold side, the anxiety and out-of-my-comfort-zone feelings keeping me heated.

We continue on, and I have the vague sense that now, as of this moment, I'm a grown-up, with a grown-up life and a grown-up date. Goren wears real clothes: a brown leather coat over a pressed button-down blue shirt, and a pair of clean, crisp khakis (with a pleat so sharp you could probably use it to cut a steak) that cover a pair of polished brown loafers. He's preppy chic, but looks completely comfortable and put together, not like the wrinkled, ripped jeans, T-shirt and muddy Converse sneakers I used to date.

And he seems to care. He's asked countless questions about me, about my favorite book and my favorite band and where I went to school, and when I told him about my father, he asked a hundred questions about blindness and Greece and the traditions they'd be using in the wedding.

The other thing is that when he talked about himself, *I* cared. He talked about his music and his favorite drummers and his favorite places to go on tour, and he told stories about Jack Mantis (all save one off the record—a story about a broken guitar string and a fired guitar tech who cried) and the bands he's played with—Fleetwood Mac and Rush and Aerosmith. And he spoke reverentially and softly of them, never once intimating that they weren't good people, never once implying that their talent was lacking or that they stole drumbeats from him.

Now a chill overtakes me. I curl in on myself, and we stop, leaning against a wooden post, the sound of the water lapping against the pier lulling me into a calm feeling. A squirrel out for a midnight walk scampers by, and I smile in the direction of the moon: plump and polished white like a pearl.

Goren's cheeks are red, the collar of his coat kisses his chin and he looks at me kindly. "What's your general opinion of after-dinner drinks?"

Now this is a question I can answer. "Positive, generally."

"I know a place."

"I'm sure you do."

And he puts me in another cab. That's two in one night. Now, yes, he's in a band bankrolled by a major label, he's the drummer on three consecutive number-one hits, yes, he lives in a penthouse apartment in Soho, yes his coat is leather and smooth like the interior of a seashell, yes, I met him at the most prestigious recording studio in Manhattan and possibly the United States. And somehow it's the fact that he sprung for two taxis in one night that really sets my stomach aflutter.

We pull up in front of an adorable coffee place in Hell's Kitchen—this is one of my favorite places to go, actually, because they make a killer carrot cake, they'll put bourbon in your coffee if you ask real nice, and their music, in a word, rocks. I give Goren an approving nod and wrap my scarf around my neck one extra time for good measure.

"It's not a bar, but I figured we could talk here."

"It's perfect."

And I'm referring to the whole night, not just Stella's, the coffee place. As we stand in the perfumed doorway of the shop, peering into a red-velvety room of sofas and bookcases and plush chairs, with feathers and scarves and other hanging sequin-covered fabrics covering the walls and a cake case fertile with goodies, I think to myself that it's going to be okay. I'm going to be able to do this, to go on, to acclimate myself to this new life, this life without my father needing me and my boyfriend draining my energy. And I know that it was hard to leave the comfort of those things, but for the first time since, well, since before I even thought to hunt down Jack Mantis, I feel like it is okay that my life is moving forward, moving to the next phase, the next big thing.

"Ready?" Goren puts that man hand on the small of my back. It makes my skin burn, in a good way.

"I am. All ready."

He's a tall guy. I can barely see ahead of him as he follows the hostess to our sofa. Stella's has no traditional tables— another reason I love it here. With the couches and coffee tables it's a great place to read. I brought my father here once, but he was so distracted by a conversation going on in the corner about whether or not Kit Marlowe was the actual author of Shakespeare's plays, that he couldn't concentrate on my rousing version of Euripides. I never brought him back.

But now I'm here. "Do you read?" I ask, unaware that

this is a concern until the moment the words filter through the air.

Goren looks abashed, and holds up his menu. "Some things I like to read. I'll read your story on us, of course."

"You'll be the star of my story," I joke, and peruse my own menu, though I know already what I want.

"Jack's the star. Don't forget that."

"How'd you meet Jack, anyway?" The menu falls to the table, and Goren waves a scolding finger at me.

"No shop talk."

"Okay. But we still get to talk about music."

He smiles and stretches—man, is he tall—and rests his arms along the back of the sofa. I track down the waitress and order a cappuccino and a carrot cake.

"So, what's your favorite Dylan album?" Goren asks, once our coffees and cakes are delivered.

"Um, this one, actually." I point in the air, where we can hear the soft twanging vocals of Dylan as he sings "Tangled up in Blue."

"Ah, the divorce album."

"Exactly. You're a scholar as well as a performer."

He moves an inch toward me on the sofa. It's imperceptible, really, except to a woman who has gone without a moment like this in three years, such a body shift resonates like a tremble over a fault line. I inhale deeply, and when the waitress puts down my carrot cake I look away, thinking that if I had abstained on these kinds of treats my whole life, my hips wouldn't be so close to Goren's now. And it's a cruel torment that causes me to want him to slide closer and simultaneously keeps me from hopping onto his lap.

He smiles softly. Have I mentioned that he's nice to look at? It must be all the corn they fed him in Iowa—that's where he's from, Iowa. And gosh his eyes are blue and his skin still looks pale like milk but not the wheyish kind of pallor that Jack has and—oh, my—he's getting closer and closer and closer and—

There. Lips. On mine. Non-Hanley lips on mine. I freeze up before relaxing for a split second (what does that mean by the way, how are seconds possibly split? Split from what? The rest of the memory? Because I want to remember this feeling forever, the split feeling of hunger and horror and love and hate all wrapped in one uncomfortable moment).

And then the whole business is over.

"Was that all right?" he asks, shy suddenly and absolutely adorable despite himself.

"It was." I'm a writer. I should have better control over my vocabulary, and the ability to string together a sentence that couldn't be diagrammed by a third-grader.

Alas, I'm out of my comfort zone.

"I thought we should get it out of the way."

"You're a romantic guy, Goren."

He laughs, moves an inch away from me and picks up a fork. "Let's try the cake."

The song changes. Now it's Marvin Gaye. Why do they play a song about sex when I'm on this date? Good lord.

And I'm self-conscious, like a girl in high school. I look at Goren, who's eating a piece of carrot cake. I smile.

And then I reach for my fork. I'm feeling something. A warmth. And I start to wonder. He kissed me before the end of the date. What's the thing to do now? Invite him back to my place? I run through my checklist of the things I did today. I wrote a bit, read, listened to some demos, tried to track Jason down. I did not clean, change the sheets on my bed, sweep the floor, take out the trash, or vacuum the couch to get out any traces of the smell of Matt Hanley. Alicia told me not to worry. She also told me to be sure to shave my legs, and I'm so glad that I listened to her on that count.

I look at him from the corner of my eye. He puts his hand on my leg. I drop my fork. We're going to make out. I know it. Right here in this coffee shop. We're going to make out.

His drummer hand comes up and touches my face. The sound of the conversation inside Stella's whizzes by my head. The legs of the walking-by waitress blur into a whoosh of black-stockinged color. Those fingers. My head pounds. Those lips. My heart hammers.

"Echo's rules for the happy man…"

His other hand brushes my hair away from my cheek, and I kiss him back and then we freeze.

"Hold him back just as you can."

I jerk away from him and tilt my head to the ceiling. "What is that?"

Goren looks around and raises his shoulders. "I don't know. The music, you mean?"

"I hope it was worth it…"

We look at each other, but my thoughts are elsewhere, frantically searching through my memory for something, a touchstone to blast away the sudden confusion I feel, my ears straining to the sounds filtering through Stella's sound system.

"Hey!" I shout. Loudly. All the annoyed patrons of Stella's look at me. "Can somebody turn up the music? What is that?"

"I hope that it hurt you…"

From behind the counter, my waitress jumps and fumbles with the remote, pointing it toward an iPod perched in front of a minispeaker system.

The song instantly takes over the room, that tiny set of

speakers doing the work of ten concert-sized amps. All movement in Stella's ceases—the chatter, the clanging of utensils to plates, the scraping sounds of shifting chairs. All we can hear is:

"And you were happiest
When I was crying.
And you were loudest
When I was trying
To echo you.
But Echo
Only broke me."

Goren scrambles over to the other side of the couch.

"Son of bitch!" I'm on my feet, the chorus repeating in my head and in the ears of all of Stella's customers: *"But Echo only broke me…She only broke me…"*

"Echo!" Goren calls and chases me to the counter.

"SHHHHH!!!!" I put my finger to my lips. Rage reverberates through me, like a pounding ocean wave. "That iPod. Give it to me!"

I don't know what I look like, but that waitress reacts as if she thinks I might eat her alive. Her hands are a bit shaky as she passes it to me.

"Is this yours?" I demand, nearly dropping the thing as I rip it from her grasp.

She shakes her head no, and says, "It's Paul's. He spins down at Beauty. He gets all the new music first."

"Get him," I bark as my thumb furiously wheels the buttons on the iPod round and round until I see it.

Goren tries to help. "Echo, I don't—"

"Matt Hanley! That goddamned— Agh!!!!"

Pressing back through the menu, I see the name of the album is *Echosongs*.

"That motherfucker!" I am shouting. And cursing. Shouting and cursing in one of my favorite local hangouts. And really, the only sound in this place, since the waitress ripped the iPod out of the dock is my screechy, swearing screaming.

The waitress appears with a guy who is apparently Paul. He's like seventeen years old, a white kid but covered in dreads, which are pinned with beads. *Beads.* Christ, I hate beads.

I shake Goren's hand off my shoulder. "Hi. Paul?"

The kid shakes his head up and down.

"Um, what are these Matt Hanley songs and where did you get them?"

Paul extends a clammy arm and retrieves the player from the psycho's grip (the psycho being me). He rubs his thumb around the click wheel.

"I just get advanced CDs from labels, you know, because I spin. At Beauty."

"I know, I know."

"You've been?"

"She writes for the *Brooklyn Art and Times*." Goren points at my head and I bat his hand away.

Paul's face lights up. "You do?! I've been trying to get you guys to come and write about me for months."

This plaintive plea stops me in my path for a second, but then I recover. "Listen, I need to know where you got this. The Matt Hanley CD. And if you know, have other people gotten it?"

"Um, yeah. I mean, I would think so. It just came in the

mail today. I thought he was dead. But he's not. Only heart-broken. The whole album's about this girl."

Goren's hand falls from my shoulder. I take a deep breath and look to the floor before peering up at the waitress and Paul. When I speak, my voice sounds freakishly, horror-movie calm. "Paul, do you happen to have the CD here?"

"Nah, I left it at home. But I can bring it in tomorrow, if you want to meet me here. Or I spin on Thursdays. I can bring it to the Beauty, if you want to meet me there. What's your name again?"

"Alicia. Alicia Campbell. You can e-mail me at the paper, okay?" Thank goodness I remembered that Jason set Alicia up with a *BAT* e-mail account. The last thing I want to do is reveal my identity as Matt's muse to these people who already think I'm a wacko. "I'll make sure one of us hits your club. Just—don't play those Hanley songs, okay?"

He scratches his head in complete puzzlement. And the waitress chimes in. "Do you guys want to settle your bill?"

Neither Goren nor I speak. He merely passes a twenty-dollar bill by my eyes. My perfect date has come to an abrupt ending.

12

On my way to the *BAT* offices, I make two emergency phone calls. One to Alicia, who I thought was going to be home, and one to Jason, who has become all but impossible to find since Alicia broke it off with him. He comes into work only after-hours and on the weekends now. I know this because every morning I get to work, there's a stack of new CDs left on the desk, with a note detailing his opinion on all the ones he's listened to.

I haven't been so diligent about going through the stacks in the past weeks, because I've been working so hard on the Butter Flies interview. But clearly, I should have been paying attention to the new CDs that have come in. And as I run in my heels down Smith Street, teetering quite literally on the brink of despair, my clutch purse being pressurized into a ball of shapeless cloth, my hair slipping out of its barrettes, my date long since left in the lower end of Manhattan with a chaste cheek kiss and a sour expression on his face, I suddenly realize the real reason Jason's been MIA.

It wasn't avoidance of heartache so much as avoidance of having to break the bad news to me.

I fish my office keys out of my bag, and seriously, in my fury, I've completely destroyed this purse. No matter. Once I explain the situation to Alicia, she'll probably take me on a shopping spree. She'll have to. She's the only one I know who will be able to afford the bill for the massive reconstructive surgery and the brand-new wardrobe I'll need once word of this CD leaks out.

I fling open the front door, and step across the threshold, only to see Jason—regally casual in his blue velour track suit—frozen in place, backlit by the desk lamp in the writing room, leg raised in the air as he was about to take a step. He looks *completely* like a deer trapped in the headlights of my rage.

"You!" I point my finger at him.

"Hey, Ec." The entire angry package of me catches him off guard, and he kind of trips in his step. And his voice goes all thirteen-year-old boy on him for a second there. "How's it going?"

"Where's Walter?"

"Um, it's Friday night, Ec. Cabaret night, remember?" As Jason speaks, he backs slowly away from me, and I notice that he seemingly quite deliberately puts the couch between us.

"So, Jase," I say threateningly as I advance, causing him to inch away from me along the back of the couch, "how you been?" I toss the purse onto the couch, and Jason flinches. He then makes a break for the desk, where he spins the chair in front of himself and throws his arms over the back.

"I've been fine. What about you? You seem a little intense right now."

"Do I, Jason? Do I?"

Jason puts his arms over his head and says, "You know, don't you?"

"Know what Jason? About Matt Hanley's new CD?!?!"

"All right. Okay. You want a drink?" He breaks for the kitchen. I kick off my shoes and start screaming.

"You are such a jerk. I've been so *worried* about you! Thinking you were going through all this pain and that being at work was too hard for you and that seeing me would remind you of Alicia, and so I was being all understanding about why you would want to stay away—"

"No, that's all true," Jason interrupts, before dragging two bottles of beer from the lowest shelf of Walter's refrigerator.

"It's not true! Alicia's right! You're a wuss!"

Jason throws a bottle cap into the sink, with a little bit of malice. "I'm not a wuss, Echo."

This stops me. "I don't know why I'm yelling at you," I say, in complete defeat. I sink down to the beanbag chair, and in my upset state, my body loses its balance, and I topple to the floor. Jason comes running, pulling me up to a sitting position.

He hands me a bottle of beer, and I chug. Like a college girl on spring break. I chug.

"You okay there? Napkin?"

I ignore him. "I was on a date, you know. With *Goren Liddell*."

"Oh. Shit."

"Yeah. And we're having this kind of a thing. On a couch. And then I'm hearing Matt sing about me."

Jason sinks to the floor next to me, and I see that he's brought the remainder of the six-pack: three empty slots and three bottles wrapped in the cardboard carrying case. "It's getting airplay already? That CD only got here a couple weeks ago."

I whip my head over. "A couple of weeks ago?!"

He makes a little motion, raises his shoulders up to his ears and shrugs. "Yeah."

"I thought we were friends. Why wouldn't you tell me about this?"

"Come on, of course we're friends. Here's the story." He takes a deep breath. "A couple of days after Alicia dumped me, I was here late, and feeling bad, and so, you know, I was just hanging out and drinking, and going through the stacks."

I sigh deeply.

"I'm really sorry. But Alicia said I shouldn't say anything."

"*Alicia* knows—wait, you're talking?"

"Yeah. We're talking. I mean it sucks, but, I'm around, she's around. We're talking."

I reach for a new beer, twist the top off, and take a long, thoughtful drink. "That's mature of you."

"Yeah, well, listen, she just thought that, I mean. Come on, how many of these CDs do we get and they never end up anywhere?"

"But Jason, this isn't some nobody guy. Magic Records has been hounding Matt for this for years. They'll play it. Unless it's really bad. Is it really bad?"

Jason's look can only be described as pathetic. He again scratches the side of his head, and zips his sweatshirt up until his chin is hidden, and then he sighs.

"I can't believe this is happening." My head goes crashing to my knees. I'm in the fetal position, and as I sit there, I start to feel all kinds of things; anger, sadness, fury, shame, guilt.

"Alicia's on her way." Jason reaches out and begins rubbing my back, and then, of course, I cry. Large, painful sobs. "I'm really sorry, Echo. I'm really sorry."

"What'd you do with it?"

"Listen, it wasn't the whole album. It was just three songs."

"What did you do with it? You didn't play it for Walter, did you?"

"Of course not."

We look at each other, and he bashfully smiles, a smile full of pity and thankfulness that it's not him having to deal with this.

"You wanna go drink for real?"

I nod my head up and down, my tears falling into my lap, where my hands are folded in a sad, desperate knot.

It's after-hours at my apartment. Alicia's come over, with a bagful of colored bottles that contain liquors from around the world. Jason and I called her with our venue change and then stopped on the way here and bought a battery of fruit juices and sodas. We're set for a long night of wallowing.

"Another round?" Alicia asks after I hand her my empty glass and press Play on the remote one more time. "No!" She swipes the remote out of my hand and tosses it to Jason, who's perched at my coffee table, surfing the Net looking to download the complete Matt Hanley LP, *Echosongs*.

I'm too tired for remote-control keep-away, and drop onto the floor, where I've been sitting for the past hour, sinking deeper into a hole of misery, worrying the nap right out of my pink bathrobe.

I'm past my initial anger. Now's on to full-fledged panic mode. At first, when Goren was kissing me and the sound of Matt singing penetrated my first-kiss nerves, I was worried, like the kind of worry you feel when you walk into a darkened room and realize all your friends are about to leap out of your closets yelling "surprise" or like when your father says he has news, then clutches your housekeeper's hand and pulls her onto his lap, while a giant—*giant*—diamond flashes you into matching father-daughter blindness.

But then we got here, and Jason brought up the Web site—Magic Records's Web site—and smeared across the screen was "Matt's Back!" And below that was a line that said, "The long-awaited, hotly anticipated follow-up to Matt Hanley's *On Top of the World*." Alicia snorted and said something derisive about the copywriters. It did nothing to make me feel better, because after Jason clicked on the screen, we were welcomed to the sight of Matt, in pictures clearly taken only very recently, wrapped in the wool scarf I bought him last winter, his floppy hair covering his ears, his sad expression betraying the tortured heart of a man skewered by his lousy girlfriend. In this case, me.

The photos were black-and-white, and I started to get really angry, remembering that damn Daisy standing in Annie's club, wielding her annoying camera, snapping photos when so clearly flash photography wasn't allowed.

Echosongs the Web page read. "Songs for a Broken Heart" the reading line said. Alicia clutched my hand. Jason brought up a list of titles. "Echo Only Broke Me," "Lizzie Borden (42 Ways to Lose the Man Who Loves You)," "Dirty Laundry," "Boston Blues," "Echo's In The Night," "Medusa's Twin," "Hippie Chick," "Emancipation Proclamation," "Where Were You Last Night?" All ten "Hot Fudge" songs now full of lyrics wholly inspired by the appallingness of me.

"Okay. Got it!" Jason has downloaded some illegal bootlegging program onto my laptop, so that he can pull the album.

My throat goes remarkably dry. Like desert dry. And my head's hurting. And my heart? Forget it.

"It's okay, Echo. Just keep drinking." Alicia thrusts a tumbler full of honey-colored liquid into my hands and I take grateful, thirsty sips.

"Thanks."

She slips down next to me and begins to stroke my back.

"I can't believe you didn't tell me about this," I say, biting the hand that comforts me.

"Here we go." She impatiently shakes her head. "This is the last time you get to say anything about it. I told you. I thought it was for the best."

I drink down the rest of the drink.

Jason looks over. "Um. Make sure that's—" he points at my empty glass "—full then come over and we'll have a listen."

"I feel sick."

"Freshen that up," he repeats, then pops a CD into my burner.

I head into the kitchen, my feet feeling like they're tied to ten-pound blocks of concrete.

Alicia glides in after me, I'm guessing to make sure that I don't slit my wrists with a steak knife.

She takes the empty glass out of my hand and opens my freezer door. "Just sit."

"Stop treating me like I'm a pregnant crazy person."

Alicia nods. "Just sit."

The tinkling sound of ice cubes bouncing into my glass momentarily cheers me. I finger the bottle of scotch that I've single-handedly put a dent in this evening.

"So, how was your date, anyway?" she asks.

"You're kidding me," I respond, rifling through the many plastic bags Jason and I brought home from the store, looking for the bag of Twizzlers.

"No, I'm not. How was it?"

"Um, well, it was great, until the part where we were making out to Matt singing about what an awful person I am." I rip half a Twizzler off with my teeth.

Alicia adopts a soldier's pose. "Stop right now."

I roll my eyes and lean against the counter, screwing and unscrewing the top of the bottle of scotch.

"Seriously. Just stop. So what? So he knows Matt and knows the song was probably about you." She takes the bottle from my hands, and proceeds to hold it in one hand and a bottle of 7-Up in the other and pour from each into my newly icy drink glass. "I bet he wouldn't have put two and two together if you hadn't made such a big deal about it."

I squint at her and drink half the drink down.

"You're going to make yourself sick," she pooh-poohs, but still refreshes me.

I look away, then back at her. "At first I thought I was dreaming, because I knew the song but couldn't figure how."

Alicia leans against the fridge and fishes a box of graham crackers from one of the grocery bags.

"It's just, I've heard it a million times, but without words, and now, it's got piano. He's always played it on the guitar."

"The piano's nice, actually."

"Yeah. It's real nice."

She laughs. "I'm sorry, Ec. I don't know what to say."

"I know. I know. This is just—"

She sucks in some air and shoves a handful of crackers into her mouth.

"Oh my God, oh my God, this is going to be so bad." I am now moaning into a dish towel.

"It'll be okay. You can always sue him. Thalia probably knows a good lawyer or two."

I drop the towel. If any of you have an older sister, you know the feeling you get when they, say, sit on you, or say, read your journal aloud to the thugs in your neighborhood, or paint your hands bright green, or sleep with your teacher. Humiliation, that sensation that only older sibs can perfectly imprint on your psyche.

"I might kill him, Alicia."

"I'll hold him down while you do."

The soft footfall of Jason's padded steps brings him into the kitchen, and he pours scotch into his glass before tossing in a few ice cubes for good measure.

"Are you ready?" Alicia asks as she grabs the dish towel and wipes up after his mess.

I'll say this: it's nice to see them on such good terms. I feel a little foolish, actually, knowing that this whole time Jason was doing so well.

"Yeah. And I found a few reviews online." Jason crosses his feet at the ankles. "I hate to say this, but the lyrics are good. And you—" he points at me "—were a very bad girlfriend."

Alicia whips him with the soggy, dirty dish towel.

Scratch what I said about them being on good terms.

"You can't hit me anymore!" he shouts, holding his arm. Then he snatches the rag out of her surprised hands and throws it into the sink, before storming out of the kitchen.

Alicia looks at me, her eyes wide. "What's that about?"

I shake my head. "Are you learning nothing from my life here? A little scuffle over a dish towel is nothing."

I walk into the living room and spy Jason removing the CD from the computer. "Okay, hit me."

"Are you sure?"

"I'm sure. Let me do the honors." I take the CD from him, put it into my stereo system, and grab the remote.

Alicia, Jason, and I sit on the couch, wedged in like matches in a book. Alicia puts her hand on my knee, Jason drapes his arm over my shoulders, and then I hit the play button.

The first strumming of a song I recognize as Hot Fudge #3 begins, and my breath catches.

"The air I breathe
Is free
And the life I'm living
Is free
I proclaim my emancipation
From the shackles of you."

"Can he *write* that?!" Alicia screeches after the song comes to an end. I can't answer. My head has fallen back, I'm staring at the ceiling, and visualizing the concentric blue-and-red circles Matt tried to paint when he should have been writing lyrics to the songs I've got on this CD.

"Let's just play it through" is all I can say.

And we do. The three of us sit there for forty minutes, listening to Matt's opus. His declaration of independence, if you will. I'll give this to him: he sure expressed his pain.

There's an entire song about the laundry, an entire song about how I spent my nights listening to bands that weren't his, a song about my preoccupation with my hips. At one point, he sings, *"They aren't that big,"* and Alicia stage whispers, "They cannot release that one." The only one that entertains me in the slightest is "Medusa's Twin," which manages to lob a few good insults Thalia's way. *"Sisters do the worst damage to the soul of the loved,"* goes the line.

When the CD runs its course, and we're once again bathed in silence, I bite the inside of my cheek.

Alicia gets up and clears away the glasses. Jason goes into my bathroom and brings me some Kleenex. They tower over me, staring, waiting, I assume to see if I'm going to crack.

"I'm okay, you guys."

They look at each other before looking back at me.

"What are you going to do?" Alicia asks, cautiously.

I wish I had the answer.

13

Yesterday, when I woke up, I was a girl whose career and love life were on track. I was working on an article for a major magazine, and I had a date with the drummer in the most famous rock band in the United States.

Today, I'm a woman teetering on the brink of total obsession. I thought stalking Jack was odd, incongruous to my neat little personality?

Well, my game's been raised. I awoke with a mission. And I won't stop. I won't rest until I have yelled, at the top of my lungs, at my ex-boyfriend.

The good thing? I'm full of energy. When I woke about ten minutes before my 7:00 a.m. alarm went off, nobody could have been more surprised than me. It's Saturday, after all, my day to sleep until eight. And today, after the night I had, I would have expected myself to put those covers over my head and just wait for God to take me.

But I have never felt so alive, so ready for battle. I was up, showered, dressed, powdered and primped all before I even had a second to drink my coffee. I took that CD out of the stereo and stomped on it—in Thalia's stiletto boots. Then I burned another one, just to have it. I called Helen and told her I wouldn't be there for either Saturday brunch or Sunday night dinner.

Fury has transformed me into a woman of iron!

And then, I sat in my kitchen, fully made up, hair perfect, PJ Harvey roaring on the CD player, and plotted my attack.

I called Matt's mother. She didn't answer. Possibly because it was eight forty-five on a Saturday morning. I left messages with his manager, and his sister and even left a rambling message on the voice mail of Frank the tattoo artist. Then, I grabbed my gear and left the apartment.

I went to the *BAT,* where Walter greeted me with pancakes. I declined. Having a song written about your hips will do wonders for the first day of a diet. I grabbed a grapefruit out of the fridge and ate it, without even sweetening it with sugar!

Then I went online, researching, researching, researching. They set a release date, a moment when a CD called *Echosongs* would be unleashed on the public, an entire album dedicated to the tyranny of me.

"Are you okay?"

I crane my neck around the corner of the screen, and see Walter, draped in a kind of Bea Arthur-esque caftan, looking intently at me.

"Of course I am, why?"

"You're banging on the keys and singing Blondie under your breath."

"Oh." I immediately fold my hands neatly and place them on my lap.

Walter retreats, and reappears in ten minutes holding a cup of hot chocolate.

"I can't, Walter. I'm on a diet."

His face betrays his disappointment. "But I made this special for you! It's from scratch. With skim milk."

See? And this is why I have hips so large they inspired a *song*. It's because of Walter and Helen and all the food enablers in my life. Don't they get that no means no? But I look into Walter's runny-eyed stare, and I can't help myself. I take the mug and sip, and sure enough, the smile that replaces his frown makes me feel a bit more comfortable.

He leaves me finally, and I'm left with the hot chocolate and my thoughts. My thoughts on life and fat and boyfriends who secretly harbor negative opinions about what you look like. I wonder if it was the sweatpants that did it. Because I tend to enjoy a good comfy-clothed evening, and my favorite red sweatpants do hang off my waist in an unappealing way. I try to remember how big Daisy Dorfman is. All I remember about her hips is the Matt Hanley–embossed belt she wears around them.

To shake that particular image, I drink the hot chocolate down, all the while knowing that emotional eating will only exacerbate my fat-hip problem.

Alicia says it's not a good sign that the hip song has me more worked up than the others, but what does she know? She can't let Jason, or anybody, in long enough to feel what I feel—the sensation of a million trapped bees in your gut, a panic derived from the fact that the person who was meant to love you unconditionally had a condition. Two of them. Hips.

Once I tongue down the remaining of Walter's homemade marshmallows, I pack up my bag and head for my next stop. Since none of Matt's family or friends will call me back, since I know for a fact that Annie doesn't know where he's living, I can think of only one way to track this loser down.

When I walk into the Silver Records's reception area, the same girl is there, in the same shade of blue, reading probably the same magazine, looking bored and also alert, if it's possible to pull off both characteristics at once.

"Hi," I say, walking up to the counter, clutching a picture of Matt that I printed from his record label's Web site. It's one of the black-and-white ones. "I'm looking for Matt Hanley."

"No stalk—"

"Yeah, I know. You got a CD player back there?"

The girl nods her head, blows a bubble and puts out her hand.

After she places the disc in the computer monitor in front of her, I say, "Go to track eight."

As the song "Hippie Chick" plays, the girl's expression changes from boredom to sympathy. "I remember you now. This really sucks."

"Yeah, I agree. It sucks and it's about to go nationwide. So if you have his address I'd really appreciate it if you could give it to me."

The girl stands straight up, and her head tilts a bit. "Men can be such babies," she says. "I know just the trick."

She picks up the phone and dials a number. The person who answers seems to give her a hard time when she asks for Matt's contact info, but this girl is a pro. She launches into a masterful bout of emotional manipulation, mentioning, over the course of this brief conversation, that she's never gotten a raise and that she's never once violated their musicians' privacy. I contemplate hooking her up with Thalia—the two seem like a good friend match.

"Okay," she says, hanging up the phone and scribbling something down on a torn corner of the magazine she was reading. "Here you go."

I take the piece of paper. "Thanks so much." When I read the address, I have to curtail the impulse to crush the paper in a ball and hurl it at something. He is living only *ten blocks* from me. I recover my composure and say, sincerely, "I appreciate it."

"He's a pig. Men are pigs."

"They're bastards."

"Is there anything else I can do for you?"

"No. Actually, is Goren here?"

"Goren?"

"Yeah, Goren Liddell from the Butter Flies? I was here a few weeks ago, interviewing him, remember?"

"Oh, right. Yeah. Let me call up."

She dials the phone, hands it to me, then dismisses herself through a doorway, leaving me by myself in the lobby. Listening to the phone ring and ring, my stomach starts that dirty dance again, the million bee shuffle. Our goodbye last night was brief and chaste and I can't remember how awkward it was because at the time my head felt like it might shoot off my body and go careening into the stratosphere. Looking back on it, Goren was acting distractedly, understandably so.

"This is Goren."

"Goren! Guess who!" Does this make me insane? Saying something lame like this? Is this how Daisy talks to Matt? Thalia to Jack? When he doesn't answer right away, I breathe deeply then say, "It's Echo."

"Oh. Hey, Echo. How ya doing?" I start analyzing his tone right away. Warm but not excited. Approachable, but not desperate. I know he's only just spoken a handful of words, but somehow, somehow, I feel there should be more subtext here.

"I'm downstairs." I blurt this out, like a tactless six-year-old.

"Really?" Okay. I'm *not* mistaking this. There's a trace of panic in his voice. I can't be wrong. It's there. That "Really" was covering an "I'm going to keep you on the phone while I search for the emergency exits."

"Want me to come down?" Or not.

"Yeah. Can you?"

"Okay—hol—" And then I hear a muffled voice in the background, just before Goren comes back on the line, "Hey, Echo? They need me in the studio. I'll call you later, okay?"

"Okay." And then he hangs up. And I look down at the crumpled picture of Matt in my hand.

I'm still staring at this photo of Matt an hour later, while I'm camped out in front of his new digs. Matt, the man of little-to-no means of support, the man who let me pay his rent for three years, has moved into a building in the posh, bistro and boutique-dappled Lower East Side district known as Nolita. The best way to describe this neighborhood: clothes sold here cost either $1000 or $2. No in-between. Also, supermodels live here. Lots of 'em.

They live in Matt's new building. Watching an apartment for over an hour, you get a pretty good idea of who it's housing. And this place, a four-story brick building with kelly-green trim and a doorman, is chockfull of statuesque ladies with prominent cheekbones, thousand-dollar hair-styles, and large, shiny jewelry.

When I first arrived, a grandé latte held tightly in my hand,

I wondered if perhaps the bead-bug girl lived here, and if perhaps Matt was just "crashing." It would be in keeping with his personality. But after spying the ins and outs of ladies whose looks embody the word *goddess* and the phrase *looks like a million bucks,* I've deduced that wherever he's sleeping in that building is being bankrolled by me. I am his muse, after all.

I sip my coffee, wrapping my hands around the paper for warmth. I'm not a complete coward, though I am trying to keep out of the line of sight of the doorman, my new nemesis. When I first got here, I asked him to buzz me up, thinking I was being all cool and slippery. But along with the 24-hour security and the polished brass door handles, inhabitants of 99 Elizabeth Street apparently buy anonymity, too, because the guy flat-out refused to confirm for me that Matt lived here.

So, I'm stalking. I like to think of it as focused waiting. I'll just sit here, and drink the java until that bastard appears. I suppose that I could have refined my plan a bit. I mean, it's around 1:00 p.m. Who knows if he's even awake? Maybe he's having filthy, beady sex with that horrible groupie Daisy.

I'm starting to think that so many caffeinated beverages aren't good for me. I text message Alicia to confess what I've become. Also, to ask for pointers and reassurances and maybe catch phrases to use when Matt emerges. At this point, I don't even know what I want to say. I just want to make him take it back. It's not like I don't know that maybe my hips are a bit on the round side. I mean, the day Helen met me she said she'd love to introduce me to a few of her nephews because I'd be good at giving birth and the women in her family traditionally had narrow birth canals.

A breeze blows, and a woman with a stroller passes by where I stand, with my back to the wall of a record store. I notice that she's wearing designer jeans, in what can be no larger than a size two. I pull my coat around myself.

And that's when I spot him.

"Matt!" I yell, and drop the coffee all over myself. Thank God it was only half full. "Yeesh—OOWOWOW!!!" I screech and start patting myself down like I was a cop.

"Echo?" Matt's voice emanates from across the street.

I look up in my frothy, heated, messy state, and see Matt poised midstep, hand outstretched and held between the two mitts of Daisy Dorfman. She's staring daggers at me, and then narrows her beady little eyes into dangerous-looking gashes. Matt turns to her and clearly gives her a stay-here motion, before dodging through the traffic of Elizabeth Street like he was in a video game.

I watch him come toward me, hair floppy but buoyant; coat a camel color with a fuzzy white lining that looks so warm, and so *new*. I'm momentarily stunned out of my coffee-burn pain.

When he reaches me, I stop breathing.

It's been weeks since I've seen him in person; weeks since he locked himself in my bathroom like a girl and I threw him out. Weeks since I walked into a sparkling house and cursed his name.

And now here he is. My Matt. My Matt in a six-hundred-dollar coat.

"You look warm." I say this as I hold coffee-covered hands to my chest. I fear that I look decidedly *not* warm; that my hour in the frosty air has left me snotty and red and frostbitten.

And then it's the smile I know and used to love that warms me a bit.

"Hey, spilla'." He digs through his pockets and I know he's looking for napkins to help me. But he comes up empty-handed.

This could be it: my big moment. I mean, the stage is set. The wind blows, the cars pass by, he could pat at the stain on my corduroy and our heads could touch and he'd apologize and grab me and pull me in, and whisper into my ear that it was all a big mistake, not the record, but the lyrics, and that he was finally going to come back and take care of me and pull his weight and clean my apartment for the rest of our lives.

But what happens instead is this:

"MMM-AAAAAATT!" Daisy Dorfman is clearly not a singer. Nasal and haughty and cords like a Wagnerian hooker.

He turns from me, and holds out his hand, telling Daisy to hold on a second. She pouts and sinks into her hip, and Matt turns back to me. He chews on his lip for an almost imperceptible second. "What are you doing here?"

The directness of the question slaps me in the face. Because there are so, so many answers: checking up on him, waiting to ream him out, hoping to get him to apologize. These thoughts cram into my skull, pushing language out, the sting of the coffee as it drips onto my stocking-covered leg barely registering as the wind whips and swirls around my runny, stuffy head.

"Why didn't you tell me?"

The proper pieces fall into place behind his eyes, like three cherries lining up in a slot machine, and I know that he knows that I know.

"I work at an *arts paper*. We got the demo."

He looks away and shrugs. "I don't know how to explain it."

"Well, I'm giving you a chance to try."

His eyes find mine, and he shoves his hands into his tissue-less pockets. And then he breathes, and removes a hand to scratch the side of his head.

"I just—I didn't know you were so unhappy."

"Because you didn't care," he says. And then Daisy Dorfman succeeds in making her way across the street. She petulantly arrives at Matt's side and ushers him from me in a blur of beads and confusion.

I don't go home. I don't go to work. I go to Annie's.

Because it seems appropriate that I should seek comfort from a glass of something not healthy.

I don't quite know what I'm most upset about.

When I find Annie behind her bar, polishing a stack of highball glasses and humming to herself, I know it's not the fact that Matt thinks I'm a little on the round side. But, Lord help me if I can figure out how to make this jabbing pain in my side go away.

Annie senses my distress. "A Saturday in November, not yet five o'clock. How 'bout a drink?"

I pull out a stool and collapse on top of it, throwing my bag to the floor and crumpling into a ball of some indefinable desire. "Have you talked to Alicia?"

Annie pushes a tall glass of Coke and a short glass of scotch my way. The jukebox plays Johnny Cash at a lonesome, tolerable level—there's something comforting about being the only two people in this bar. This is always kind of how I picture my mother spending her days, anyway.

"Yup," she says.

I drink the soda first. Then I sigh and put my head on my wrist.

"I feel like it's kind of a mean thing to do."

"It's harsh." Annie leans over the bar; I can see down her white blouse to the white tank top beneath it. "Did I ever tell you about my friend Sharona?"

"No." I cringe at the story before she even tells it.

She blows her bangs out of her eyes. "Oh, honey. There were bumper stickers. It ruined the poor girl's life."

And then a thought occurs to me. "Annie, what if these songs make radio play?"

She nods and pouts her lower lip for a second. "You should prepare for that."

14

Annie knew what she was talking about. I should have prepared for that.

Poor boy choices notwithstanding, I'm a bright girl. I may not always know the right thing to say, I may regularly embarrass myself in front of bouncers, but I happen to have graduated from Emerson College, a most reputable establishment of higher learning—with honors. Also, if pressed, I could probably recite most of the works in the classic Greek canon from memory, and that would be sure to impress the most close-minded person of my intelligence.

But for some reason, with all that going for me, I didn't see this one coming. It never occurred to me that if a guy is prominently featured on a major record label's Web site; if there have been "Where is he now?" speculative articles written about him for the past three years; if he still gets a stack of fan mail delivered every month by his manager, that maybe the public was expecting, nay!—anticipating—his next album. And that when said next album dropped, that it would, of course, get airplay.

I was disadvantaged, unfamiliar with the reality of how in demand Matt was, because to me this person was a creature who lived in holey underwear, who trailed Froot Loops behind him like he was in a fairy tale and I was a warty witch. He was a man who scratched himself on his inner thighs often and without bothering to unzip to reach his itchy spots. This was the man who would spend three days painting a mural, only to decide that his work sucked in any medium and that the right thing to do would be to cover it all over with large circles of color.

But despite all these personality traits, the man has written an unquantifiable, undeniable hit song. And it's taken me completely unawares, blindsided me like a drunken hockey player ramming a guy into the boards.

"Echo Only Broke Me" is everywhere: on the radio, on television, in the background at grocery stores and restaurants.

The first time I heard it independently of the CDs I'd burned, I was in my father's little backyard, escaping the smells of Saturday-morning brunch—the pungent odor of frying bacon. Helen ran out holding her little radio in one hand and her head in the other, the very image of classical mourning. It was all I could do to keep her from yanking out her own hair. I sent her back into the house to compose herself, and leaned against the brown stones of my dad's house, holding the radio to my ear, a tear falling down my face, freezing on my cheek in the winter chill.

The first week "Echo Only Broke Me" was released it registered at number 242 on the Billboard charts. I honestly wouldn't have thought twice about looking for the song on this list, though Jason and I do make a habit of checking the charts every week if only so we can make fun of what songs are popular. But Jason wisely thought that we might want to keep our eye on the movement of this particular ditty. He heard it in a cab on the way home one night and he says that if you hear a song like that at 4:00 a.m. on a Friday, it's an up-and-comer. I remember this so clearly partly because of the stricken look on Alicia's face when we both realized that Jason had been on a date.

So now we have a new Tuesday tradition at the *BAT.* When Jason gets to the office—I've been getting there notoriously hiding-from-your-problems early—me, Jason and Alicia, if she's there, gather impatiently around the beanbag chair. Jason nervously shuffles the papers back and forth, reading through the list with his finger, his mouth moving as he recites song titles inaudibly to himself. Alicia clutches my hand until I can't feel it anymore, and the only sound to be heard is the nervous pacing of Walter, who waits for the bad news from the kitchen.

The second week, "Echo Only Broke Me" jumped nearly 200 spots to number 54. My response was to spend the next week searching for Jack. Because, despite all the personal turmoil in my life, my Butter Flies interview was basically done. All I was waiting on was a sit-down with my future brother-in-law.

I was also pretty busy fielding all the phone calls from Dick Scott, who made it his daily habit to call and harass me for the Butter Flies story. It had been hard to explain to Dick that Jack was under Thalia's spell and therefore unreachable. Every time I tried, Dick would hang up. I'd get a call five minutes later from Stan, begging me to tell him where Jack and Thalia were, I'd say I didn't know, and then five minutes after Stan hung up on me, Dick would call again.

This week, it's been harder for me to bury myself in my work. Because it's become pretty obvious that Jack Mantis is ignoring me. And also, *Disc* has been suspiciously quiet. No bothersome phone calls. In fact, for the past week, the situation's been reversed. I've been calling Dick and Stan like a spurned ex-wife, begging for any news, any feedback on the Jack-less version of the interview I'd sent over. And they've been quite obviously not returning my calls. Neither, for that matter, has Thalia. It's all looking a bit fishy, if you ask me.

Because of this stagnation, I've had little else to do but listen to the CD stacks and write reviews and collect a pile of "first" memories like a squirrel gathering nuts, or a first-time mother. The first time Matt's song was playing on the radio. The first time I heard someone humming it to themselves. The first time Walter started to cry over it. The first time someone said, "Echo? Like in that song?"

The first time I heard the song in public was at the Starbucks near my dad's, where I was waiting in line for my favorite drink. But then the song came on. I felt like I had just been caught with my skirt tucked down the brim of my panty hose, or the way I did when a teenaged Thalia showed Johnny, the seventeen-year-old Mafioso-in-training who lived on our block, my color-coded underwear and training bras. After that incident I didn't leave my house for the remainder of seventh grade, and now I don't know if I'll ever go back to my Starbucks. It's bad enough that I recognize the song, but here's the thing: They write your name on the side of the cup at Starbucks. My name is Echo, not exactly Alice or Mary or Jane. Randy the barista's face fell thousands of feet in disappointment when he caught himself singing the words "Echo Only Broke Me" and looked down at my name.

I'm drinking a cup of Walter-brewed coffee on this late

Tuesday afternoon, sitting at the typing desk, staring at a Web page belonging to this girl from Queens who's started her own record label. Strewn about the desk are her first CDs: one of her own, and two additional ones of bands from Astoria and Jamaica, respectively. I run my finger along the edge of my coffee cup and peer at the picture of the girl named Maggie Brown, a girl that Annie Lee and Jason have been talking about for months. Maggie Brown stands alone, in black jeans and a white button-down shirt; androgynous chic, with her guitar by her side and a wreath of flowers in her long, stringy, Patti Smith hair. I trace her image with my other hand, thinking about what it must feel like to be so strong, so independent, so free that you could do things like start your own record label without so much as a second of doubt in your own ability to succeed.

I'm about to start an article on her, when Jason asks, "Are we ready?" He walks up to me and angles the computer keyboard toward himself. I nod, and take my position by the beanbag chair, while Jason brings up the Billboard site and prints out the list.

Alicia joins me, sitting and propping her feet up in my lap, I think to anchor me in case Matt's song appears in the top ten. She cracks her knuckles and adjusts the strap of her tank top. It pisses me off that Alicia can wear a tank top in winter and not feel bad about it. And it doesn't reach all the way down to her pants, either. Her midriff shows. Her perfect, small, narrow, tanned midriff that never inspired any songs. She must know what I'm thinking, because as I reach for a blanket (which I intend to use to cover my hips) she leans forward and stops me. "You have nothing to hide. You're a hot, sexy woman."

I grunt in response and see Walter leaning against the

kitchen doorframe. "I'm so nervous. I feel like it's Christmas. A perverted, backwards Christmas," he says, almost literally biting at his knuckles. He wrings his hands.

"Make another pot of coffee, Walter."

"We're out of coffee? Okay! You sit right there! One fresh pot of coffee coming up!" And he retreats into the shell of his kitchen.

"That was nice work," Alicia says, reclining. I hear our archaic printer kicking to life like a rusty, 1920s car.

"He needs to keep busy. He's stressing me out."

Alicia snorts. "He's the least of your problems."

She couldn't possibly be more right about that.

"Okay," Jason says, joining our knitting circle.

Alicia sits up and wraps her arms around my neck. I wrap my fingers around her arm, holding on so tight I'm surprised she doesn't say anything.

"I can't find it," Jason says, shuffling through the pages.

"It has to be there." Alicia loosens my grip and peers over the tops of the pages in Jason's hands. "You're not looking on the right page!"

"I am, too!" He raises the pages in the air, where Alicia can't possibly reach them. "Seriously, sit back, or I'm throwing these away."

"Oh, for crying out loud, Jason, like we need you to find these."

"All right! Kids, stop! The anticipation is killing me!" Walter cries from his hiding place in the kitchen.

Jason sighs dramatically and deeply and shifts his weight from sneaker to sneaker. "Okay." He resumes his shuffling, focuses on something and then lifts his eyes to mine. "Number 9."

"Number 9? Ooh." Alicia looks at me. Apparently my

face conveys the turmoil that my body feels, because instead of trying to soothe me or convince me that number 9 isn't that high or that impressive, all she says is, "We need wings."

She means chicken wings. But for a second, I do wish I had wings, the flapping kind, so that I could take off and leave this nightmare behind.

Two hours later, Alicia and I are at our favorite wallow joint: Just Wing It, in the West Village. I'm not sure when or how this tradition started, especially since I don't eat meat, but whenever we're feeling ugly or without prospects, we go to this down-in-the-basement dive by the West 4th Street subway station.

We've ditched Jason, and didn't have time to change, so despite our normal Just Wing It rules of no makeup and elastic-waistband pants, we had to come dressed up. Not that it matters; I'm long past my attraction point. It's, as they say, the witching hour, and we haven't even cracked noon.

I dip a carrot stick into some hot sauce and chomp down on it, then refill my plastic beer mug with the last drops in our pitcher. Alicia grabs the empty pitcher, raises it above her head and waves it at the bartender. He winks and begins to pour a new one.

"My mother heard your song today," Alicia says, polishing off a wing in lightning speed.

"It's not my song."

"It's kind of cool actually. I mean, who knew he had it in him? This has to be the best ex revenge of all time, don't you think?"

I just stare at her, and say nothing.

She looks at me pitifully and advises, "You've just gotta go through it, that's all."

"Thanks, Dr. Phil," I say grumpily.

"You *did* dump him."

"Yes. And all of a sudden he's a creative genius, and a hit-maker to boot."

"Well, you always said he had what it took to make it."

"And I was right." I throw a carrot onto the floor and smash it into tiny shards with the toe of my boot.

"I think you need to learn from my example."

"What example?"

"I'm confronted with Jason all the time. I'm fine."

"You're not fine. You're irritated with him. And it's not the same thing." I dip a carrot into a container full of blue-cheese dressing and bite down on it, trying not to let my meaner instincts kick in.

But Alicia's not going to let this go. She sits back in her seat and tilts her head. I know that head tilt; it's her bring-on-the-argument head tilt. "What, your breakup's more important than mine?"

I take a deep breath. "No. But I was in an actual relationship."

Alicia's mouth shuts and a small muscle bulges out from the side of her face. She crosses her arms and cocks her head. "What's that supposed to mean?"

I'm in no mood to pacify anyone. "You weren't very nice to Jason."

"Well, when you're too nice, you run the risk of being a doormat." Her delivery is soft and sweet, but the meaning is still deadly accurate.

"I *wasn't* a *doormat*."

She throws her napkin down on the table and scoots her chair in. "Echo, you're my friend and I love you. But you lived your whole life for that guy, then got pissed at him for it. And I hate to tell you this, but you didn't even want to break up! You just wanted to get your way! You can barely stand to be in your apartment without him!"

I feel like I've just been punched in the gut. She can tell that she won that round, but she looks as stricken as I feel, and she scoots back from the table, dabs at her fingers with the napkin, throws the napkin down again and looks at me.

"That's not true," I grumble to the table.

"It is true. What he says, about you changing the rules and punishing everyone who hasn't got a clue. That's totally true. He's got y—"

I'm about to call Alicia some serious names but the bartender plunks the refreshed pitcher down before I can, and anyway I'm distracted by the way her face suddenly falls. She stares intently at a spot above my head, and I turn, following her gaze, realizing as I do that I can hear the intro to Hot Fudge Sauce #1, or as it's now known, "Echo Only Broke Me."

Mounted on the wall behind me is a huge flat-screen television—when we first got here there was a college hockey game on, so I am at first shocked to see a grainy, romantic-looking clinch between a shaggy-haired man and a short-haired, chisel-cheeked supermodel in the stead of sports.

I don't realize what I'm looking at until Alicia says, "That had to be the fastest video shoot in the history of MTV."

I can't respond. I'm transfixed by the sight of the shaggy-haired guy (who I'm guessing is supposed to be Matt) wrapping his hands around the face of a young model.

"Holy shit. That's you." Alicia's right. The girl in the video has brown hair exactly my length and thick black eyeliner and a choker. She's even wearing an Elvis T-shirt and a corduroy jacket.

"She's got really pretty eyes," Alicia says, in an apologetic tone. I shush her with my hand and stare transfixed at the screen.

"Can you turn that up?" I stand and shout to the bartender. He nods and reaches for the remote control. Soon the entire interior of Just Wing It is flooded with Matt's song and the sight of Video Matt caressing and kissing Video Echo. When the chorus starts, VM kisses VE's forehead, but she disappears, leaving Video Matt to grasp at the empty air around him. Then they cut to a sweaty, panicked-looking Matt Hanley sitting up in mussed sheets, as if he was awaking from a nightmare. I hold my head in my hands and Alicia exclaims on a giggle, "Oh, no."

Then the video cuts to Matt strumming his guitar on the Brooklyn Promenade, still in grainy black-and-white. Over his singing, the camera pans across a panoply of Brooklyn Promenade minglers. Daisy's there, as are Matt's mother, and his sister and his friend, Frank, from the tattoo parlor. Frank makes more than one appearance in this travesty: there's a lovely scene where the shaggy-looking Matt stand-in gets the word Echo tattooed on his arm.

I look back at Alicia and reach for my beer. "I feel sick."

The bartender approaches to clear the empty pitchers and stands beside us, watching the end of the video. When Matt's name appears with the closing credits, he says, "God. That guy's back, huh? Good song."

15

So, it's been proven—by me, in the past couple of days—that when you most need a life raft is when you are sure to keep right on drowning.

The humiliation of being the subject of a heartbreaking ballad and an unflattering video is nothing compared to the panic inspired by the prospect that, not only will you be left with no love or companionship or self-respect, but that you have no imminent source of income (I don't count the *BAT* at this point).

There are only so many phone calls a desperate girl can make. I've fried Thalia's machine leaving her messages, but she hasn't called me back in just under a month. Dick Scott only called once, to ask if I'd be interested in giving a statement about Matt's album. I declined, because I have nothing nice to say, and now he hasn't called back, no matter how many times I've e-mailed with New Tunes ideas. Stan Fields won't call. Neither will Goren, and, for obvious reasons, I've given up on him (but he *did* earn an afternoon of in-the-bathrobe tears and ice cream). Jack Mantis? Forget it. I'd have better luck reaching him if I scrawled a note, shoved it into an empty Seagram's 7 bottle (as of this morning, I have one) and sent it sailing into the East River.

All I've got to my name these days is a spick-and-span apartment, a ninety-nine percent finished article on a rock-and-roll god, and a boss who wants to take me sympathy shopping.

This is not to say that *nobody's* called, because that would be a lie. In fact, my phone's been ringing off the hook.

People are desperate to get the inside scoop.

My dry cleaner, the TA I dated and was jilted by in college (I can't believe *this* is how we were reunited), and four girls who went to my high school and who I hadn't heard from in years, including Sherry Howard, my junior high school nemesis, have called. Sherry now grows lettuce in Portland, Maine, and has three children (over the course of a twenty-minute phone call you learn a lot about a person). Two guys I casually dated in college have e-mailed me, my music teacher from fifth grade called, Alex Paxton has called twice and dropped by Annie's three times (I've avoided him successfully, at Annie's advice).

Even my mother called. I hadn't heard from her in about six months; she was living in some collective out in Oregon where they had no phones. So, on a Monday at three, when I should have been at the *BAT* but instead was writing insults in Froot Loops on the kitchen counter while listening to *Echosongs* at full volume, I was shocked to answer my ringing phone and hear my mother's voice.

I dropped a handful of Froot Loops on the floor.

"Echo! I'm the most popular mother on the fruit farm!"

She went on to say that normally they try to ignore the

media on the farm, but that every once in a while she has to have a music fix and so sneaks out to the nearest town and plants herself in a Virgin megastore for a couple of hours.

She heard Matt's song standing at a listening station, and said she about fainted.

Then she asked if she could come stay with me, since it seemed like I was living such an exciting life.

Ha! An exciting life, indeed.

The good thing about my mother is that she rarely follows through on her plans, so I'm betting that she'll never actually make it out to visit or stay with me. Besides, I filled her head with stories of Thalia and Jack Mantis, and so I think she now realizes that her older daughter is the one with the exciting life.

But it's not just the folks who've known me way back when who've been calling. The media has been in on the action, too. Now, I don't know how people have found me; I can only guess that either Matt or his manager have let word of my existence out of the bag (though I have been mentioned in some of the "Where's Matt?" articles throughout the years, so maybe the more enterprising of these folks have merely done their research). Well, no matter how they found out about me, the vultures are circling. *Rolling Stone,* MTV and VH1 all called, as did *Spin,* several college papers and Matt's hometown Pennsylvania newspaper.

I had to change my number.

That could be why Jack and Thalia aren't calling me back.

My dad sure is getting a kick out these events, in a macabre way. He should try harder to keep the truth out of his words, though. When he says things like, "I always wanted you to accomplish something of note," it's not hard to find the double and triple meanings.

My hairdresser, my doorman, my mail woman, the pizza guys who work in the shop beneath my apartment: they all look at me now. It's a look I can only describe as sweeping. I can't leave the house without a full face of makeup and a world-class outfit, that's for sure. Even over the phone, I'm having problems. The other day I had to call a record label that keeps sending the *BAT* duplicate CDs, and the pause the person on the other end of the phone took when I revealed my name was terminal.

But the only person who is wearing their distaste on their sleeve is Helen.

Take tonight. I've come over to work on her wedding dress. (When you're called out nationally as a bad girlfriend and have little in the way of a career or social opportunities, sewing a wedding dress becomes as good a way as any to spend your time.)

Helen and I sit in what used to be my mother's record room—all through high school I kept my music there, too, in addition to the Casio keyboard I would practice my scales on. But Helen's transformed this room into a practical paradise that would make Ma Ingalls weep with joy. The room has been painted pink and decorated with prints of flowers and young girls in bonnets and flowery dresses. Helen's reupholstered all the chairs to match the walls, the sofa that my mother dragged home from one of the dorms at my father's university has been covered over in a pattern of large flowers that are yellow as the sun. And there are knitting needles, and crochet hooks, piles of yarn spilling from every surface: the floor, several baskets, the shelves.

"Echo!" Helen yanks the pale yellow silk from my hands. "You ruin the stitch! You'll make me look like potato sack."

I shift my weight while Helen undoes the three or so of my cross stitches. "I'm sorry. You'd think after so many months I'd get the knack of this."

"You'd think." She pulls her needle in and out of the material she's stolen from me and shows me the results.

"Yeah, I can't do that."

"I know." She *tsk-tsks,* and hands the piece back to me. "You have to do anyway. If you help me, then there's no time to mope, yes?"

I grunt ironically and smile at her, and resume my faulty stitching.

We sit in silence for a couple of minutes. Helen's eyes peer over my work often enough to start making me really self-conscious.

Soon enough, Helen takes a deep breath and runs her fingers over the stitches. She looks at me.

"What?" I ask, dropping the fabric to my lap.

Helen sits back in her chair and resumes her work. "Echo, when I met your father, he was a blind man with daughter who was a hanging around."

"What??"

She looks up at me and purses her lips, as if to say, "It's true! It's true!"

She goes on: "But I know your problem as soon as we meet. Not enough inner light. So I say to Jamie, you let that girl go. You let her have life."

I just stare at her. I have no idea what she's talking about, but I'm vaguely intrigued. Or insulted. I can't tell the difference anymore.

"And then, we kick off chain."

"Helen—"

She puts her fingers to her lips. "You listen. We kick off chain. Like when one cow lies down, soon all cows are lying down. You get?"

"I'm a cow?"

She *tsks-tsks* again. "You are not a cow. We put you on your own. Soon after you kick Matt out. You grow up."

I slump back in my chair. "Great. How do you explain his revenge album?"

Helen puts the fabric to her lap and raises her shoulders dismissively. "He's mean."

I let out a short burst of laughter.

"Boys are mean when their hearts are hurt. They aren't tough like girls." Then she rattles something off in Greek that I expect is a quaint adage about men and how they suck.

"He's got a new girlfriend already. He can't be too hurt."

"Bah." Helen dismisses this. "Any boy who cleans an apartment for a girl will love her forever."

At this I laugh for real. I never thought of Matt's cleaning the apartment as a gesture of conciliation, and though I appreciate what Helen's trying to say here, I don't know if I buy it. I mean, if Matt loved me so much, shouldn't he have cleaned my apartment when I asked him to? Or offered to pay the rent on a regular basis when he knew how much I hated asking my dad for the money?

Speaking of which. "Helen, is Dad upstairs?"

"Yes. You can bring him his tea. Say hello."

I do as told. After Helen brews my dad a pot of honey-lemon tea, I walk up our old staircase balancing a blue ceramic teapot upon a saucer. At the door to my father's library I knock loudly, because the sound on his Olivier *Hamlet* record is raised to amphitheater decibels.

"Hey, Pop," I say as I gently open the door.

My distinguished father twists in his seat and lowers the little voice recorder Thalia bought him. His dark glasses cover the handsome blue eyes that used to make his female students swoon.

"Hamlet?" I set the tea down at his right hand and pour into the waiting teacup on his reading table.

"Ah, yes. The Prince of Denmark. A circumspect fellow, he."

"Won't that drown out your notes?" I point to the recorder nestled between his leg and the arm of his chair as I walk to the record player and pick up the record jacket.

"I'm working on my vows for the wedding. I don't want Helen to hear." His gorgeous voice sounds warmer than normal.

I smile at him though he can't see it. Then I turn the volume down on the record player and remove the needle from the vinyl. "You have to get a CD player, Dad. It's a very hip thing to do."

"Posh, Echo. I shall spend my golden years in the Greek countryside with a wind-up Victrola by my side, the sheep gathered to hear the dulcet sounds of opera and Shakespeare."

"You're a man of days gone by, Dad."

"Yes. Are you here for a visit? Or merely a tea delivery?" He holds his teacup delicately, his pinky extended in an act of gentility.

"Dad, can I ask you a question?"

"Of course, honey. Get my checkbook." It's a wry attempt at a joke, but it hits its mark.

I'm glad he can't see my cheeks flush, because though he's kidding, this visit eventually is going to end with me asking for money. Until Dick Scott or Jack Mantis get back to me, I'll have to continue my status as welfare daughter. "Later. First, well, I know you know what's going on with Matt."

"Ah!" My father puts the cup down and takes his glasses off. Yes, the attractive blue Paul Newman eyes are covered over in a milky residue. I inhale deeply, still unable to look at him this way. It's incredible the way being in this house renders me a complete child. "All right, Echo, ask me." He reaches for my hand, which I take gratefully.

"When Mom left—" I look to see if this topic will be tolerated. My father and I have never really discussed my mother's leaving before. I assumed he took it in stride, seeing as it had nothing to do with anything he seemed to have cared about in his life: books, work, success.

"Go on, Echo, dear."

"When Mom left—" I'm not sure why it's so difficult for me to put into words what I want to say "—I mean, Matt and I broke up, and he did this awful—" My voice breaks and I release my father's hand to cross my arms in front of my chest. "Well, he did just this mean, mean *awful* thing, and I can't even talk to him about it."

My father places his hand on my arm, and smiles a sad little smile.

I breathe deeply. "I guess what I want to know is, how did you do it?"

My dad picks up his teaspoon, which he begins tapping on the rim of his teacup. "What's that?"

"Go on. When Mom left, why didn't you ever want to hurt her? Because, well, I feel like I could *kill* Matt." I'm left breathless by my confession. A girl who's grown up with her dad and a less than available older sister to turn to for things like puberty and first-kiss advice doesn't take sharing her fears lightly.

But my father appears to take me in stride. He again reaches for my hands. "Echo, Echo. *Medea*."

"Dad, I—"

"No, now Medea was so distraught by her husband's infidelity that she killed her own children, just to strike into the heart of the man who had wronged her."

I don't know what to say, so I crack an inappropriate joke. "I've been meaning to thank you for not killing me and Thalia."

He laughs, and I'm grateful.

"But she never won back Jason's love."

While he's spoken he's focused at a spot just to the left of my ear, but now he looks on my face. "Lean closer," he says.

I comply.

"I have a confession to make, dear daughter."

I swallow hard.

"When your mother left, I was angry for three days. Three. And then you and Thalia had to go to school, first day, remember?"

I nod, and then remember that he probably can't see the motion, so I say, "Yes, I remember."

"It was the queerest thing, Echo. But you were beginning fifth grade, and Thalia seventh, and I was teaching, and I remember when we all got home after our schooldays, thinking how easy it had been to go about our lives without her. Without your mom."

I take a deep breath. My dad does, too, and then sips his tea. "So, what you're saying, is that you were happy she was gone."

"I'm not proud of it," he says.

"And that's why you didn't want to kill her. Or find her. Or make her come home."

He sips his tea, and rests the blue cup on his lap.

"But—"

"You're reacting differently than I did," he says simply.

I take in the sight of my father, my aging father, with the failing eyes, the inquiring mind, a man of books who married a woman of spirit, and is about to do the same thing again. "Dad?"

He smiles.

"I'm happy for you. With Helen, I mean."

He chuckles. "That's very magnanimous of you, dear."

"No, no. I mean it. And, and I'm sorry if I've been bratty about it."

"I understand, honey."

We sit in silent companionship for another minute, the only sound in the room the soft clunking of the spoon hitting the side of my father's teacup.

"Dad, if Matt wasn't happy about breaking up, he would've tried to do something, change something, so that we could move forward, wouldn't he have?"

The whiny, pleading tone to my voice, and the way it cracks, makes me realize that it was absolutely naïve of me to think that I was ever anywhere near over him.

"But didn't he?"

I think about this as I leave my father's library, and wonder if I'll ever be able to answer.

Normally, when I spend time with my father, I leave feeling secure, sure of myself and the fact that I have something to fall back on. But tonight, I don't feel that way at all.

I feel naked, vulnerable, sad. To cover up these feelings, I stop in at Starbucks, and give my name as Alicia, even though the girl behind the counter's seen my face a thousand times and knows I'm hiding something.

I take my drink and nurse it the entire walk to the *BAT.*

I'm such a sad case. I'm a human boomerang, bouncing back and forth from my apartment to my father's to the *BAT* to Annie's. It's my square of comfort, the places I can be sure that I won't be confronted with images of Matt or the sounds of my bad girlfriend-ship.

But even that's not guaranteed, really. Matt's songs are cropping up everywhere. Some girl's cell phone rang at Annie's the other day, and I instantly recognized it as "Echo Only Broke Me."

It's getting to be so that there's no escape anymore.

I'm thrilled to find that neither Walter nor Jason is at the office. I throw my stuff onto the ground, place my empty Starbucks cup into the garbage and head into Walter's kitchen, where I know I'll find at least two tins full of homemade cookies.

The diet I'd embarked upon after my date with Goren Liddell has long since been dispensed with in favor of comfort eating. My reasoning is that I'll never have a date again for the rest of my life, and therefore can let myself go. An old maid at twenty-seven.

I never imagined my life would turn out this way.

I open cabinet after cabinet, the watchful pinup eyes of Judy Garland on me while I raid. Finally I find a Tupperware container full of homemade pinwheels. I pour myself some milk and mix in some chocolate syrup and then head to the desk.

If only I kept slippers and sweatpants here, I'd be set for a night of spinsterhood.

After turning on the computer, I put an *Echosongs* disc into the stereo and crank it all the way up. I figure a) that none of our business neighbors are probably at work at this hour, and that b) if somebody does call the cops and they show up, I'll just show them my driver's license and turn up the volume on "Echo Only Broke Me." They'll totally let me off the hook.

I plug in the lava lamps, and sink into one of the beanbag chairs, before forwarding to "Lizzie Borden," my favorite of Matt's songs. It's my favorite both because it's the most artfully written and the most painful to hear.

The darkness envelops me. I take a bite of marshmallow—that Walter should get a job at Stella's café—and listen.

"The only one who's strong
Doesn't have to be you
Forever
Just for now.
Then it'll be my turn.
But I forget
I'll be gone before you fall down."

I let out a large puff of air and shove two cookies into my mouth. I hit the back button on the remote so that I can listen to the song again. Then I head to the desk and pick up the phone.

Of course, Thalia's not going to pick up. I haven't heard from her since she started dating Jack. I can only hope that she and Jack are in some faraway land feeding pandas or jumping off of skyscrapers, and that she hasn't heard about Matt's album yet. Because if she *has* heard it, then she's obviously avoiding me.

"This is Thalia. You may recite your wishes now." Beep!

"Hey, Thal. It's me, Echo. I'm just—I promise not to ask about Jack, okay? Just call. I'm in dire need of a big sister."

I hang up and put my head in my hands. "Lizzie Borden" ends and begins again—the prolonged, sweet agony of the single-song-repeat function. I eat another bite of cookie. My throat constricts. And then the phone rings!

"Thal!?!?"

"Wrong. Guess again, Hippie Chick."

"I didn't realize the devil had my number," I say with venom.

Alex Paxton only chuckles. My negativity endlessly fascinates him. He seems to feed off it. "Why the tooth? Being the most notorious lady in the world not working out for you?"

"And I'm not hanging up why?" I ask through a mouth stuffed with marshmallow.

"Meet me at the Kentucky Cocktail. We'll two-step and I'll tell you what I know."

"Hmmm. Let me think."

"Echo. You can't hide the rest of your life."

My hand freezes with a marshmallow puff in midair, chocolate drips down my fingers, and I catch a sudden reflection of myself in the window.

"Echo? You there?"

"Barely."

He chuckles again. "Okay. Just meet me at the Cocktail. I'll probably be a perfect gentleman."

And he hangs up before I can remind him that nothing about him is remotely gentle.

But let's face it. What else do I have to do with myself? Matt's off with that Daisy, counting the money he's made off my inabilities as a girlfriend, my father's writing his vows to my stepmother; Thalia's busy being in love. And who knows where Alicia is now.

So I go home. I shower. I brush my hair, and cover the hips that launched a thousand words with the widest belt I can find. I gloss my lips. I paint my cheeks. I cover my lids in purple. But no matter what I do, when I look in the mirror, I see an awful, selfish, shrewish girl, a girl who forgot that money and a career don't mean a thing without love.

16

Saturdays at the Kentucky Cocktail can only be described as New Yorker Halloween. While Tuesdays and Thursdays bring actual fans of bluegrass, among them always some genuine folks from south of Jersey, on Saturdays this place is always packed to the brim with yuppie posers.

Tonight is no exception. The ten-gallon hats and bright, never-been-through-a-washing-machine button-down shirts are the tip-off. But also, the way the guys here just stand around the bar, and play the same Garth Brooks and Toby Keith songs over and over again on the jukebox. Right now, I'm watching a pack of idiots—probably bankers by day—pound shots and chase them down with cans of Pabst Blue Ribbon. There are four of them, all respectably tall, all lanky and goofy, all none-too-reserved about leering at the blond girls in the corner.

It's a sad state of affairs when a club of losers not noticing me can make me depressed. But, I mean, I'm standing not two feet from them, staring at their shenanigans, looking as nice as I can in my denim miniskirt and purple Highwaymen T-shirt. And not even so much as a drunken leer is thrown my way.

"Want me to shoot a hoop, and maybe you'll get to take one home?"

I jump a mile and Alex laughs. "Don't do that!"

"I couldn't help it. You're staring like you're smitten."

"Heh," I mutter, and lift my half-warm and three-quarters full bottle of Bud Light to my lips.

Alex swings around to my front, blocking my view of the frat cowboys with his huge, goofy hat, and his bright red shirt, which is covered by a really lame leather vest.

"Nice outfit."

He gives me a two-gun salute, and I think to myself that he couldn't possibly be cheesier. "So, what's a pretty girl like you doing in a place like this?"

I shake my head. "You tell me. You're the one who invited me here."

Alex pops a handful of popcorn into his mouth and opens his stance; he looks momentarily like Fonzie. "Hey. I'm just trying to show you a good time, Brennan. I imagine you need it."

"Why? Why would you imagine I need it?"

He smirks and shakes his head.

"You know what I find funny?" I straighten the cowboy hat that sits askance on his head. It's docked on that pointy noggin like a Macy's Thanksgiving Day Parade float.

"What's that, pardner?"

"What I find just so amusing about you, is that I haven't

really heard from you since Alicia's and my party. Then Matt's record comes out, and—*bam!*—it's four calls in a row. And then a date." I scrunch my nose up, to make the word *date* sound cozy.

"A date, huh? Do you think anybody's ever going to want to date you again?" He drinks his newly arrived beer and sneers at me.

I really have no response to that. Because I've been thinking for a good couple of weeks now that no, nobody will ever want to date me again. But that's only half of it.

"Actually—" my voice comes out sober, serious, which fits, because I am about to speak the truth "—I don't think *I* am ever going to want to date again."

"You're a drama queen."

"No. It's true. I mean, what's the point of it? When it starts, all that happens is that you shut out the people you love, or spend so much time with the person you're falling in love with, that you don't pay attention to other things, like your sister or your career. And then, when it ends, it's *always* awkward. You either see them at work, or on television, or you have to stare at the murals they've painted outside your favorite bars because you're not allowed to paint them over. And whenever your heart feels as though it's about to heal, something will happen, something will come along to rip the scab off your heartbreak and make you bleed all over the floor."

When I look up from my little speech, Alex, the four frat cowboys behind him and the bartender are all looking at me with horrified expressions on their faces. Alex and the bartender exchange a look, and all of a sudden a brand-new bottle of Bud Light plops down in front of me.

"I don't think I need that," I say.

"Probably not," Alex agrees and checks his watch. "But take a drink, then let's you and me go two-step. If you know how."

I follow his instructions. I drink half the new bottle of beer down, and wipe my mouth on the back of my hand. When I leave the bar to follow Alex onto the dance floor, the bartender raises his eyebrows (I think in relief at my exit) and gives me a halfhearted salute.

The same band plays the Kentucky Cocktail every Saturday night. Alex and I move to the front of the stage, and watch as the band warms up. They play only covers, if I remember correctly, and three of the members have day jobs on Wall Street. But they get a groove going on, especially when the tall guy who plays the mandolin starts riffing.

Before I have a chance to catch my breath, Alex Paxton grabs me by both hands and wheels me around. He pulls me close for a moment then releases me, and I can't help but let a giggle escape my lips. He pulls me right back in again, and grins at me. "That's more like it." He affects a corny accent. "A purdy gal like you shouldn't be all frowny."

And then I just let it go. I let go the worry and regret and angst and fear, and I burn a hole in the hardwood floor with the shortest guy here.

It's late, but not at an hour I couldn't tell my father about. Alex and I walk home along First Avenue, and when we're about ten blocks from my apartment, we stop in at one of those juice and hot dog places that appear every thirty or so blocks in Manhattan.

Alex saunters in, and I wait outside, leaning against an empty bike rack. I wish I could take my shoes off and walk home barefoot. I wore a pair of cowboy boots, to get into the spirit of the evening, but after two hours of high-stepping with Alex and another pair of fine-looking Manhattan gentlemen, I've about worn my poor feet to the bone. I'm bruised, probably, and blistered, definitely.

But it was worth it. In fact, I'm still a bit breathless. I haven't danced that way in ages. My makeup's all but gone and my hair's a mess, and even though Alex and I have walked through the winter streets of a midnight Manhattan, my T-shirt's still sticking to my back, damp with perspiration.

It was just what I needed to shake the cobwebs from my brain. And who would've thought that I owe all the peace I'm feeling to Alex Paxton, my complete mirror image, as can be attested to by the fact that he comes lumbering out of the hot dog place carrying three dogs, piled in sauerkraut and mustard, for him, and a small cup full of papaya/carrot/orange juice for me.

"You sure that's all you want?" he asks, handing me my cup.

"I'm sure, cowboy Joe."

He nods his head and fits half of one of the hot dogs into his mouth. "I gotcha. I thought a couple hours of dancing to America's music would put you in the mood for a little red meat."

"I hate to tell you, but that ain't red meat," I say, pointing to his paper tray of dogs.

"Duly noted." The other half of the first dog disappears. "Hey."

"Yes?"

"Thanks." I gesture emptily in the direction of the Kentucky Cocktail. "I needed that."

"Feeling sorry for yourself, huh?"

"Yeah. I guess a lot of that."

"I'll say this for him—Matt sure knows how to launch a comeback."

"That he does."

"You gonna sue him?"

I laugh. "Nah. Just haunt him a little. Make his life a living hell," I taunt, speaking in a ghoulishly evil voice.

"I like it. I like it a lot. Revenge is always best served piping hot, right?" He brushes his hands together, and throws his dirty napkins into the trash can by the street corner. "Shall we?" He bends his arm at the elbow and gestures for me take it. It's too bad that he's so short and round and unattractive. Because being with Alex is the happiest I've been in days. Weeks even.

I slip my arm in his and we resume our northerly journey. He's still wearing his cowboy hat, and it's saying something that we get not so much as a glance or a yell as we walk down the street: him a country cowardly lion, me a tarted-up, denim miniskirt-wearing Dorothy.

What I decide to do here is try a little friendliness. I want to shake myself out of the habit so lyrically put in "Echo's in the Night," where Matt sings, "back of the bratty pack back talking, making sure your friends sound bad while I'm left gawking." I realize how much of my Alex Paxton thoughts fall on the mean side of things, and really is that fair? Is that kind? Is that the kind of girl I want to be?

So, I just try to enjoy the moment. I try to stop all the mean thoughts in my head, the little voice (that sounds suspiciously like Thalia) that keeps noting how I can see down onto the top of Alex's cowboy hat, with the assistance of my cowboy boot heels. I ignore the fact that his shirt is wet to the touch. I stop my thoughts midmotion when I start to smell something funny. It's the city, that's all. The city.

"Thanks for walking me home." See? Screw you, Matt Hanley. I can too be nice just for the sake of being nice.

"Not a problem." He turns his head to look at me, and hits me in the chin with the bill of his hat.

"Ow."

"Sorry," he mutters.

"Hey, listen. I'm sorry if I've been bitchy to you in the past. I know we're kind of in competition, and I hope you don't ever take anything personally."

"Huh? Oh. Okay." He shrugs my confession off like a dog shaking his coat after a bath. Such a boy reaction.

I take a deep breath.

Alex smacks his lips together. "Some of those lyrics are taking some poetic liberties I'm sure."

I'm surprised that he understands what prompted my apology. "I don't know about that."

"I know it feels like it's all true, but it's not."

"Some of it is." We come to a stop at the curb, and wait for the light to change.

"Well, you can always change the parts you don't like."

"Yeah—" We continue our walking, scooting past a rushing taxi that looks like it wouldn't stop for a parade.

"What?"

"I was just going to say—" I put my arm back through his "—that it's not easy to have a mirror held up to yourself like this, you know? I can't help but question if it isn't all true."

"Yeah," he says, touching his free hand to the brim of his obnoxiously big hat, "but anyone can do that to another person. You always see somebody you're close to much more clearly than they see themselves, especially the bad parts."

I look at him. He's a surprising little fellow. *Argh*. I meant to think, he's a surprising fellow. "You're pretty perceptive."

"Don't sound so surprised."

"Sorry."

"You know, you could probably easily fill an album of vitriol about Matt, but you don't."

"That's true. I could. I mean, he wasn't the easiest person to live with."

He looks at me sideways, without turning his head. "Like what would he do?"

"Huh?"

"Like what?"

"Like what? I don't know. He'd walk around in this pair of navy blue underwear that had a hole right where you don't want there to be one. And speaking of underwear, he never wears any when he performs."

Alex takes a tense little breath, and pulls his hands out of his back pockets before shoving them right back in again.

"I'm sorry. That was mean of me to say. I shouldn't say that stuff about him. Especially to a music reporter."

Again, he tenses, and depockets and repockets his hands.

And that's when I get it.

I yank my arm back out of his, and stop dead in the middle of First Avenue, and pivot on my heel. I almost fall backwards, and my mouth definitely droops until it's hanging wide.

Alex steps back from me, and smirks, and he's such a Napoleonic little bastard, that I can't see his face underneath the brim of his dorky cowboy hat.

"I don't believe this."

"Echo—"

"You have no soul."

"Echo, come on. Don't you think it would make you feel better to air some of these grievances in public?"

I spin around and storm off down the street. He chases me, calling, "Echo! Wait, come on! Echo, don't go!"

I stop walking and turn back around and we collide. "You are such a bastard. I take back not thinking all those bad thoughts about you."

He flinches backwards. "Huh?"

"Forget it. Lose my number!" I shout this, and a few drunken people passing us on this crowded winter New York Saturday clap and cheer. I distinctly hear one, "You go girl."

"Echo!" Alex continues to shout at my back, but I keep stalking off toward home. Until I hear this: "Echo! Dick's not gonna run your Butter Flies article, unless you give us an exclusive."

I turn, slowly, like I'm in a movie, like I'm in anesthetic, like my entire world is in slow motion. "What?"

Alex jogs to where I stand, panting and sweating while he catches his breath. "I didn't want to have to tell you like this. Dick's holding your article hostage."

I open and close my mouth without saying anything. I don't know what to say. I have no words for this development.

"*Dick's* holding my article *hostage?*"

Alex hems and haws. "Well, maybe that's an overstatement."

"Did he *say* that he's holding my article hostage?"

"Well, I guess not. I guess he just said he was bumping it."

This shocks me. I mean, it's true that Dick hasn't returned my calls, but it never occurred to me that he was going to cancel my article.

The look on my face must speak volumes, because Alex raises his hands in a calming pose, and says, "It's not being canceled. It's being bumped."

"What does that mean? Bumped?"

"It means the January cover always goes to the most promising, exciting act of the year. Dick's decided that *that* act isn't the Butter Flies. You haven't heard from Dick, because Stan Fields and Jack are throwing a fit that the article's being pushed back. And they're pissed that January's going to—" He shuffles his feet, takes the hat off his head, and runs his sweaty hand over his greasy hair.

"Matt." I say it calmly and softly.

Alex can barely look me in the eyes as he says, "Yes. The next cover of *Disc* is going to Matt."

I spend the next day in my apartment, back in the pink bathrobe, back in pure grieving mode. Honestly, there's little else for me to do except laze around, stare at my white ceiling, imagine how it looked with the primary color wheels on it and think about how many cats I should start out with. I suppose I can't just walk into a shelter and adopt fifty cats. So I'm thinking I'll start small. Maybe I'll go to the ASPCA and adopt a litter. Let the cat ladies of the world know there's a new spinster in town.

I've spent the past weeks doing late-night research and writing. Clipping articles was fun, printing out factoids about Jack Mantis and his band, taping them to my wall, imagining my name on the cover of *Disc*. I passed entire evenings thinking about headlines, fonts, colors. But now, of course, those dreams are shot, and I've long since packed away all the Flies info. I know, I know. Alex said that it's not being canceled, but come on. Something else will come up. I wasn't born yesterday. Bumped today, canceled tomorrow.

So I'm back to commandeering my couch and making googly eyes at my bare ceiling. And I've lost more than my career and my boyfriend and my dignity. I can't even listen to music anymore. What was once my own true love is now my mortal enemy. Every song, every lyric, every note of *any* song reminds me of Matt, of Jack, of my dying career.

I call Alicia. I ask her to bring me a dozen donuts.

"Who is this?"

"Just get over here." I'm bitchy in my misery.

Alicia coughs and moans, not sounds you want to hear over the phone.

"Are you still in bed?" To the best of my knowledge, she hasn't suffered humiliation so debilitating that she should be hiding out in her apartment.

"Oh, I'm up. I'm up." And then I hear the squeak of her bedsprings as she, I assume, gets out of bed.

"Okay. Now come over."

She guffaws, and gives me what amounts to a pep talk. "Why are you letting these bastards get you down? It's not like you."

"I know, I know," I moan.

"Here's what you're gonna do. You're going to call Dick Scott on Monday, and give them the hard Echo Brennan sell on why he should just give you a permanent job already."

"I'd be happy to give him the hard sell. But that requires him taking my call. Which nobody does anymore except for you."

It's true. Even my own sister has turned against me.

Thalia still hasn't called. And now that I know about this development with Jack and Matt at *Disc,* I'm having a hard time believing that Thalia doesn't know about any of the things that have been happening lately. It's not like she doesn't know I'm trying to track her down. Last night, after Alex left me devastated in the street, I took a cab to her place. The lights were off, but I stood outside her door crying for a good half hour, before her elderly neighbor Millie took me in and brewed me a pot of tea. She rubbed my back a bit and gave me a piece of paper so I could write Thalia a note.

I shoved it under her door.

I'm still waiting on her reply.

Forty-five minutes later, Alicia, intuiting that I'm glued to my sofa and therefore won't be able to answer the door, just lets herself in.

I can feel her eyes boring holes into me when she walks into the living room.

"What have we here?"

I can understand her disapproval. I'm wearing boxer shorts I pulled out of the dirty clothes, and a ripped T-shirt with yellow stains on it. A pint of soy ice cream has melted over the sides of its container and is dripping onto the coffee table. The television's tuned to a church show, and a Texan preacher gesticulates wildly if silently, as I have the volume turned all the way down.

"Wha'cha watchin?" she tries again when I don't answer the first question.

"I need spiritual guidance."

"You need a shower and a shopping trip," she says, picking up the carton of ice cream and the spoon and walking toward my kitchen.

"No, thanks." I burrow deeper into my cushions.

Alicia comes back into the living room, sits by my side and hunts around for the remote.

"Don't do that."

She ignores me, turns the volume up ever so slightly and begins to surf my cable. "You need a shower."

"You said that already."

"It bears repeating." During her flip, she passes by the video for "Echo Only Broke Me." She realizes what it was only after she's moved on but quickly turns back to the channel.

"See, that's why flipping the channel is bad," I mutter, before Alicia and I both slip into silence and watch the pitiful display before us.

Matt's standing on the pier again, in black-and-white again, the wind ruffling his hair the way I used to do when he was sleeping. But then Video Echo comes up to him and puts her hands all over him. This is the part of the video that I always have to turn away from. Don't get me wrong, the entire thing is very hard to watch, but this moment, seeing the affection between him and this pretty, tiny girl, really gets to me.

I attempt to wrest control of the television from the sprite currently sitting cross-legged on my couch and drinking a cup of Starbucks coffee, but it is next to impossible. She merely hits me when I reach across her lap trying to grab the remote and then I give up.

"He really sold out, huh?" she asks, licking the foam from her lips.

"There's an entire fleet of ships coming in for him right now."

"What's going on, anyway?" She turns the volume button down, and then turns to me.

"He's the January cover for *Disc*."

"Oh." Her face falls.

"It gets better."

"How?"

"Alex is writing the story."

"You really need to let me take you shopping."

"It doesn't matter anymore," I moan.

"Hmmmm. I don't know if that's true."

I roll my head over (it's leaning on the back of the couch for support) and look at her.

"Will you buy me breakfast, too?"

She smiles and cocks her lip at me. "You got it, honey."

Two hours later, Alicia and I are barricaded into our booths at Showtime Diner on 23rd Street by six huge bags of goods.

We bought out Chelsea. Books, bags, shoes, belts, three tops, four skirts. I'm not clear on which items are for me and which are for Alicia, but the act of selecting whatever I wanted and watching her pay for it all was, I'll admit, a bit therapeutic.

"Give me that bag," she says, putting her Coke glass down, and reaching across from me.

"Which one?"

I rifle through them while she yells at me, "No! *That* one."

I finally pass her all of them in rapid succession, until, on the fourth bag, she finds what she was looking for—a pair of Coco Chanel sunglasses that cost about $240.

"Put these on," she orders, and I agree without asking why. "Now sink down."

"What?" I ask, ripping off the sunglasses and reaching for a fry.

"Just put them back on, all right?"

I squint at her, and shake my head.

"I should've insisted on a makeover."

It's now that I notice her eyes flicking above my hairline. I follow her vision and turn around, and over my left shoulder, sitting at the counter, thumbing through what appears to be a knitting magazine is Daisy Dorfman.

I whip my head back around and throw on the sunglasses.

Alicia shifts in her seat and speaks out of the side of her mouth. "Too late."

And before I can respond, a shadow casts its pall over my diner table, over my veggie burger and my fries, and my Coca-Cola. A frizzy-haired, bead-wearing shadow.

"Echo Brennan."

I have no choice but to look up at her. But I do not take my sunglasses off. And before I can defend myself, Alicia pipes in with, "Scram, bead-girl."

Haughty righteousness descends upon Daisy like a cape, and I deflate. Sometimes my friend could really use a little tact. And I'll never know if Daisy was going to be polite now, because Alicia came out swinging.

"Good to know you're every bit as bitchy as Matt said you were." She throws something onto our table, and stalks off.

I reach for it—a beaded black spider.

Seeing Daisy Dorfman really ruined my day. Not that it was hard work to ruin it. But whereas I used to burrow into my work, avoiding my problems like a worm shying away from sunlight, now I feel formless, adrift. I go into the *BAT,* and willingly bake cookies with Walter. He's thrilled to have me as his helper.

Jason peers at me from one of the beanbag chairs, his legs

extended, feet crossed at the ankles, large can-style head-phones on his head.

"Anything good?" I ask, walking to him and taking a chip out of the tube of Pringles by his hip.

"Nah," he says, taking off the right ear. "Alicia here?"

"Nah." I eat another Pringle. "We did heavy-duty shopping, and she needed to get the spoils home, and also to rest. We pushed it pretty hard today."

"That's Alicia. Spend, spend, avoid, avoid," he scoffs, and then replaces the can on his head.

I return to the kitchen where Walter has pulled out a clean apron for me.

"Sugar cookies today, cupcake."

"I'm down with that," I say, tying the white apron around my waist.

Walter's chubby face lights up like a flashlight, and he claps his hands. "I wish you were depressed more often! It's less lonely!"

I hoot in disgust and request instructions. We proceed to measure and pour and sift and stir until my hands are sore. Jason soon joins us, and we nearly drive Walter out of the kitchen with our talk of Maggie Brown and all the other bands he's discovered in the past weeks.

"Getting dumped sure has been good for my productivity," he says, ladling teaspoonfuls of sugar-cookie dough onto a heart-shaped cookie sheet Walter got from a Betty Crocker seminar.

"I'm glad it agrees with you."

"Though I wish I was Matt Hanley."

I drop my dough on the floor.

"Sorry, Echo, but it's true. I do. I'd love to humiliate Alicia the way Matt did you."

Walter throws his spoon into the sink and a sob escapes his mouth. "OH!" And then he's gone, running out into the living room, sinking down onto one of the fuzzy chairs and putting his hand to his lips. "I just need a minute!" he croaks out.

Jason and I return to our work. My focus is on the cookie dough, but I notice Jason looking at me.

"What?"

"I'm okay, you know."

"Huh?"

"Without Alicia. I'm better off."

I stand up and look him in the eye. "Jason, I love Alicia, I do. But you *are* better off. She didn't appreciate you."

He looks at me thoughtfully, his blue eyes popping with the aid of his navy sweatshirt. He returns to his work and then looks at me again.

"Matt's playing Righteous Hall on Friday."

I didn't know this, because of my self-imposed media blackout. I look down and then up again. "Really?"

"Yup."

I drop a cookie onto the sheet.

"Wanna go?"

We lock eyes for a moment. And I ponder. But not for long, because before I know it, a door slams open and Walter screeches.

Jason and I rush into the main room, only to see my long-lost sister, Thalia, covered in layers of fabrics: purple and orange pashmina over a batik gypsy skirt, which is layered over white thermal underwear. She's in a large belt and a pair of boots, and her hair covers her neck like a halo.

"Ec!" she exclaims, and widens her arms to hug me. "I've missed you!"

"She scared me," Walter cries.

"Where have you been?" I demand, conscious that I'm covered in flour and an apron.

She walks over and hugs me so tightly I can barely breathe.

"Do you have any idea what's been going on?"

She releases me and gives me that Norma Desmond look. "I'm sorry, Echo. But I'm *involved* now. I went a little mad. I needed some time away."

"So you *did* take a trip?"

"Of course! I brought you back a Patagonian rock."

I jut out my hip and cross my arms over my belly. "Did Jack go with you?" My voice sounds hopeful, yet strained.

"We need to talk." Thalia puts her arm over my shoulder and tries to steer me into the kitchen.

I shrug out of her grasp. "No. Let's just talk here, okay? Walter and Jason don't care."

"No—" Walter peeps from the beanbag chair "—please go elsewhere."

Thalia turns an impatient glare upon him.

"What? You scare me!" Walter says.

"Everybody stop," I exclaim and hold my arms out wide. "Thalia, tell me what's going on."

Thalia cups the bottom of her curls in her hands and flips her hair over her shoulders, before leaning against the edge of the sofa. "Echo, Jack and I were getting along great, just wonderfully, and it started making me question things. My life. And you seemed to be doing well. And Dad's always fine, so I took a vacation. Some me time." She cocks her head, as if she's expecting me to make a crass comment.

"And?"

"And I get back and hell's broken loose. My sister's the most famous ex since Ivana Trump, my new man's a basket case."

"How long have you been back? You couldn't call her?" Walter scolds. Jason quiets him by placing a hand on his shoulder. I give the shush sign, my finger in front of my lips.

"I'm sorry, Echo, I just, I didn't know what to do. I'm not good at taking care of people like you are."

I look to the ceiling and exhale loudly before crossing over and sitting next to Jason on the sofa. "I'm not that good at it either, apparently."

Thalia scoffs, and she and Walter and Jason all say "You are" at the same time.

Then Thalia joins us on the sofa. "So what's the plan?"

I look first at Walter, then Jason, before I realize that she's talking to me. "Huh? What plan?"

"To fix it. What's your plan?"

I'm about to answer, I'm about to tell her that I'm no longer in the business of self-improvement, that I've resigned myself to a life of cat-sitting, preacher-watching and cookie-baking. But before I can get a word out, Thalia reaches for a cookie.

As she does so, the three of us on the couch simultaneously screech:

"Jesus!"

"Yowza!"

"Ouch!"

I yank my sister's hand so hard, upon which sits an engagement ring with a diamond the size of Plymouth Rock and a diamond-crusted wedding band alongside it, that she drops the cookie and tries to push me away out of habit.

"Echo, for crying out loud!" She again attempts to pull her hand from my grasp, but I'm holding on for dear life.

"Did you—you—"

"Oh, yeah, I forgot to tell you that part. Jack and I, in

Italy. They're both nice rings, huh?" She succeeds in re-claiming her hand and spreads her fingers to give the three of us a better view of her bling.

"Dad'll be crushed."

"Dad'll be fine. He stopped getting upset over me after I was arrested that time."

Jason and Walter look to me for explanation. "She was doing yoga in Washington Square Park naked."

"It was art!"

I refuse to have this argument with her again, and anyway, now I'm too tired to try.

"You know what the best part is?" She takes a bite of cookie and finishes talking before she swallows. "He's Jack *Brennan* now. We took each other's last names."

Jason cracks, "Well, that's just what your family needs. More wacky name problems."

"Echo's name isn't her problem," Thalia says, eating the rest of her cookie. "*Matt's* her problem."

I sigh and look at her forlornly, hoping she'll get the hint. She does. She inserts her fabric-laden body in between mine and Jason's, and runs a hand through my hair. It takes just this simple gesture for me to melt into her side, and I tear up a little. "Thalia, I really needed you here."

"I'm sorry, honey. But I listened to that album. Now, first of all, I can't believe that idiot had it in him. Second of all, those songs turned out great. Really."

"You do suck at comforting people," Jason says. He gets up and walks to the kitchen. "I'll be baking if anybody needs me."

Walter sighs heavily. "I'll help him. He always burns the cookies. Glad to see you, Thalia, and congratulations." He rises, pats us each on the cheek, and leaves us to our sisterly bonding moment.

"I'm glad you're back. I'm not doing so well, Thal."

"Echo, I meant what I said before as an apology." When I look at her questioningly, she continues, "You were the one who always said Matt had it in him. Nobody else believed it. You were right."

I look at my hands, my fingers, my cuticles, the polish from that manicure I got long gone. "That doesn't make me feel any better."

"Echo. You're not a bad person, you're shapely and lovely and sometimes you're a little judgy, but really, Matt's feelings were hurt. He's not the most motivated guy, but he was crazy about you. And you did good by him. You got him to get his act together. That's the greatest gift of all time." She kisses my forehead.

"Thanks, I guess."

"No problem."

I breathe in, my head comfortably on Thalia's shoulder, like it was made to rest there.

"You realize, though, that you can't stay down forever."

"I know."

"You've got to fight back."

"I know. I just haven't known how."

"No problem. I'm here to help. And while we're shaping up your life, we'll have to figure out how to fix Jack's, too. Before *he* writes an album about you."

17

In retrospect, I should have realized that any plan hatched while eating two dozen cookies is bound to be faulty.

I mean, have I learned nothing from my twenty-seven years on this planet?

And when I run a plan by Alicia, and she thinks it's "ballsy and vengeful," I should *definitely* know it's a bad idea.

In fact, my only voice of reason, Annie, counsels that revenge never ends with the score even. She tells me this on the heels of a long story about Jimi Hendrix and a guitar that never played correctly again. All fables I am ever told, it seems, have to involve the mistreatment of a guitar. I guess that's what I get for hanging out exclusively with musicians.

Anyway, back to my revenge. After Annie advises against it, after I obliquely get Helen's opinion over a long run of cream hemline, I change my mind.

I call Thalia, who is back to picking up her phone, and tell her our plan is off.

"No it's not." She's not even talking to me, I can tell. Her voice sounds like she's got the mouthpiece on her phone covered and is speaking to somebody else.

"What are you doing?"

"Huh? Oh, Echo, right. Sorry. Jack and I are looking at sheets. Back to you—you're going through with this. He deserves it. I gotta go." And then she hangs up on me.

Even if she and I are in disagreement about how I should go about living my life, it's nice to have her back. It's especially nice to have her back and *occupied*.

Thalia and Jack are too wrapped up with settling into their new married life to pay me much mind. Jack's pain at losing the *Disc* New Year's cover seems to have subsided enough so that he finally answered some of my interview questions, albeit via e-mail. And aside from having a few dinners with Helen and my father (I haven't been invited because Thalia wanted these dinners to be "couples only") they've been busy looking at apartments, and planning their move. Also, the Butter Flies began recording their next album, and Thalia has been preparing illustrations and concepts for their cover design.

So that is that. I am continuing on in my slothful, adrift life. I'm not going to do anything to try to change it. I putter around my place. I eat lots of ice cream. I have become Alicia's constant shopping companion. I let Jason start writing some articles for the *BAT,* which, I'll admit, he seems to show a knack for.

One good thing that's happened: Jason has started dating Maggie Brown, the singer-songwriter from Queens. The two of us went to her show, and I could see right away that

Jason was smitten with her. Even I had a bit of a girl crush on her; she was a bad-ass knockout with black hair and a T-shirt that said Queen of Queens. She fronted her own band of gangly musicians, who all looked upon her as if she were a goddess. She, in short, was a girl who would never let a boyfriend paint her ceiling at twelve-thirty in the morning. When I mentioned this out loud, Jason said, "Well, Echo, neither are you, as we all know."

I spend my nights helping Helen sew her dress (which seems to be taking an awfully long time). It turns out that every morning she rips out the stitches I've done the previous evening. I can't blame her, though it's nice to see that she's accepting the truth about my sewing ability. I read to my father. I've stopped giving my name at restaurants, at coffee houses, on the phone when I order food.

On the plus side of things, coming up with a steady stream of aliases has been a fabulous exercise for my creativity. Sure, there are the old standbys, Liz Phair, Aretha Franklin, Bonnie Raitt and Stevie Nicks. But I play with it. I'm not afraid to go with Paula Abdul. Or Debbie Gibson. Last week I went through a Motown phase. One day I played each of the Supremes. And if I'm feeling really daring, I'll pull out the old Celine Dion.

In short, I think I'm coming to terms. I am going to live out my whole life like this, in hiding, doing my family's bidding, not watching television, not listening to the radio. I am contemplating moving to Greece with my father. I don't think he knows Helen offered the invite to me. Immediately after she did I dismissed it, but then I started thinking about it. My career is dead and dying. Jason is more than eager to pick up my slack, and he is so happy with the work, the *BAT* wouldn't suffer at all if I left permanently.

And it is unfair to make Walter pay us both when I'm not even really doing work there anymore.

I am okay with it all.

Until MTV has to go and ruin my inner peace.

Here's what happens.

Matt Hanley is on *TRL.*

Yes, normally, even if I was regularly watching television, I wouldn't watch *TRL,* but in this case, Walter and Jason are playing hooky on a Monday afternoon. The three of us are lazing around my apartment, eating ice cream and bouncing from talk show to talk show. I have been feeling fairly strong all day, buffeted by my two girly-men. When we hear Matt's name announced as the guest on *TRL,* I am calm. Walter confesses to having some morbid curiosity, and truly, I have been keeping myself from all media for so long that I don't mind watching.

And also, I, as I have said, have come to terms with the fact that Matt is now famous, thanks in large part to me, and that I am now a pariah and always will be.

So we watch it. Walter holds on to my hand like it is a life raft. The nubile, pierced hostess, a girl barely able to fill her halter top, introduces Matt. And when she says his name, there's squealing—squealing!—among the girls in the audience. Walter squeezes my hand, but my upper lip is stiff as a dead body.

There's banter. There's laughing. There's more squealing. Then they show the video. I am still calm as can be—human Zen, in fact. After the video, they cut back to Matt, and he looks appropriately abashed. He talks a bit about the album, says that "Lizzie Borden" is going to be the next single (this, I'll admit, cracks my Zen just a bit) and smiles a lot more.

The hostess is beside herself. She makes suggestive comments a few times, nothing to be too upset about, until one moment where she literally shakes her nonexistent cleavage at him. Walter squeaks. And Jason says something about being embarrassed for her and that he hopes Matt can't be arrested for attracting this particular piece of jailbait.

To his credit, Matt *does* look uncomfortable. I recognize the signs—the nervous laugh, the redness near his hairline, the way he keeps clasping and unclasping his hands. He steps away from the haltered-hostess, and says, "Whoa, there. I have a girlfriend. She'll kill me."

Walter drops his spoon.

Then the hostess says that she hopes Matt has dumped that Echo.

Jason slumps down into his seat. "Uh-oh."

"Oh, yeah, Echo's gone," Matt mutters in that bashful, adorable way of his. His eyes get all crinkly and his hair flops around, and he shoves his hands in his pockets, and he kind of "aw-shucks" a few times toward the floor. You can see the girls in the studio collapse in pools of adoration.

I grip the couch until my fingertips hurt.

The interviewer girl flips her hair. "Right on, right on." Matt beams a handsome smile at her, and she asks who the new lucky woman is. And then the camera pans over to Daisy, who is planted on the edge of the stage, just off the area the camera catches with its lens. She waves and giggles demurely, and runs a hand through her stringy, filthy hair. It snags on one of her hideous rings.

"She's heinous!" Walter hurls his retrieved spoon at my screen.

I chew my lip.

Jason gets up to retrieve Walter's spoon. "You know, Ec, she's not that pretty."

"What about those hips? Nice, though, huh?"

Walter and Jason tilt their heads at the same angle, and say, almost simultaneously, "I guess so."

The camera finds Matt again, and he launches into this awful spiel.

"I'm really doing good, you know. It's such a blessing to have this record doing so well, and I'm just really, really jazzed about the songs. They've been such a labor of love—"

"For FOUR years!" I shout and throw *my* spoon at the screen, which Jason dutifully fetches.

"—and no growth comes without a little pain, you know?"

The studio audience audibly sighs.

Then, the part that really seals Matt's fate and my destiny as a spurned and humiliated ex-girlfriend: the hostess claps her childlike hands together and lectures, "Well, I hope you've learned your lesson, and will only date *nice* girls from now on." And then she turns to Daisy, whose grin threatens to consume her entire face. "You look nice."

Daisy responds as cheerfully as a cheerleader on uppers, "Who couldn't be nice to that?!" And then she gestures to Matt. And the studio audience sighs, again.

I reach for the remote, and Jason, sensing that I'd like to lob it at the television, wisely extends it above his head, into the air. I am too lazy to reach for it.

He shuts off the television. "Oh, Echo."

Walter turns to me and takes a big-boy bite of ice cream. "What'cha gonna do?"

Here's what I do.

I call Alex Paxton and ask him to arrange a meeting between me and Dick Scott, which he does, happily. And when I get to the offices of *Disc,* big beautiful offices adorned with flat-screen TVs on the wall and metallic ergonomically correct furniture and blissed-out employees happily chatting and walking the halls and reading magazines and listening to music, I walk to Mr. Scott's office.

Mr. Dick Scott is not wearing an apron when I meet with him. He isn't baking or listening to show tunes. I see no pictures of Liza Minnelli upon his desk, there are zero framed playbills or autographed Barry Gibb records on the wall. No, Mr. Scott is impeccably dressed in a three-piece suit, with a red tie and a diamond-chip tie pin. The only chink in his otherwise pristine professional armor is the twitch underneath his left eye when he gets a load of my escort, Thalia, who has dressed to slay in a leather top and the tightest jeans I've ever seen on a person.

And the twitch in his eye comes *before* she introduces herself as Thalia Mantis.

Alex Paxton is a preening idiot. He falls over himself trying to make sure that Thalia and I are comfortable. He even leaves Dick's office and returns with two hot cups of tea for us. And though I haven't forgiven him for pulling a fast one on me, for preying upon my emotional weaknesses, I am fortunate to be able to use his greed and ambition against him.

My sister and I are here for a purpose: torpedo the story.

Okay, really we don't torpedo anything. We go in hoping to have Matt knocked from the cover of the next issue of *Disc*.

Mr. Scott is titillated by Thalia but no fool, so he won't budge on making Matt the cover boy of the first issue of the New Year.

But we get a guarantee that Jack gets the *next* cover. As a matter of fact, Thalia gets Dick to sign a document drawn up by one of her ex-boyfriends attesting to such.

I know, I know, you're dying to know what we gave up to secure this.

We don't give anything up.

I merely agree to give an exclusive interview to Alex Paxton, to be run alongside Matt's story, to be advertised on the cover of the New Year edition of *Disc,* a coming-out, if you will, a chance for me to tell what really happened, to tell my side of the story.

Echo's Sidebar, Alex keeps saying he'll call it, and Dick Scott keeps hushing him.

Thalia grins like she's just swallowed a canary, and struts out of there like Lauren Bacall.

When I'm leaving, Mr. Scott pulls me aside. "They're not really married, are they?"

"I'm afraid so, sir."

"It's too bad. Yes, sirree, too bad." And he smacks his lips as he watches Thalia's backside sashay away.

On the following Friday, I primp as if I'm going in for a job interview or a blind date. I wake up early, and take an especially long shower, using the exfoliant and shampoo Alicia bought me on our previous shopping trip. I moisturize and perfume, and style and color. I look at myself in the mirror, and practice a variety of smiles and speeches.

"We met on a cold day in Boston…" I mold my features into a maudlin arrangement of wistfulness.

"Matt Hanley is the love of my life…" I frown and fake cry.

"He's a fucking bastard." The truth doesn't look so flattering.

I sigh and open the vanity door, reaching for my hairbrush. Then I walk into the bedroom and proceed to pull out every item of clothing I own. Skirts, pants, dresses, long-sleeved shirts, vests, baubly halter tops, before deciding on a pair of slimming black pants and a silver T-shirt Alicia gave me two weeks ago.

Alex Paxton said repeatedly that there'd be no photo of me in the magazine, but I don't know. It's important that I look good for this, and as slim as possible. I've read Alex Paxton's work before and he can be, um, honest. Brutally so. Our hateship was cemented by his scathing review of Matt Hanley's first CD, so I have firsthand experience with his brand of merciless writing.

And the last thing I need is a description of me in *Disc* as "plump" or "mousy" or "ugly." So I'm beautifying myself to the best of my (and Alicia's) abilities.

When I'm ready, I grab my "be fri for" keys, and let myself out.

I'm meeting Alex at the *BAT* offices, because I wanted to conduct this interview in a professional environment. Not that I'm afraid of chickening out, but I feel that if I'm in my apartment, staring at the furniture and the walls that witnessed Matt's slovenly ways for so many years that I'll get really, really nasty.

But at the *BAT*, I'll be reminded of why I'm doing this—to escape the art you can touch and the smell of baking cookies.

And to get revenge.

When I arrive, Alex is already situated. There's a tape recorder on the desk, and he's got two notebooks out and a box of blue Papermate pens. There's a plate of chocolate chip cookies in front of him, and two glasses of milk—clearly the sign of Walter's hospitality. The late morning sunlight streams into the room, and Alex looks up at me as I walk to him. He's wearing his work outfit—black jeans and a black Anthrax T-shirt.

He smiles and waves a notebook in the air. "Ready?"

I sit down across from him, and fiddle with the tape player. "Where is everybody?"

Alex looks over his shoulder, as if he expects Walter and Alicia and Jason to be behind him. "Jason and Walter went to the park. Alicia just ran out to get some beer."

"It's eleven o'clock," I say.

Alex shrugs his nonexistent shoulders. "She thought you'd need it."

I nod my head and recline in my chair. "Lizzie Borden" comes on the stereo and my head falls.

"This is your favorite of the songs, huh?" Alex surreptitiously presses the record button on the tape recorder, but I see him do it.

"Yeah. I guess."

"Tell me why." He pushes the recorder toward me.

I pull my legs up cross-legged and rest my elbows on the insides of my knees, and my head in my left hand. "I guess because Matt's had this tune written for four years, since he was on tour the first time. He played it for me over the phone one night. It was like four o'clock in the morning, and I remember it because I was disappointed when I went to bed that night—I hadn't heard from him and he'd promised to call. Anyway, the phone rings in the middle of the night, and usually I'd be mad to be woken up, but I was so happy that he remembered. And he played this tune over the phone on the guitar, and said that someday he'd dedicate that song to me."

Alex writes something down on the first of his yellow notepads. "How'd you meet?"

I answer his question. In fact, I tell the whole story, about the T platform, and the songs he played me at that party, and how we were together that first night, and how years later he had forgotten me, but lied and said he remembered. And I tell him about our "Name That Tune" courtship, and how he would send me a magnet from each state he visited, and how when my father went blind he bought him a custom-made armchair and a recording of John Houseman reading the *Iliad*. I tell him how when Matt got off tour, he took me to meet his mother and his sister, and how my spine felt tingly the first time he called me his girlfriend.

I'm so engrossed in my story, I don't even hear when Alicia comes in and sits on the couch. And I don't register when *Echosongs* comes to an end. I tell Alex about how Matt painted the exterior of Annie's for her birthday one year and how I had to run all over town finding the exact color yellow, and how Annie's husband Fred didn't realize what Matt was doing and leaned on the side of the building and came away as yellow as a banana.

I start to laugh and then reach for a cookie. Alex presses Pause on the recorder.

"Let's just take a little break, okay?"

He walks over to the kitchen, and Alicia brings me a bottle. She twists off the top and hands it to me. "How you doing?"

"I'm fine," I say and swig down half the beer. My throat kind of hurts, actually, probably from all that talking.

Alicia grabs my hand and leans on the desk. "Are you sure this is a good idea?" Her face is open, plaintive, her hair pinned back with three black bobby pins, her eyes lined in sixty-dollar powder, two of her fingers wrapped around the neck of her Bud Light.

She squeezes my hand, and the ache in my throat intensifies. I look away, and drink my beer, and look back to her. "I'm fine. I haven't thought about that stuff in a while."

"Yeah. Me, neither."

When I finish the interview, Alicia offers to take me to Annie's. But I decline. I'm tired, my throat is in serious pain, and my stomach's twisted into knots. I think I'll feel better later tonight—Jason and I are going to Righteous Hall to see Matt. I made him get press passes, because there's no way I'm spending money to hear Matt perform; though now I'm thinking maybe I should have paid. Then I could get my anger back.

As it is now, all I feel is regret, which didn't descend upon me right away. But as I was walking to my father's house, this small nugget of something started growing in my chest. It started while I was remembering how smug and happy Alex looked, taking notes for what is sure to be a momentous article. Matt Hanley's the top-selling artist in the country right now, and I'm public enemy number one. The issue of *Disc* that carries both of our statements is going to sell like hotcakes.

A few months ago, all I wanted was to write an article on Jack Mantis, and now I have. Now they'll run it; it'll be on the cover of the February issue of *Disc,* Jack's happy and now my brother-in-law, Thalia's happy and strangely quiet.

I should feel good. But as I let myself in to my father's brownstone, and shout, "Hello? It's Echo," I feel anything but.

I strip off my coat and let it drop to the floor. "Hello?" I shout again. No answer.

I trudge up the stairs, and stop in to the sewing room.

Helen's dress is on a dummy, a headless mannequin with a really nice figure. The skirt of the dress hangs low, spread out on three chairs, so that it's elevated. I walk in, and touch the hemline, running my fingers over the soft cream fabric. Helen's sewn small beads into the hem and they catch the dim light of the room. I take a deep breath, sink into a nearby chair, and pick up a needle.

When Helen finds me, I've been sewing for a half hour.

"What you do?" she exclaims, standing in the doorway, like a sentry.

"Hey!" I twist in my chair.

Helen stands still, her hands on her hips, her hair in a bun and her mouth in a frown. "What happened? More bad news?"

I lower the fabric into my lap and start to cry. It only gets worse when Helen approaches and settles into the chair with me and puts her arms around me. "Aw, little one, it's okay."

Walter will be so mad that he missed out on the opportunity to comfort me.

18

All my tears are dried by the time I meet Jason at the Dublin House, an Irish pub around the corner from Righteous Hall.

As a matter of fact, I think I left all my emotions back in Helen's sewing room. I'm a bit on the empty side. My anger and guilt have swallowed each other up until there's nothing left but nervous agitation. I was looking forward to hanging out with Jason, drowning my thoughts in talk of new bands and how we'll handle a transfer of my writing duties to him once I'm officially out of the *BAT,* but no such luck. Because as soon as Alicia found out where I was going tonight, she insisted on coming, and unbeknownst to me, Jason brought his new girlfriend, Maggie Brown.

Sitting at a table with these three people hardly helps the twitchy mood I'm in. And to make matters worse, Jason and Alicia, in an attempt to avoid the *huge* white elephant at the table, keep making my interview with Alex Paxton the main focus of their conversation.

"And then, and then, she told him about the million versions of 'Hot Fudge Sauce' and how she'd have to lay out his clothes in the morning if she wanted him to wear clean ones. And how he sang nothing but cover songs for a year." After Alicia announces this, she leans back in her chair with a smug look on her face. "Now *that's* how you treat an ex-boyfriend." What's funny is that during the interview she was acting cagey, like she thought I was making a mistake. But now, for Jason's sake, she's all bravado and vengeance. It's enough to give a best friend a mixed signal.

But Jason knows what she's up to. He narrows his eyes and slings a casual arm around Maggie's shoulders. They're in the booth side of our table, and Alicia and I sit opposite them in two heavy, wooden chairs carved with Celtic crosses. Normally, the Dublin House is a cozy, warm establishment. They make an excellent plate of garlic mashed potatoes and serve a tasty pint of ale. But now, it's absolutely frigid, it's like having a drink in the middle of the Antarctic.

I will say, though, that I'm enjoying seeing Alicia have to work so hard to remain calm. It's this damn Maggie Brown. She's just so *cool*. Take now, for instance. She's looking at Alicia with knowing brown eyes, her hair tumbling over her shoulders and her luminous skin looking like she just had a facial. She's unflappable. She wraps her finger around a curl, and reaches for her beer. I wish I could handle Matt and Thalia and all the freak shows in my life as well as Maggie is handling the blond bundle of anger seated to my left right now.

"How about you, Maggie?" Alicia scoots her seat forward

just an inch. "How many scathing songs have you written about *your* exes?" Jason catches my eye from across the table.

Maggie only smiles politely, her class far outmatching Alicia's desperation. "No, no. I've never met a guy worth a whole song." Again, that finger finds a curl, and she turns to Jason. "I think I'll write you one, though." And she smiles at him, revealing a row of perfect teeth.

"Oh, man," Jason says, clearly enjoying himself. He starts zipping and unzipping his sweatshirt, until I'm ready to reach over and bat his hand away.

"Hmm…nice. I need more beer. Jason? Why don't you come with me?" Alicia ups Maggie's smile with a nasty, petulant wink.

The zipper flies. "Um, n-no, that's okay," he stammers.

"No, it's cool, Jay. Go ahead," Maggie tells him.

He looks at her in confusion, then at me. I merely raise my shoulders, as I have no idea how to act in a situation like this. Alicia stands and holds out her hand for him.

"Um, okay. Do you guys want another round?" He stands, and ducks out of Alicia's reach.

I check my watch. About thirty minutes before Matt goes on. "Yeah, you know what? Bring me two. I'm going to need fortification."

Alicia pats me on the arm as she walks away.

"Hey," I immediately say to Maggie. "I'm so, so sorry about Alicia. And this—" I point to the two empty chairs and then to Maggie and me "—I had no idea Jason was inviting you."

Maggie Brown bashfully smiles at the table. "It's really okay."

"It's really not. Alicia, well, I'm actually surprised she's this upset. She's not usually like this."

Maggie swallows and waits a beat before speaking. "Well, Echo, nobody knows better than you how poorly people handle breakups, right?"

I'm suddenly embarrassed to have my dirty laundry aired so honestly, *and* by somebody I want desperately to like me, and so I lower my head and run my fork through my pile of mashed potatoes. "That's true," I mutter to my potato pile.

"It's the human heart. It's not rational," Maggie says matter-of-factly, scientifically.

"How can you be so calm?" I raise my eyes. She meets them with perfect poise and a half smile.

"What should I do?"

I smile at her and lift my head. "I've found that playing dirty works pretty well."

"No, Echo. You never walk away unscathed if you hurt someone on purpose." She looks at me kind of knowingly, and raises her eyebrow, and reaches over and takes a bite of my potatoes.

I know she's not talking about Jason or Alicia. A small, odd part of me wants to beg her to forgive me for sinking down to Matt's level.

A half an hour later, Alicia and I are bulldogging our way to the front of the jam-packed crowd at Righteous Hall.

Righteous Hall holds about four thousand people on a good night, and the way the crowd is packed in here like sardines, I'd say that Matt is quite the draw. It's mostly girls here, though there's a range of ages. Alicia just elbowed past a cool thirtysomething mom who was here with three fourteen-year-olds, and as we push our way to the front, I can tell that all the young, pretty misses here would die to become Matt's next muse.

"Keep up!" Alicia screams back to me and grabs my elbow, yanking me toward her. It's going to be a long night. Seeing Jason happy and paired off with a girl who'd make the most secure of women feel like a failure has put Alicia in quite the bad mood. The only upside to her state of mind is that every time I've expressed even an iota of regret at spilling the beans to Alex Paxton, Alicia's been angry enough to tell me that I absolutely did the right thing. I take comfort in this, even though I know she's not talking rationally.

As we make our way closer to the stage, my eyes lock on to Matt's guitar—the guitar *I* bought him. It's sitting in its stand on the dark stage, awaiting the beginning of the show.

This nervous, nauseous feeling in my gut intensifies. It's a teenager feeling, that sensation you get when you've done something you hope your father never finds out about. It's not like Matt could have heard about the article in the hours since I was interviewed, and hopefully, he won't find out about it until after he's left town on this tour. If Matt finds out how I ratted on him while he's in Detroit or Santa Fe or Seattle, there's very little he can do to me. Actually, I think as I step on the foot of a very large man and apologize profusely, there's not a lot more he could do to me anyway. He's already ruined any chance I'll ever have of finding baggage-free love, and he came about ninety-nine percent close to closing the lid on my career.

Alicia looks back to me. "Hanging in there?"

"Yes!" I shout. "I'm getting a little angry, actually."

"Good!" she shouts back. "You'll need it!"

She ducks around a girl in an orange halter top and through the conversation of two preppy-looking kids, causing one of them to spill a beer all over his pale pink button-down T-shirt. "Sorry about that," I yell as I continue to follow Alicia, keeping my eye on the stage.

My eyes keep landing on that guitar, that damn guitar Matt wanted for over a year and that I scrimped and saved to get for him. Now it's commanding the Righteous Hall stage and being used as an instrument of evil, helping Matt spread the word of his vindictive, torturous girlfriend.

I exhale angrily and throw an elbow, just for good measure. The dude I poke jumps back, and I dart past him, trying to keep up with Alicia.

We continue to move to the front, and I recover from the sight of the guitar long enough to be able to take in the other details of the setup. There's a drum kit, and a bass guitar and a grand piano off to the left. There's a set of bongos and a tambourine lying on the floor just in front of the drums. Three mics, and various amps and pitchers of water are set out, too.

I'm also aware of the crowd. People teem out on the balcony above us, and the box seats that align both sides of the hall are crammed full of people. And in the one I pass by to my right, farthest from the stage but clearly affording the best view, sit Stan Fields, a host of bodyguard-looking guys, and Thalia and Jack Mantis, who's hovering around her like a host of angels. It stops me for a moment. It's the first I've seen them together since they've been married, and it's jarring to see the mutual affection between them. Her hands are all over him, and though they're far away, I can see from here that she's making him *blush*.

"Hey!" I shout, loud enough to be heard over dozens of chatting people. "Jack! Thalia!"

The only one who hears me is Stan. He rolls his eyes, and pokes Jack in the ribs, who turns his clear eyes on me. His arm is around my sister, and he's clearly massaging her neck.

As Thalia lifts her hair up, I assume, so that Jack can get better traction, he whispers in her ear.

Thalia follows Jack's eye line, and when she sees me, she jumps up and leans over the side of the box. "Echo! Get out of here! Right now! Go home! Go *home,* Echo!"

I'm sure you can imagine the reaction of the crowd when they hear my name. Thalia realizes what she's done and covers her mouth. Stan's eyes go wide, and the people who are in my immediate vicinity all turn on me.

"Echo??"

"Like the girl from the album?"

I look for Alicia, but she's missed this entire turn of events, and is lost to me, swallowed up by the crowd.

I feel a sharp poke to my back and three girls stare like they're about to issue a challenge to a date at the flagpole after school.

"Thanks a lot, sis!" My voice is carried away on a cloud of anger, but Thalia's not alarmed. She cups one of her curls and shakes her head.

"Get out of here!" she mouths, as Alicia appears from nowhere to save me from the approaching mob.

As she yanks me up to the front, I feel a wave of eyes turning on me, and hear a few less than complimentary phrases tossed my way. Alicia finally can't take it anymore, and pushes me in front of her. "You're like my own tiny bouncer," I say to her, but she just tells me to concentrate on walking.

Finally we find a spot up near the front, and it appears that we outran the knowledge of my name. We land just off the right side of the stage, but behind two ladies in professional-looking clothes.

"I can't believe she did that," I seethe, my fury making my face hot.

"She didn't do it on purpose," Alicia responds. She puts her hand on my shoulder and pats me. "We can always go, if you want. I don't know why that idiot thought this was a good idea, anyway." She's taken to *only* referring to Jason as "that idiot" since we left the Dublin House.

I ignore the baited chance to start dishing about Jason, and examine how close we are to the stage. "Do you think Matt'll see us from here?" When they hear my question, the two ladies in front of us turn to us, huge smiles on their round, bland faces.

"If he looks in this direction, he's mine! I called him!" the brown-haired one shrieks.

Her friend shakes her head and pokes the brown-haired lady in the ribs. "She's in love with Matt Hanley."

"So's she," Alicia responds, pointing at me.

"Shut up!" I hit her. Alicia's shocked that I would resort to violence. "I don't love him," I say turning to the two women. "I'm over him." They look at me like I'm crazy, and then turn back away from us.

"Thanks!" I say to Alicia, who stares at me like I've lost my mind.

"I'm sorry. Just take everything I do with a grain of salt tonight." She digs into her purse, pops a piece of gum into her mouth and hands me a mirror. "That idiot's got me off my game."

"Do I need fixing?" I open the compact and peer at myself. There's really very little I can do at this point, and anyway, I don't expect that Matt will see me. Which is good, because my eyes are still puffy from my crying jag with Helen, and my skin's a little splotchy from the trauma of having to outrun an angry crowd of concert-goers. All the stress of being America's most famous ex-girlfriend is wreaking havoc on my complexion. I run my finger underneath each eye, to keep my eyeliner in place, and click the case shut.

Alicia replaces the compact in her bag, and turns to me suddenly. "So, do you think he really likes this girl?"

It doesn't immediately connect that she's referring to Jason and Maggie. "Um, do we really need to talk about that right now? I feel like we should focus on the matter at hand."

She nods her head and turns to face the stage. But after a moment, she turns back and repeats, "So, do you think he really likes her?"

"Yes. I do. And I think she really likes him."

Alicia pouts a little and scrunches up her nose. "I don't like her."

"I'd be surprised if you did."

Thankfully, I'm saved from having to declare my fondness for Maggie Brown by the simultaneous dimming of the house lights, surge and roar of the crowd and the piercing squeal of all the girls around us.

"How many covers do you think he'll play?" Alicia screams over the din of the roaring crowd.

I raise my shoulders and shake my head, but of course Alicia can't see me do this. And then, all the lights in the whole place go out, and my attention's on the stage. A shadow passes in front of my eyes—it's the band heading for their instruments.

The stage lights come up to half, and a short, squat guy wearing a shimmery blue suit and matching tie heads for the drums. He taps the snare once, twice, three times with his sticks before hitting the cymbal once. A girl in a plaid, tulip-style skirt and a button-down white shirt that's basically unbuttoned picks up the bass, and puts the strap around her head, pulling free her long, light-brown ponytail as she does so. And an older gentleman, a man about medium height and with a slight paunch, sits at the piano. He has pattern baldness and chews gum, and is clearly old enough to be either the drummer or the bassist's dad. He runs his fingers through a few arpeggios, and then folds his hands in his lap, waiting for Matt to appear.

"Who are these dudes?" Alicia asks, her face contorted in confusion.

"I have no idea," I reply flatly through a constricted throat.

Alicia looks at me. "Oh. Weird."

She gets what I can barely put into words. For four years, I was Matt's entire support system, his lifeline, his method of socializing and interacting and surviving. And now, in the space of a few short months, he's got himself a band full of creatures I have never even met before.

It's crushing.

He's moved on. Without me. In fact, it seems the only way he was ever going to move on was without me. Just like he sings in "Emancipation Proclamation."

The drummer starts a bass beat, and the schoolgirl bassist joins in, and the screams of the crowd intensify. I look around behind me. Sheer ecstasy can be seen on everyone's face, except for the collection of folks in Jack's box, who look plain pissed off.

"I hope he doesn't choke!" Alicia calls out.

I know what she means. Despite the many new things in Matt's life, all I know is that only months ago, if confronted by a crowd like this, he'd be seriously terrified to go on.

And come to think of it, this vamp the band's doing is going on an awful long time. I stand on my tiptoes to see if I can see any activity in the stage wings.

And sure enough, as soon as I elevate, out comes Matt, strolling, sauntering, in dark khaki pants and a green T-shirt. He gives the crowd a jaunty little wave, and gets a wave of squealing, adoring sound in response. He smiles that Matt smile, the one with the crooked upper lip. Alicia clutches my arm, and Matt picks up the guitar, the fruit of my and my father and his mother's labors, slings it around his shoulders, and steps up to the microphone, launching into "On Top of the World."

Matt played only one cover song, a respectable number for any musician. Even Paul McCartney plays a cover (well, not a whole one, but he is known to sample a Carl Perkins bit in the middle of one or two of his songs).

But back to Matt. He played all the songs from *Echosongs* and most of the tracks off his first record. He played two new songs, and dedicated one to his mom. The only time he mentioned my name was when he sang it; he never alluded to me in between songs or spoke about what his Echo songs meant. He referenced being from New York City and that he was leaving soon to start a new tour. He thanked people for coming out, and asked folks to cheer if they'd seen him at Annie's Punk in the past year.

The crowd cheered and sang along, and clapped and screeched his name, and demanded he come back for an encore, which he did. His encore was "Echo Only Broke Me" and before the end of the song, the band cut out and Matt held the microphone up to the audience, and four thousand people chanted, "Echo only broke me, Echo only broke me, Echo only broke me," over and over until Alicia was biting her nails and looking for the exits.

I remained calm, picturing my name beneath a headline reading, "My Side of the Story."

Thalia and Jack left early. Their box was empty after Matt's third song.

Jason text messaged me after "Lizzie Borden" to say that he thought Matt was off his game. He was trying to make me feel better.

But he was lying. Matt was great. Confident. He vaulted around the stage like Springsteen, engaging the crowd, encouraging sing-alongs. And his voice—brilliance. He nailed every note, every inflection—he sounded exactly the way he does on the radio, in his videos, in the shower. Rich. Complicated. Emotional.

When the concert ended, the crowd continued to cheer even when the houselights came on, and only stopped when the roadies appeared and began to coil the wires, to put away the mics, to break down the drum kit. Alicia, who tried not to communicate to me too much during the show, hugged me. And she held my hand while we watched everybody mill out, while we listened to everyone proclaim what a great show they had just seen.

Alicia squeezed my hand, and said, "They won't love him so much after they read the thing in *Disc.*"

Again, I tried to picture my byline, and the nasty way Alex would be sure to spin my stories.

Now we're on the street. Jason and Maggie text messaged me to say they'll meet us at Annie's. Alicia's on her cell phone, telling Peter the *BAT* plant-waterer to meet us there, so she doesn't look like she's single. Which is ironic, because for the year she dated Jason, she got angry whenever anyone tried to tell her she *wasn't* single.

"What are you staring at me for?" she asks when she gets off the phone.

"Do you think that's a good idea? When was the last time you saw that guy?" I pull my coat tight around me, the winter chill in the air smelling like Christmas and feeling like ice.

She pouts. "Our party? No. I saw him at the *BAT* after that and ignored him. He was surprised to hear from me just now."

"You realize you're freaking."

"Okay, pot."

"Oh, kettle, be nice."

Alicia eyes me, and leans up against the wall next to me. "God, I'm pathetic. I didn't even like him until Maggie Brown showed up."

"The human heart's not rational." My breath appears on the air in a solid, vaporous stream. The street's gone quiet, most of the Matt-lovers long gone, seeking warmth in a variety of surrounding bars.

"Who told you that?"

"Maggie Brown." I start to laugh and Alicia punches me in the arm.

"You're so awful." She's giggling. "And I'm a wretched mess."

I rest my head against the wall. "Naw, I'm the wretched one. I'm actually waiting to see this guy, after he has the world singing about me."

She pushes off the wall and pulls her bag up around her shoulder. "Well, come on. Let's get this over with."

"Yeah. Let's."

And we walk around the block to the backside of the Righteous Hall, where a crowd of about thirty people is gathered around a large, metal, red door. A couple of bouncer types guard the door, and fend off the crowd, who start a Matt Hanley chant while Alicia and I approach them.

I tug on the sleeve of a twentysomething girl who has a tiny heart drawn underneath her left eye. "Did he come out yet?"

"No! And I'm dying! But he leaned out the window a minute ago." She points up to the second floor of the Righteous Hall where you can see into the dressing rooms. Alicia and I crane our necks as the girl hollers at the top of her lungs, "Come out, MATT!"

Alicia makes a face at her and tugs me along. The chant continues, and only abates momentarily when the drummer sits in the sill and smokes a cigarette. He enjoys the screaming girls so much that he throws a pair of drumsticks down to the crowd.

"Where's Matt?" one of the crowd shouts.

The drummer looks over his shoulder into the dressing room, then leans back out the window and shouts, "He'll be down." This is met with a resounding cheer.

Alicia tugs me over to the door, where the bouncers are all gathered around a small handheld television, watching the Knicks game.

"Let's just duck in here." She pulls me into a small indention in the wall, where there's a little delivery area. I shove my hands into my pockets and peer at the crowd. They're dancing, drunk, happy to be alive.

"At least we know he's still a dilly-dallier," she says.

As soon as these words leave Alicia's mouth, the red door swings open, and the bouncers abandon their game and adopt a protective stance. Out comes Matt. I step forward, but Alicia stops me. "Just wait."

It's good advice. Matt's immediately swarmed. A collection of girls forms a circle around him, shoving various shaped pieces of paper and an assortment of pens in his face. Matt's looking a little overwhelmed, actually, I can tell even from my stance behind him. He's shifting his weight a bit too often and looking around him, and then he drops a pen, and jumps back when one of the girls grabs his hand and kisses it.

I take a step forward, feeling like I should help him, but again Alicia stops me by grabbing on to the sleeve of my coat. "You don't have to."

She's right. Taking care of him isn't my job anymore. I shiver, mostly from the cold, but also from the sight of watching Matt stand on his own two feet.

Well, almost on his own two feet. When Matt drops his pen the second time, Daisy emerges from in front of the red stage door and hands him a new one. He kind of does a double-take when he realizes that she's at his side and nods at her.

"God, I hate new girlfriends!" Alicia wails.

I close my eyes in panic, because my girl Alicia has a *loud* voice. Much louder than you would expect her to have. And this particular utterance was loud enough to get everyone's attention. The bouncers, the crowd around Matt, Daisy and yes, even Matt Hanley himself.

"I don't believe this!" Daisy sneers snidely and stomps off to the bouncers. When she gets their attention, she points at me and Alicia and is clearly ordering them to have us removed.

Matt stoops to pick up the piece of paper he dropped when he saw me, and turns to Daisy who strides over to me and Alicia with one of the bouncers. "Daisy, it's fine. They're fine."

Then Matt looks at me for a moment and doesn't smile and blinks his eyes sadly and purses his lips and turns back to his adoring fan base.

"All right, ladies, let's go." The bouncer reaches for my elbow, and Alicia slips in between us.

"We're not going anywhere. We're friends of Matt's!"

"Not anymore, you're not!" Daisy snaps. She's got an array of dippy-looking beaded flowers lining the buttons on her winter coat.

I push Alicia out of the way, say, "No worries, sir," to the bouncer and head for Annie's.

When I'm halfway down the block, I check to see if Matt's still signing autographs, but he's gone.

19

Though I participate in the festivities at Annie's, watching the pitchers she keeps plunking down on our table come and go, I remain completely sober.

It's amusing to me how all the people in my life, including the new additions like Maggie, expect me to be falling apart. Jason keeps rubbing my back, and playing "Divorce Song" by Liz Phair on the jukebox. Alicia, when not shooting eye-daggers at Maggie and attempting to get me to commit to not liking her, books me for three solid days of shopping. Annie hasn't charged me for a drop of drink. Even Thalia's on full alert. At about one-thirty, she shows up looking fresh as a newborn babe, her new husband on her chiffon-covered arm. Jack's dressed head-to-toe in black (the shirt's a button-down, of course) but still he manages to pull focus from all Annie's revelers as he struts through the bar on his way to my table. Fortunately for him, he's got a pit bull of a wife, and after she sends the first autograph-seeker away in tears, nobody bothers Jack for the rest of the night.

Now I'm sandwiched between my sister and my new brother-in-law, who I've only spoken to over the phone since his marriage. "Did you enjoy the show?" Jack asks now, as he compulsively cracks peanut shells open and drops the nuts onto the table.

Thalia reaches across me and slaps Jack's hands just as he's balling them into fists and crushing the peanuts into a fine powder. "Darling. We don't do that anymore," she says, her voice full of concern. When she sees me staring at her, she scrunches her face up in a smile. I can't believe I ever for a moment doubted the perfection of this pairing. Maybe that could be my new career—matchmaker. I'm one for one. That's batting a thousand.

I turn to my brother-in-law, and respond, "Yes. I thought he was really good."

Thalia narrows her eyes into slits. "You're not having second thoughts, are you? You have every right to air your grievances."

I shake my head back and forth. "I know. I'm okay."

"Really?"

"Really. Matt's done what he had to do, and I'm doing what I have to do."

I'm getting stares from around the table.

"Seriously, guys." I take a draining sip from my beer mug. "I feel good."

Then I talk to Thalia the rest of the night about what we're getting for Dad for Christmas, and what we expect from his and Helen's wedding. Once I talk her out of bringing me a date, she lets me go home.

★ ★ ★

I walk. Yes, it's three o'clock on a Friday night, but it's Manhattan. The city's still hopping at 3:00 a.m. here, and Christmas is a week away. Nobody will attack me during the Christmas season. Besides, I need the air, and the chance to clear my head.

I pass a park decked out in tree lights, big floppy red bows and a large plastic statue of Rudolph. A young man swings his girlfriend in the air and lands her on Rudolph's back. Last year, Matt forced me to enjoy my Christmas by leaving me messages of him singing various Christmas carols, and for the past three years, he's taken me to the lighting of the Rockefeller Center Christmas tree. This year, I didn't even remember it was happening, and now, here it is a week from the holiday, and I haven't yet bought a single gift.

I open the door to my apartment, anxious to bathe in the warm mustiness of my radiator-heated home. Peeling off my coat, and removing the barrettes from my hair, I kick my shoes off one by one and stare into my domain.

Empty.

Clean.

White-ceilinged and quiet.

I moan, and pad over to the stereo, slipping in *Echosongs* quietly. I wish there was a device whereby I could distort the lyrics, yet still be able to hear Matt's voice. Then I remember something.

Thirty seconds later, I'm on my hands and knees in my bedroom closet, sorting through crates and boxes, searching for the tape I made of one of Matt's recording sessions at Silver Records. At the time, I got kind of mean looks from the producer. Matt had exhausted everyone's goodwill that day, with a marathon recording and rerecording session

of "Hot Fudge Sauce #11." He tried about a zillion different arrangements, instruments and backing vocal combina-
tions before the producer finally was ready to cancel the
whole project. I bribed one of the engineers to lay everything down for me on a tape.

Finally, underneath a Matt Hanley T-shirt from his first
tour and three undeveloped rolls of film, I find it. My legs
are tingly and falling asleep, but I push to my feet, pull the
T-shirt on, replace my jeans with sweatpants, collect my hair
into a ponytail, grab a blanket to cuddle with and head back
out to the living room.

I replace *Echosongs* with my homemade recording of the
Hot Fudge Sauce opus. Keeping the sound low, so as not
to disturb my neighbors at this ungodly hour, I don't even
make it to the couch. I lean against the coffee table, facing
the stereo, letting Matt's scratchy voice wash over me. If
only *Echosongs* could've been released this way, I could
enjoy them.

But hey, let's face it. Without his singularly ingenious act
of revenge, I'd have no hand in terms of *Disc*. And so, the
irony of this whole situation is that without Matt, I really
would've amounted to nothing.

Because I'm sure something else, someone else would've
cropped up on the music scene to displace Jack Mantis
from his cover story. Until Jack and the Flies release their
new album, they're at the mercy of whoever's hot at the
time.

"Emancipation Proclamation" comes on. It was always
one of my favorites of Matt's tunes. Matt wrote it in a
minor key, on a rainy day. I look to the spot on the windowsill where he sat, strumming his guitar, humming the

tune. I remember sitting cross-legged in front of him, listening to him while he worked, watching him pick out the notes while he looked into my eyes.

My memory is shattered by the soft, plunking sound of a knock on the door. I shoot to my feet, look around madly for a robe, realize there's none, wrap the blanket around my shoulders and run tippy-toed over to the door.

"Hey, I'm sorry!" I say with my cheek pressed to the door. "I know it's late. I'll turn it down. Sorry." I lean my head back to catch a glimpse of my kitchen clock. It's almost 4:00 a.m.

"Echo? It's me."

My stomach spasms and my throat goes dry. I open the door a few inches, blocking my wide-hipped body from view, and see Matt Hanley, rock superstar, on my doorstep—hands in pockets, head sheepishly tilted to one side. "Hey," he says.

I don't say anything. I open the door wide enough for him to walk through, which he does. He stops in front of the couch, looks around and passes a hand through his hair. He also shifts his weight twice, a sure sign of his nervousness.

I attempt to disappear inside my blanket, and I'm really hoping he doesn't notice that I'm wearing his concert T-shirt. "It's late." Not the best first line. But what should I have gone with? "Dude! I nailed you to the wall and you don't even know it yet?"

Matt points to the stereo. "What are you doing?"

Flash Gordon has nothing on my speed, racing to the stereo to shut off the most embarrassing sound of Matt's demo. My fingers fumble with the buttons, and for some reason, in my late-night haze, I take the tape out, and then throw it behind the stereo, of course there is no behind the stereo (there's no backing to the shelf) so the tape clatters to the floor behind my credenza.

Matt looks at me warily. "Smooth as chocolate, lady."

"Yeah, some things don't change." This might have been the worst thing I could have said. We're both left feeling incredibly awkward. So I cover by cutting to the chase. "What are you doing here?"

Nice. Venom. I was afraid for a moment there that I'd forget to be nasty.

Matt hooks a thumb toward the couch. "Can I sit?"

"Sure." I sit on the corner of the chair farthest from him. And take the opportunity to be nasty again (of course I do). "Is Daisy on her way with the angry mob?"

Matt's expression softens, and his fingers begin drumming a syncopated beat on the coffee table. "Yeah. I'm sorry about that." He scratches his head, runs his fingers through his hair and returns to his drum practice. "She was surprised to see you there."

Matt needs a haircut. I'm caught up in trying to decide how many inches of his floppy brown do should go, and realize too late that it's my turn to talk. "Did you see me at the show, though?" I slip from the arm of the chair into the cushion, and swing my leg over the side. "I was up front."

His hands still. "You were?"

I draw my knees up to my chin. "Yeah."

"I didn't see you."

"Well, you were good."

Matt tilts his head as if to call me out, as if to say, "Tell the truth." Then we descend into silence, a quiet so still that even our breathing seems loud. He looks miserably uncomfortable, and if I pull the blanket any more tightly around myself, I'm going to cut off my circulation.

"So, what are you doing here?"

"You could have called, to let me know you were showing up tonight. I could've gotten you in for free."

"I did get in for free. Jason paid."

"Oh."

"Matt—"

He stands up and shoves his hands in his pockets. "I'm leaving tomorrow."

I don't immediately grasp what he's saying. I think for a moment that he means he's leaving my apartment tomorrow.

He must read the expression on my face, because he jumps in with, "On my tour. It's only smaller venues at first, but then I'm hooking up with some big name or other."

"You'll be the big name soon."

He shakes his head in disbelief. "Maybe. Not anytime soon, though."

My gut twists a bit. "Don't sell yourself short."

Matt looks at me for a minute, and then steps forward. "Well, I guess I'll get going."

"Oh. Um, okay. Yeah, it's late." I hop off my perch, and face him; I'm supposed to walk him to the door now, but he came all the way here for a reason, and I'm dying to know what it is, and I don't want his gun-shy bullshit to keep me from finding out. So I stare at him, until he spills it.

"Yeah, I—"

"Why'd you come?"

"I just—" He looks at the floor then at me. "I'm sorry."

I don't know what exactly he's sorry for, for the little things like showing up at four in the morning or the big things like smearing my name in front of the entire world.

He takes a deep breath. "Listen, I came over to tell you that not all those things in the songs are true."

My eyes immediately get wet—from embarrassment, I

think, tears accumulating and threatening to spill down my cheeks, and so I look away. This has the undesired effect of prompting Matt to walk closer to me, which in turn sends a tear careening down my face.

"Most of them are totally lies. Complete creative license."

I shake my head to communicate that it's time for him to stop talking, but he ignores me and plunges ahead.

"I was just pissed off, Echo. And the words poured out of me, I wasn't even thinking."

I look at him, and he sighs and tilts his head. I look away again.

"The night you kicked me out I walked straight from this apartment to Silver Records, and had everything laid down by that Sunday night. I didn't even remember half of what I sang until I heard the first playback on Tuesday morning, and then everyone was so excited and *psyched* to finally have a record, I couldn't exactly take my lyrics back."

"But the name, couldn't you have changed the name?" I sob, still facing the wall.

He makes a move toward me again, and then stops. "I— yes. I could have. And I didn't. And I'm sorry. I'm really, really sorry. And not about just that, but about everything. And I guess, well, I just came to say that I—I'm sorry that everything went down the way it did. Honest."

My incoming breath makes my ribs hurt, my chest shudder.

He smiles at me, a crooked smile.

"I'm sorry, too."

"I know. You did the best you could. I wasn't easy. I was kind of a mess there for a while."

I laugh a bit. We look at each other.

And then I say a really stupid thing:

"Wanna sleep over?"

★ ★ ★

Nothing ruins a good breakup like spending the night together. And confessing all your sins (minus one important revenge-type one).

Matt does indeed sleep over, and in the morning, when Thalia calls to check on me, and asks me what I'm doing, the look of sheer terror on his face is priceless.

But he doesn't stay long. He's bound for his first tour in a couple of years. We wake up, I brew a pot of coffee and we sit in the kitchen and drink our cups in mostly quiet— although Matt does take time out to read the article I wrote for *Disc.* His face is full of pride as he does.

This, as you can imagine, makes me feel awful, as I withhold the bargain I had to strike to get this article on the cover.

We don't talk about Daisy, or the fact that everyone I've ever met has called me since his album came out; we don't talk about anything other than his tour and my article. The rest of our conversation is filled with Thalia and Jack anecdotes, which could change the mood for even the saddest person.

Matt takes a shower, and puts on the clothes he showed up in. While he's in the bathroom, his phone rings three times. I'm shocked, because he never, ever had his phone on while we were together.

It's one more thing that's different about him. Since he showed up last night, my mind's been awhirl trying to keep track of everything new about him. Little things like rinsing out his coffee cup when he's done, or taking calls on his cell phone. But big things, too, like the way he's standing a little straighter, and not avoiding answering my questions, and the way he looks me in the eye without averting his gaze after three seconds. He's confident, but also, he's *happy*. And this is a side of him I haven't seen in ages.

Then, as he must, he leaves. When he goes, he doesn't say he'll call or that he loves me or that he had a good time. I don't say any of these things, either. He kisses me on the forehead, mock cuffs my chin, and then tips his pretend hat. He spins on his toes, and walks off down the hall.

It's nice like this. An amicable parting of the ways, a goodbye that doesn't involve door-slamming, and tears, and neighbors shouting at us to keep our business behind closed doors.

Before Matt disappears behind the door leading to the staircase, he pivots and gives me a little goodbye salute.

Not the big moment I had envisioned.

But nice enough to send my heart into a panic. Because in less than a week, there's going to be a nationally distributed article detailing what a lousy jerk he is.

In my defense, I *do* try to get the article pulled, at great detriment to myself as a journalist, but tremendous gain as a human being.

My first attempt is with Alex, who I invite to Annie's for an afternoon of pleading and bribing. The bar is mostly empty, as it is four o'clock on the Thursday before Christmas. Bruce Springsteen's rendition of "Santa Claus Is Comin' to Town" fills the silent space, and Annie gets into the holiday spirit by hanging plastic reindeer ornaments on the small, fake tree propped up amongst the top-shelf liquor bottles.

When Alex walks into the bar, wrapped in an ugly homemade blue-knit scarf and a weird puffy pair of earmuffs, I greet him holding a pitcher of beer and an autographed-by-Lou-Reed first pressing of a Velvet Underground album.

He takes the beer, but leaves the album, citing the fact that I overplayed my hand.

"If you'd come with a nonautographed copy of an import or something, maybe I would've taken the bait. But this is too much. Hey, Annie."

I throw the album down and pour myself a mug of beer. Annie walks over, says hello, picks up the album and brings it down to the opposite end of the bar, where she proceeds to slip the vinyl from its protective sleeve and look lovingly at both sides of the record.

Alex takes the pitcher from me and leans forward against the bar. "Have you lost your mind, anyway? Do you really think Dick would pull this?"

I exhale and drink.

"And if he did," Alex continues, "you know you would have to kiss your future there goodbye."

I lean on the back two legs of the stool, sending my front end teetering in midair. "He never committed to giving me more work, anyway."

"Oh, come on," Alex scoffs. "You know how it works at *Disc*. He's already run those stories for New Tunes. You know you're in. Dick's got this weird idea of making the magazine like a family."

I eye him. This sounds suspiciously like Walter's MO, too.

"Besides," he continues. "You're cute. Dick loves cute."

"Hmmm...." I knock my fist against the bar.

He turns his body toward me now. "Why the sudden change of heart?"

"None of your beeswax."

Alex chuckles condescendingly. "You're a real catch. Somebody should write a song about you."

I scrunch up my nose and fight the urge to pour the remaining beer in my mug all over his black acid-wash pants.

"You're too late anyway. The issue's done. Don't you know anything?"

I grimace.

Alex reaches below his stool and pulls his bag up to his lap.

"You have a copy with you?"

"No. But I have the article. Read it and weep."

He pulls six notebook pages from his back pocket and spreads them out on Annie's bar.

"You couldn't bring a typed version?" I say derisively, picking up the first of the sloppily composed handwritten pages.

"Not how I work," he says, reaching around the bar, placing the empty pitcher underneath the Yuengling tap and pushing the handle down. Annie sees what he's doing and doesn't even bat an eyelash.

I read. And my worst fears are confirmed. "'Dating Matt Hanley was like babysitting a mentally challenged child'????" I hit Alex in the arm with the paper as I scream this out loud. "ALEX! I didn't say that!!!"

He ducks and covers his head with the crook of his elbow. "You heavily implied it!"

I keep hitting him. Jesus. I barely skimmed the second sentence, but see how this article is already bad as can be. "Retarded? RETARDED???? You can't use that *word!*"

Annie rushes over. "Kid. Kid. No fighting at Annie's Punk. What the hell?" She pulls me off of him, stops the overflowing tap of beer and pushes Alex for good measure. "What the hell, kid?"

I can barely string together enough words for an entire sentence. "Read it!" I thrust the page under her nose. "Read it!"

She takes the page, exhales in exhaustion like an over-worked kindergarten teacher and begins reading. Her face goes from annoyed to aghast faster than you can say, "Sue me."

Then she begins to read aloud. "'I'm amazed Matt had it in him,' scorned girlfriend Echo Brennan states over coffee at her office in Brooklyn. 'He's been kind of creatively challenged for the past couple of years, spending more time staring at the bottom of a whiskey bottle and in his under-wear than working on his career. I got tired of taking care of him all the time.'" Annie raises her head in disbelief, then hands me a dirty dish towel. "Hit him with this, hon."

I can't even oblige her. I'm so leveled by how harsh this sounds.

"I don't get why you're both so upset! It's all true, isn't it? Everyone knows his life was going nowhere until she dumped him."

Annie shakes her head and then hits *me*.

"Ow!"

"I'm sorry, sweetheart. But you deserve it." She lowers her eyes back to Alex's childlike chicken scrawl. "'Echo is in her late twenties, aptly described by the song "Hippie Chick" and feels frustrated that people only know of her as a shrew.'"

"A shrew?" I drop my head into my hands.

"You've got to do something about this," Annie advises.

My second, more urgent attempt to get this article pulled comes the very next morning. Yes, I know going in that it's all but futile at this point, but still, I have to do something.

So I just pop on in to *Disc* headquarters, fully expecting to be able to catch Dick Scott there, though it is the Friday before Christmas. Sure enough, he's there, as his assistant, who confirms my notions of what a nationally distributed magazine head's work ethic should be by saying that as long as it's a workday, Dick'll be there.

I do as instructed. I sit in the pleather chair outside of Dick's office, and watch his assistant do some last-minute gift wrapping. I stare at the framed *Disc* covers on the wall, all signed by their respective cover subjects. My eyes land on the one from last January, with the picture of Lindsay Lohan and the large, off-set, green headline, The Next Big Thing…" This year Matt will have that slot. I wonder if Daisy took the photo they're using.

The door to Dick's office swings open at that moment, and he peers out, every silk-suited, gray-haired pound of him. "Echo!" his voice bellows. "Is your sister here with you today?" He cranes his neck, looking to see if Thalia's hiding anywhere.

I stand up, smooth out my coat and grab my hat and gloves, which I had rolled into a ball and crammed into the cushions of the seat next to me. "Nope. Sorry."

"No problem, no problem." He ushers me into his office with that meaty paw of his. "You can't blame me for hoping for an early Christmas present."

"No, I guess I can't." I seat myself opposite his great big slab of a desk, a piece of furniture vomiting up different piles of paper and CD cases and photos.

"Well." He chuckles warmly as he situates himself in the chair that looks more like a motorized toy than a functional piece of office equipment. "Maybe we'll see more of her once you start doing more work for us." He folds his arms behind his head.

This comment punches a hole in my composure, and I'm momentarily unable to think of anything except the consequences of his meaning. "Once I start doing more work?"

He rocks in his chair ever-so-slightly. "I'm sure you know that *Disc* is really one big club. And now you're in. When we get back from Christmas break we'll be divvying up the stories, and of course I plan to use you. You did a great job with the Jack Mantis article. And the other little stories, too."

Well, there it is. The confirmation of all my expectations. I am now a writer for *Disc*. The entire time I've dreamt of this outcome, I always imagined myself feeling a lot happier.

"Do you want to see the cover shot we're using of him?" Dick's avuncular tones rouse me from my thoughts.

I nod and he begins sorting through the various piles on his desk, knocking over papers and pens and paper clips as he continues plowing through the clutter on his desk like a dog searching for a bone. "Ah! Here!"

He passes a glossy picture of Jack toward me, and my immediate response is to look away bashfully. It's Jack all right. In the altogether, with a pair of lady's hands covering up his, um, manly regions. I thank all the various powers-that-be that my father's vision is so bad. Seriously, I give thanks to the gods of all religions just to cover my bases: God, Allah, Buddha, Shiva, Zeus.

"It's a takeoff on that old Janet Jackson cover, remember, the topless picture of her with her then-husband's hands covering up the parts we wanted to see?"

I close my eyes, and open them again. Unfortunately, the sight of those hands keeps me fixated, and the suspicion that I'm related to those hands fills me with a curious combination of morbid fascination, somber disappointment and acute nausea. I tear my gaze away long enough to check out the entire photo. Jack's body is so skinny you can count his ribs.

"It was air-brushed of course. You can see through him otherwise."

"Well, it looks great."

"Oh! And of course, you'll be getting some from my assistant, but here's a copy of the Hanley edition."

And Dick produces it from out of nowhere, with no fanfare or opportunity for me to prepare myself.

I don't reach for it. I just stare.

"Oh, I—"

"We're proud of this one!"

Matt looks at me. He's, mercifully, clothed. Wearing a T-shirt with a red, shattered heart on it. A sad, pathetic, heart-wrenching expression on his face. A bouquet of dead flowers in his hand and a tissue in the other. The headline says, Will Matt Hanley Ever Love Again? And underneath that, it reads, How Music Saved Him From Heartbreak And Obscurity, by Alex Paxton. Next to this is a box set apart from the rest of the cover's text. Inside it are the words: Echo Speaks—Hanley's Muse On Matt, Layla And Dirty Breakups. I hate that I'm immortalized in print with the most infamous woman in all of rock and roll.

"Doesn't that look great?" Dick turns the issue so that he can leaf through it. He finds my piece, and affixes a sticky to it, I assume so that it'll be easier for me to locate. "It's going to fly off the shelves!"

Dick raises his shoulders in fiendish, happy, capitalist delight as he hands it to me.

I open to the marked page, and look at the page-long article, see my name in bold type and the ornate flowers that decorate the article. "I guess it's too late to ask you to pull my statement, huh?"

20

Well, the holidays are officially on the list of things that have sucked this year. I'm so on edge, no amount of presents, good cheer, or towering plates of delicious food can cheer me.

In fact, when it snows on Christmas day and my sister and almost-mom, Helen, run into the backyard to have a snowball fight, all I can do is lean against the back door with my nose pressed against the glass, my breath fanning out in front of me like spilled liquid.

Thalia dislodges my pose with a sharp, sailing snowball that splats *thwack!* against the spot I'm in.

My father's hand lands on my back. "And, what merriments are my ladies enjoying?"

I take his hand in mine and look out at the goings-on in the little box-shaped yard. "They're making snow angels."

"How appropriate!"

I steer my father back into the kitchen, which is bursting with plates of cookies, sweet rolls, oddly shaped chocolates with unusual fillings like orange liqueur and figs. My father finds his chair, sits and takes the Hugo Boss sunglasses courtesy of Jack Mantis's fortune, from the table. He holds them up to the light, which is odd, because he can't really see them from that distance.

"I'll be the hippest professor at the school."

"Yes, you will," I say, placing them on his face and kissing his forehead.

The Brennan family made out like bandits this Christmas, thanks to our rich new family member. Though the wrapping is different from the previous parade of Dressers to court Thalia's favor, Jack's bank account is right in line with what she prefers in a life partner. And she certainly put Jack's hard-won funds to use, procuring for my father two first-edition works of Ezra Pound, a complete Hugo Boss wardrobe including the sunglasses now perched on his nose, and a honeymoon trip to Italy (which is a combination Christmas/wedding present). Helen received a kitchen makeover, which makes no sense to me since my father and Helen are but one semester and one summer away from their semipermanent move to Greece. Thalia says that they'll be spending their summers in Brooklyn, and that a new kitchen is an appropriate gift.

My spoils? A week at an upstate spa. A thousand dollars in iTunes gift cards. Three Chanel outfits, a haircut at a salon of my choice, an appointment to consult a lawyer about changing my name...and a car. A *car*. I opened the small gift box, expecting to see a pair of earrings or a necklace, or, you know, something normal. Nope. There were a set of keys fastened on a "Drive Fast" key chain. Then, after I looked up in puzzlement, Thalia squealed and Jack procured a Mercedes brochure from his pocket. It was folded up sixteen times, but when flattened out, my new car was laid out for the world to see.

"It'll be leather, Ec, with a multiple CD-changer, because of the music obsession. But we can go to the dealer next week, and you can trick it out the way you want." I looked up during this speech to see Helen's shocked expression.

"Guys, I—"

Jack's words on the subject were, "Now you can interview people based outside of the city."

I didn't quite follow his logic, but the fact remains that this Christmas, I got everything I want. My father got to enjoy an article with my name on it in a national publication, Matt Hanley got his life together and his career on track, my own career is right where I want it to be, Thalia's free time is now used up in running Jack's life.

But as I sink down at the kitchen table, ripping a piece of green-frosted cookie into a thousand little pieces, the feeling of unsettledness I've had since spending the night with Matt reverberates throughout my body.

"Your mother called today," my father says, his hands folded in his lap.

I drop the cookie to the table. "She did?"

"Don't worry. I don't think she realized it was Christmas. She called to congratulate me on my marriage. And to tell me that she's proud of the job I've done with you girls."

My father's expression remains placid, and his eyes are covered by hundreds of dollars' worth of sunglasses, so it's impossible for me to read how he's feeling.

"What did you say?"

"I said I was proud, too."

I bite my lip and rap my knuckles against the table, grinding the cookie remnants into so much powder as I do.

"Echo? Twenty-five words, please."

"Dad—"

"Make them festive. It is Christmas, after all."

I lean back in my chair, stretch my legs. "I'm melancholy, I guess."

He looks in my direction, expecting more out of me. But I barely know how to verbalize what it is I'm feeling. "I'm antsy. Adjusting still. I think I sold my soul to get revenge."

My father slides forward in his chair. "Cookie, please."

I hand him the tissue-paper lined box of sugar cookies that he's been visiting all day long. He reaches for a colorful, round Santa and bites off his red cap. "I put pressure on you, Echo. I wanted you to work at a school like me, but you're like your mom. Music, music, always music."

I laugh a little.

"But rarely does one make it overnight. I know that."

"Some people do." I sigh, thinking of my MIA ex-boyfriend.

"That wasn't overnight," he replies, apparently having read my thoughts. The rest of the Santa cookie disappears.

"No, it wasn't."

"But I'm proud of you, and I'm relieved."

I reach for a cookie of my own—a silver-and-gold decorated bell. "Yeah?"

"I'm relieved to know that I can relax in Greece, knowing you'll be taking care of yourself."

"Yeah."

"And don't worry about Matthew, dear. He'll forgive you. He's crazy about you."

At this, I choke on my bite of cookie, kiss his cheek and leave him in the kitchen, where he's cozying up to his box of cookies and his new gazillion-dollar bottle of scotch (another gift from the newly affluent Mrs. Mantis). I wander into the den. Jack sits on the floor, sorting and re-sorting the gifts into piles, first organizing by recipient, then by size, then by usefulness, then by color.

"Hey." I fall to my knees and try to rescue some of my gifts from his manic reorganization. "Thalia's gonna yell if she sees you doing this."

Jack doesn't even look up. "Some habits I'm finding it hard to get rid of. Did you like your presents?"

"Yes. You spent too much." I take my iTunes gift card from the pile of Christmas cards, gift certificates and other green items.

This gets Jack's attention. "You're my only sister-in-law. And my favorite reporter."

"Well, I hope so."

"I heard from Goren today."

"Really?" I drop the boxes I'm holding. I don't know if Jack knows about my and Goren's brief and pathetic dating history.

"He's in Buffalo visiting his family." Jack looks at me expectantly.

I have no idea how to respond to him.

"Cool?"

"He went to a Christmas Eve concert. Matt Hanley."

"Oh."

"Matt is telling his audience that his songs are about the love of his life."

He must see my face fall, and he must enjoy it, because his white teeth appear from behind two grinning lips. "You're in such trouble."

★ ★ ★

Matt's issue of *Disc* hit the stands two days before Christmas.

But then there was the matter of the holiday, and so when I didn't hear from him, I was able to convince myself that he hadn't gotten a copy yet. Or that he was similarly busy with holiday festivities and hadn't thought to call me.

At Walter's annual day-after-Christmas dinner party, Alicia and Jason let me know how stupid this assumption was.

"Dude. He totally read it. He's pissed," Alicia said, with a mouthful of bread and a face full of disdain. "You're never going to hear from him, until his next album comes out and all the songs are about your vindictive nature." Maggie Brown kept Alicia from continuing her spiel by asking her to pass the green beans.

Walter took a different tack, pushing his plate away in frustration. "It's like *Romeo and Juliet*. Or *Days of our Lives*. You keep hurting each other, when you really want to love each other. Poor pookie, he's all alone on the road, nobody to comfort his dashed reconciliation dreams."

I throw my napkin down. "Nobody's dreaming of reconciling."

"Walter is," Jason says to his plate.

"You knew this was going to happen, Echo. He's on tour anyway." Alicia jumps right back into the fray. "Every night he's probably got a dozen babes ready, willing and able to comfort him."

"Guys. He's dating Daisy. No reconciliation, no comforting. He's gonna be momentarily pissed, but he'll get over it, count the money he made off of me, and move on." I take a hearty bite of mashed potato to end this conversation.

But this niggling, nagging worry, the worry that's been

planting its seeds since Alex Paxton showed me the article he wrote at Annie's Punk, chews at me the whole next day. Nothing can assuage my feelings of worry, guilt. Nothing. Not spending Thalia's money on the most expensive haircut a girl has the right to get. Not planting myself in front of the computer and downloading a thousand dollars' worth of CDs. Not eating a tub of soy ice cream and watching the Texan preacher.

"Don't forget to call! Call now! Reach out, let Him know you need to confess. Your load will lighten, and the help you need to get through will come. It'll come. If you call."

Now, I *know* the preacher's talking about God. I *am* a writer—I know a metaphor when I hear one. But for some reason, this is the final straw.

I leave my pint of green-tea soy ice cream defrosting on the living room coffee table, hunt down the cordless phone and bravely punch in Matt's number, simultaneously hoping that he's still answering his cell phone and that he's back to ignoring it.

After the sixth ring, I'm about to abandon my mission, but a click followed by a breathy, definitely feminine, "Hello?" grabs my attention.

"Um, oh, um, is this Matt's phone?" I check my watch, see that it's ten to seven, and then remember that I have no idea what time zone he's in.

"Yes, you've reached Matt. This is Livvie, his assistant."

"Huh? Really? Oh, okay." I realize that as I'm talking to this unknown person, I'm spinning in circles, like I'm hoping to find someone in my apartment who'll help me figure what to do next. But, of course, I'm on my own. "Um, is he there?"

"He's doing a sound check. Can I leave him a message?"

"Oh, yeah, okay." I sink down to the couch, play with the ice cream spoon. "Can you tell him that Echo called?"

There's a two-second silence after I say this, and I slap my forehead. "Yes," I snap, "it's *that* Echo. From the album. Can you have him call me? It's not that urgent, but I do need to talk to him."

"Um. I'll tell him."

I have no way of knowing whether or not Matt's new assistant tells him that I called. All I know is that by eight o'clock, I still haven't heard anything from him. I get annoyed that he's not calling, like he's a doctor who should be checking in as soon as he's paged. I look into the mirror and say, out loud, "You're not the boss of him. You're not his girlfriend anymore." Then I listen to "Lizzie Borden" three times to remind myself where we stand.

Then, because neither mirror pep talks nor Matt's music do much to combat my ratcheting nerves, I dress, put on a little makeup, listen to some Pavement and head out.

When I board the subway, I'm unsure of my destination. And usually, when I don't know where I'm going, I invariably find myself ensconced in the primary-colored womb of the *BAT*'s offices.

Walter is thrilled to see me, as he's in the midst of planning an elaborate New Year's party and needs my opinions on a variety of topics including napkins holders (yay or nay?), to crudités or not to crudités, and whether or not to let Maggie Brown's band play. After an hour of poring through recipes and searching for the right color combination napkin and tablecloths, I remind Walter that I'll be unable to attend the party, as I'll be helping Helen prepare for the wedding. He pretends that he knew this all along, but I can tell by the puffing out of his face that he completely forgot. Then, he's so distraught that he disappears into the kitchen and whips up a batch of homemade butterscotch brownies.

Accustomed to feeling grateful when Walter seeks solace in the kitchen, I pick up my bag and plop myself down in front of the computer. I reach for the stack of CDs and leaf through Jason's notes, which he's professionally left on an array of different-color and size Post-it notes.

A clanging racket of dropped pots, framed by Walter's frustrated screeches, distracts me before I can decide which CD to start with; I abandon my task and fly to the kitchen, only to find Walter on his hands and knees, desperately trying to clean the batter, which has spilled out of the bowls and landed on every surface in this tiny kitchen.

"Walter! What happened?"

"Oh, Echo! I need your help!"

I roll up my sleeves and tiptoe my way into the room, though it's essentially impossible to find a spot that isn't covered in tan, lumpy batter.

"Oh, you won't miss this at *Disc,* I know it!" Walter exclaims as he transfers three dripping paper towels into the trash can.

I grab a sponge from the sink and fall to my knees. Walter looks at me, and we break out into simultaneous laughter. He has a spot of uncooked brownie on his nose, which I wipe with the sponge. He puts his hands to his face immediately, looking for more food fallout. "No, no," I say amid giggles. "You're clean. You're good."

"Hee!" Walter squeals, brushes a tear from his eye, and holds his stomach.

And sitting there, in the middle of a brownie mess, Walter red-faced and emotional and at a loss for words, I know I have to tell him something.

"Walter, Dick Scott's going to be giving me work now."

An odd composure grips Walter when I say this. He sits up straight, the excess color drains from his face, and his voice emerges sounding in control, fatherly and calm. "I know that, Echo, and I'm happy for you." He reaches out and pats the top of my knee.

I look to my lap and then up into his face. "Well, if it's okay with you, I thought I'd still work here. Write *Disc* articles as they come, but keep my job here."

Now Walter's eyes fill with tears. "Oh, cookie!" He launches himself, landing on me like a frantic puppy, wrapping his arms around me and squeezing me until I feel like a balloon about to pop.

"Yeah, this is the club I want to belong to," I say, hugging him back.

I have to explain this turn of events to Alicia, who agrees, after three right-in-a-row phone calls from me, to meet me at Annie's for late-night beers and continued avoidance of the fact that I've received no phone calls from Matt all day.

"So you'll stay at the *BAT,* and write for *Disc* as needed?" Alicia asks, over a plate of wings she ordered from the joint across the street from Annie's.

"Yeah. You know, Walter doesn't care if I write for other papers, and Jason's there. I think I thought that other jobs wouldn't be, I don't know, *weird* like the *BAT,* but from what I see of *Disc,* it's weird there, too. And I have a good thing going at the *BAT.* I don't need to change it."

Alicia makes a funny expression with her mouth, an expression that says to me that she's pleasantly shocked by my decision. "I embrace your fear of change. It's good for my social life." She tosses a small chicken bone into a bag. I grimace and she sticks her tongue out at me.

"I'm not scared of change. I just think I didn't appreciate what I had."

"And all of a sudden you do?"

"It's amazing what being held up as an example of being a bad human being can do for your capacity for self-reflection." I nod my head once, hard, to punctuate what I'm saying.

Alicia polishes off a wing and raises her shoulders. "Matt's CD was the best thing that happened to you."

"Ha!"

"Well, I'm glad. I'm glad you're not going full-time at *Disc.* I'm having a hard enough time as it is. I don't need to lose contact with my best friend on top of everything. You and I can be single broads together. We'll shop. We'll have one-night stands and bad dates. It'll be chic and worthy of a TV series."

Before I can laugh at this, Annie appears with two pitchers (one beer, one ice water) and enough empty glasses for all three of us. "What's worthy of a TV series?"

I respond, "Our new life as quasi-successful singles."

"Hmm." Annie sets down her paraphernalia, sits, then pulls a chair out from under one of her other customers, and slides it over to make it her personal footrest. This is why Annie's the coolest; here it is the middle of a busy work night and yet she still has time to put up her feet and talk to me and Alicia.

"Girls, tell me more. Remind me about being young." She pours three waters and passes them out.

Alicia swallows her bite of celery and says, "Where to

begin. I'm single and hating it. This one—" she uses a wing to point at me "—is single and seemingly well-adjusted."

Annie arches her eyebrow at me. "That can't be right."

"*Seemingly* well-adjusted. She's freaking about the *Disc* story."

And I seemingly don't even need to be here for this conversation. "What time is it, anyway?" I ask, grabbing for a carrot stick.

"See? She's waiting for Hanley to call. It's like a flashback to four years ago, waiting for him to check in from the road."

Annie laughs at Alicia's assessment of my situation.

"Don't laugh. It's the one square peg in an otherwise serene life."

"Really? Despite the fact that if I turn on a radio right now, I'm bound to hear about you within the hour?"

I inhale. "Yep. I've completely adjusted to the fact that this is my reality now. There's Layla. There's Sharona. There's me. It's just the way it is."

Annie raises her glass. "Power to you, honey. I think that's great."

Alicia and I raise our glasses to clink Annie's and I smile, and drink my water.

Then get hit in the head with my bag. "Ow!"

Alicia covers her mouth with her hand. "Sorry!"

"Jesus!"

"It's your phone! It's ringing!" Alicia points at my bag, and I look at her for a moment before understanding what she means.

"Oh! My phone!" I dig frantically through the pockets searching for it, and sure enough, the panel flashes, "MH."

I'm so nervous, I can barely flip open the phone, never mind find the right button to turn it on. And when I hold it to my ear and finally speak, my voice comes out breathy, barely there, insecure. "Hey! Matt?"

"Yeah. Hey."

"Did he see it?" Alicia shouts. I throw a napkin at her.

"Hey, Echo, you there?"

I get up and back away from the table, covering my free ear with my palm and walking away from the jukebox. "Yeah. Listen, thanks for calling. Will you be arou—"

"Can you hear me?"

"Yeah!"

"Okay." There's a brief pause, but I distinctly hear him run his hand over his guitar. Then he commands, "Name this tune."

A thrill runs up my spine; it's so pathetic of me, I know. But this is our *thing*.

I face the wall and fold my elbow over my head, so that I'll be able to hear. He starts strumming his guitar.

I recognize what he's playing within three chords.

My heart sinks, the air rushes out of my system, I slouch against the wall.

It's the intro to "Bitch" by the Rolling Stones. He plays through it twice before hanging up.

21

The old year passes into the new one with a few milestones.

"Echo Only Broke Me" is listed as the number 23 song of the previous year. This announcement kicks off a new rash of analyses of me and my shortcomings. There are discussions about my personality on the Web, on the radio, on television. I can't even get angry, feeling complicit in this affair now that I've gone public with my statement. So, to preserve my sanity (such as it is) I impose another media blackout on myself for the entire week before my father's wedding. I turn off the radio, keep the TV tuned to news stations, never even switch on my Internet connection. I conduct my affairs in a bubble, and all the people I need to talk to (Walter, Dick, Annie) are instructed to not mention Matt's name. They indulge me the way you capitulate to a crazy grandparent—they do what I want, all the while letting me know how crazy I am. Crazy I may be, but my plan works. For an entire week I'm able to keep myself from thinking of Matt, of how he hurt me, of how I hurt him.

My friends help keep me busy and otherwise occupied. Jason buys Maggie Brown a ring. No, not that kind of ring. Just a simple gift really, a statement to let her know that he's committed to her and only her, and wants to start the New Year off right. Anyway, he presents it to her at Walter's New Year's party, which, though I wasn't there, is described to me in vivid, vivid detail by…

Alicia. She officially breaks down. On January 2nd, after a late night of helping Helen with last-minute wedding-gown alterations, I'm called to Alicia's place. When she opens the door, I see reflected in her sad countenance a vision of myself a few months earlier. She's wearing baggy navy velour sweatpants, which are clearly Jason's, and her face is streaked with tears. These are the details I collect in the three seconds before she launches herself at me, attacking me in a teary, snotty frenzy. I spend the night with her, and most of the next day, commiserating, giving pep talks, making promises of a great year to come. And though I hate seeing her so sad, part of me is glad to see her heart crack open a bit, glad to see that she can accept having been in love with a great guy and glad to see that she's willing to own up to the fact that only her hard-heartedness got her in this position.

Not all of my January is downtrodden and brokenhearted, though. My father gets married on the first Saturday of the New Year. The wedding is simple, only I and Thalia and Jack and a few of Helen's sisters go to the small chapel in Astoria for the ceremony. The reception, however, is a knock-down, drag-out fiesta. When we step through the doorway of the hall in Queens, I'm convinced that Helen's invited everyone she's ever known.

All of my father's colleagues are there, as is the whole of Helen's family (which I'm guessing is as populous as, say, the state of Rhode Island), Thalia's invited a roster of her acquaintances (there have to be as many of Thalia's ex-boyfriends here as Helen's second cousins, and that's saying something), Jack's entire entourage (including Stan Fields and Goren Liddell), and a few of my own people. Helen and my dad told to me to invite anyone I wanted, but I kept my guest list small, just Alicia and Walter, who keeps himself busy by dancing with Helen's chubby cousin from Boston all night.

Alicia's done her best to primp for the occasion, and I will say that she looks lovely. Her light hair is parted on the side and secured with sparkly diamond clips. She's wearing a green dress that has flowers embroidered down the front, but to combat that girliness, she's wearing a black choker and black earrings. She looks like an angry, edgy nymph. Already three of Jack's buddies have asked me about her.

For my own part, I was well aware that bringing Alicia as my date would make me feel round and unlovable. I did my best to look presentable, choosing a cream pantsuit over the purple dress I bought for the occasion (it reminded me too much of Matt) and pairing it with a silk, expensive, barely there pink camisole. Alicia blew my hair out, so I look pretty damn good, if I say so myself, though I should have thought out the whole "wear pants and bring a girl" thing. Two of Helen's aunts have shaken their heads at me, and an uncle gave me his phone number.

My father, the only man who counts for me now, pulls me aside just before the first round of toasts to tell me how pretty I look. It's the sweetest of gestures, despite the fact that he can't really see me.

And it's going fine. My father looks happy, joyous, even, and it's funny for me to watch how people approach him. He's in his chair, just on the edge of the dance floor, and there's a parade of people milling by him, clasping his hand, sharing a joke, kissing Helen (who stands just beside him with her hand on his shoulder). He looks *happy,* and I am happy for him. Helen's not what I would've picked for him, but somehow she's woven a magic spell on me, too. I suppose hours spent sewing with a person really show you their true colors. And Helen's true colors are brilliant, soothing, maternal.

In short, I'm able to maintain a lighthearted mood throughout the evening. My cheeriness doesn't waver, even when Goren Liddell asks me to dance, and uses the opportunity to apologize for basically avoiding me since Matt's song broke. For a moment, I'm suckered in. But then I catch Thalia observing this exchange, and I realize that she's put Goren up to it. I politely accept his apology, and excuse myself from his clammy dancing, seeking solace in Walter's more exuberant bunny-hop dance moves. When I tell Walter to make sure that I'm not alone with Goren for the rest of the night, he accepts his commission with devious glee in his eye.

And so the evening goes. Speeches, eating, dancing; it's all very pleasant. Alicia and I are in the same kind of mindset—both feeling sad about our prospective love lives but observing Helen and my father's exchanges and allowing them to fill us with hope.

Of course, our calm mien is shattered by Thalia, who after an hour of dancing, sees fit to round the two of us up like cattle and herd us toward the corner by the dessert table.

"The two of you look like the stinky kid from the Peanuts cartoons. There's a cloud around you," she says, crouching down and reaching for something underneath the table. "But I have just the thing to help!" Alicia pokes me in the ribs and rolls her puffy eyes.

I lean against a table full of minicheesecakes and individually wrapped baklava, and cross my arms. Thalia produces a bag from underneath the table, and begins to search through it. Her hair floats upon her back like a fluffy cloud, she's put small pink rosebuds in it, to complement her sheer organza-and-tulle dress. Helen mercifully let Thalia and me dress how we wanted, but my white power-girl pantsuit blends in nicely with Thalia's demure fairy look. If only she could keep her mouth shut so I could keep on thinking she's beautiful.

Soon enough, Thalia stands and thrusts two small booklets into each of my and Alicia's waiting hands. The cover on the books says, You Don't Have To Be Lonely! By Thalia Mantis.

"What is this?" I shout, holding the book out like I'm about to throw it at her. I check to see if Alicia's appropriately annoyed, but no. Unfortunately, my little friend's been laid so low that she's actually thumbing through this mini-manifesto.

"I know it's Dad's day and all, but I'm so excited, I couldn't wait!"

"What is it?"

"I self-published a book! Jack's therapist thinks that I have a lot to offer, and that the world would benefit from listening to my advice. It's my new career!"

"It does look pretty nice," Alicia offers.

"Of course it does," Thalia says, putting her arm around

Alicia's shoulders. "What you'll find in this book—" and she taps the cover, before retrieving and leafing through the pages "—is a ten-step program that will guarantee you love again. And in no time!"

My poor sister. She obviously spent an entire afternoon on this. I look at her; her arms still slung around Alicia's shoulders, and her round, glittery face pulsing with busybody concern. "Thal, this is great. Thanks."

My sincerity throws her for a loop and she, for a moment, looks unsure on her feet. "Oh, well. You're welcome. I want you to forget that you-know-who and find a nice guy. Like I did."

At that I follow her gaze out onto the dance floor where Jack Brennan is doing a minimalist version of the robot, while Helen giggles at him like a schoolgirl.

"He looks like that Sprockets guy from the old *Saturday Night Live* skits," Alicia commentates.

"Yeah. God is he hot." And because she can't keep her distance from her "hot" husband, Thalia leaves me and Alicia with our books in the corner and runs to join her goofy, pale life partner on the dance floor.

Alicia and I fall in line, watching the shenanigans. Helen dances around my father, who stands still as a maypole. Walter dips one of the Greeks, clapping his hands wildly above his head and spinning on his toes like Michael Jackson. Jack and Thalia tightly press to each other like spoons.

"Ain't love grand?" I say.

"I guess I don't know," Alicia replies.

"You will." I grasp her hand, squeeze it and drop it immediately when I spy Helen's uncle nodding smarmily at us.

Alicia and I make it through the rest of the evening with actual smiles on our faces. It's the dancing. You can't disco and be sad. It's a scientifically proven fact. Or so Walter says.

The three of us relive our dance floor glory on the G train, a little-used but highly treasured subway line that will take us right to the *BAT*. Why the *BAT* is the after-party destination, I have no idea. But Walter keeps insisting that he's got the perfect nightcap planned, and being dateless, manless ladies, we'll follow our fairy godfather wherever he goes.

When we get there, Alicia's troubled to find the door unlocked.

"Oh, chickpea, it's fine. It's fine! Who'd want to break in here?" Walter admonishes and glides through the open door. He's got the music in him tonight, that's for sure; every movement he makes is like a choreographed dance piece.

Alicia enters suspiciously, and kicks off her shoes. "I'm checking the bathrooms."

I follow Walter into the kitchen, where he's wrapping himself in an apron, and pulling champagne flutes from the cabinet above the oven. "I saved an extra bottle just for this occasion. In the fridge, honey."

I do as instructed and fish a chilled bottle of champagne from the refrigerator.

"Oh! I wish Jason was here! I hate popping that thing."

"It's okay, Walter." I walk into the main room, kick off my own shoes and pop the cork. Champagne rushes out, spilling onto the floor. I sip from the bottle to stop the flow, and Walter quickly appears with the glasses. Alicia joins us and I pour us each a flute full of the sparkly liquid, then set the bottle down on the desk.

"To me and my girls. I'm lucky to have you both." Walter raises his glass in the air, and takes a long drink. Alicia and I clink and say, "To Walter" before we drink.

"Okay, girls, one last surprise for the evening."

Alicia looks at me quizzically. I raise my shoulders to tell her that I have no idea what's coming next.

"Just don't ask any questions, okay?" Walter looks like a spinning top right now, frenzied with some kind of excitement. There's clearly something *up*. And only one way to find out what it is.

Alicia and I re-shoe, and follow Walter out to the sidewalk with nary a word. He keeps squealing and clapping his hands together, and I can't help but wonder what the hell he's got up his sleeve. It's one o'clock on a Saturday night; long since past his bedtime. But he's full of vim and vigor—no matter how many questions Alicia peppers him with while we're in the cab (which crosses into Manhattan) he refuses to answer.

Finally, the taxi pulls up in front of Annie's Punk. "This is the surprise location?" Alicia asks incredulously. I whisper to her to go with it.

She passes the driver a twenty and shuffles out of the cab.

Walter gets to the door first, and flings it open ceremoniously, only to be disappointed when he sees how *packed* it is. Truly, Annie's is quite the Manhattan destination, but it even seems extraordinarily crowded to me.

"Who's playing tonight that there're so many people here?" Alicia asks as we cram ourselves through the doorway.

I check my watch. "Whoever it was, they should be done by now."

Walter jams himself in behind me and stands on the balls of his feet. "Where's Annie?"

"Let's go," I instruct, and proceed to tunnel through the packed, crammed-in crowds of people. I notice Ted K. and the House Band from the Kentucky Cocktail in a corner, and Maggie and Jason on stools at the bar, all over each other.

I turn to warn Alicia, but she hits me in the back. "I see it, I see it," she says. "Just keep going. Keep moving."

I do as told, elbowing folks and darting past people and reaching back to hold on to Alicia, who in turn is clutching on to Walter. Finally, with brute force and a few well-placed knees, I make it to the side of the bar. Annie rushes back and forth, racing to get everyone's orders. Her bartenders are hustling, a bar back crawls along the floor refilling the ice containers and the beer fridges.

Annie sees me and salutes.

"Hey!" When I call out, Jason sees me, and his face gets this odd expression on it. Then he hops off his stool and disappears into the crowd, Maggie Brown hot on his heels.

Walter sidles in next to me, and shouts above my head. "Annie Lee! We're here!"

Annie scowls. "I see you're here. Thanks! Now get back there! I can't take this any longer." Then she reaches up behind the bar and rings the bell hanging by the Galliano. She only rings this bell on very special occasions.

"What's going on?" Alicia asks Walter.

"Yeah, what are we doing here?"

Walter doesn't reply, but the words are visibly on the tip of his tongue. He's chewing on his fingernails and bouncing up and down on the pads of his feet. Then he steers us along with the rest of the crowd into the back room.

"Seriously, just tell us who we're seeing," Alicia begs.

Walter, again, won't say anything. He prods me along, pulls Alicia behind him, and I hear Annie bringing up the rear. "Go to the sound board!" she bellows.

I'm getting tired of being jostled by bodies, and am pleased to have a destination. Again, fighting my way through people, I finally lead my party over to Fred and his sound booth.

"Hey, girlfriend!" Fred kisses me sloppily on the top of my head, and hugs me close to him. He's a bit on the sweaty side, and I wish for the tenth time since we got here that I had changed before Walter sprung this surprise on me. At least I'm in pants and close-toed shoes. Alicia looks like she's ready to kill somebody; she's holding up her right foot and complaining about squashed toes.

"Fred, what is going on?"

"I think it's a surprise. Right, Walt?"

"Right, Fred!"

Walter can no longer contain himself. He picks me up, and hugs me tightly, then swings me from side to side while I whoop, "Put me down! Put me down!"

Alicia wedges herself in between us once I'm back on the ground.

"Oh, Liccie, you little bon-bon!" He kisses her forehead and she wraps her arms around his gut, laughing at his joviality.

Then Fred presses his headset to his ear, fiddles with a few knobs and snaps in our direction. "It's time."

The lights go out, and the crowd screams. Walter pinches my bottom. "Ouch!" I turn on him, and mean to scowl, but his excited face stops me.

Annie flounces out to the stage, which is bathed in a soft half light. This is new. She has stage fright—she hates introducing the acts. But you can't tell from how poised she appears right now. Actually I think she's so relieved to have this crowd out of the main barroom that she could care less about being nervous. She pulls the hem of her white blouse down a bit and reaches for the mic stand in the center of the stage.

"Hey, y'all. Thanks for being patient here tonight."

The crowd whoops. Walter squeals.

Annie continues, "We're happy to welcome back an old friend tonight. He was kind enough to take time off from his world tour to do a brief set here, and we're thrilled that he calls Annie's Punk home."

"Holy shit!" Alicia exclaims.

And before Annie can say the words, "Matt Hanley," Walter's jumping up and down, screeching like a horny, excited owl.

My breath catches as the lights black out. I claw Walter's arm. "What's going on?"

He removes my hand, and, God help me, the grin on his face is as wide as I've ever seen. "Just watch! He's here! He drove up from D.C. It's his night off!" Then he turns me back to the stage, in time to see Matt's band, the band I saw at Righteous Hall, claim their places in front of their instruments.

"This is your surprise? Making me listen to these songs live??"

Walter covers his mouth coquettishly.

Alicia holds my hand. "I've got your back. You want to storm the stage, just give the signal."

I lean into her ear. "This could be very bad."

Alicia gives me a knowing look.

And then the drummer starts the vamp, the same vamp that he played at Righteous Hall to welcome Matt onto the stage. And Matt strolls out, his guitar in his hand. He gets to the mic, pulls the guitar over his neck and looks out to the crowd.

"Hey, New York." His voice is quietly confident, and his eyes twinkle when the audience *roars* back at him.

"What's that song?" Alicia turns on me suddenly. I look

at her blankly, trying to figure out what she's asking for a moment before realizing that she's right; the band's begun the chords of a song that I know, but can't place. Walter interrupts our conversation by putting his hands on each of our shoulders.

"We're gonna try a few different things here tonight," he continues to banter over the throbbing bass and piano, the band cranking out this song that is just on the edge of my consciousness. "And if we do it right, before the end of the night, I'm gonna win back my girl."

And then they kick into "In Your Eyes" by Peter Gabriel.

I gasp, and hold my hand to my heart.

Alicia stage-whispers, "I think he forgives you."

I remain transfixed throughout the entire minishow. Matt plays most of his famous songs, most of which have to do with me, but he peppers them with covers, all of a theme. There's "I Want You Back" by the Jackson 5, and "Starting Over" by John Lennon and "Until You Come Back to Me" by Aretha Franklin.

It's an effective display.

When the show is over, after I've cried probably six sets of tears, after Walter has tired himself out and is drinking Shirley Temples and getting in Annie's hair, Alicia and I make our way backstage.

When we get there, there's a flurry of activity: black-clad men are packing up amps and drums and instruments, coiling wire and storing the microphones in velvet-lined cases. A girl with a clipboard and a harried expression on her face hurries by us. I reach for her, and at the same time Alicia yells out, "Hey!"

The girl turns a laserlike gaze on us, and barks, "I don't think you're allowed back here."

This immediately gets Alicia's ire up. "We're good. Thanks. Where's Matt?"

"I'm Matt's assistant. What do you want?"

"Livvie?" I ask while Alicia points to me and says, "This is Echo. Let him know we're here."

Livvie, who I spoke to on the phone that one clipped time, and may or may not be a reliable message-taker, looks at me appraisingly. Then she shyly smiles. "Echo. Nice to meet you. He's waiting out by the bus."

Alicia stays behind, and I run, skip, scamper out the back door. When I get outside, I immediately wish that I thought to bring my coat. I look anxiously up and down the street, and see a large bus double-parked in front of a hydrant on the corner. I break, running in my pumps, clutching my suit jacket closed, the wind and cool chill of the three o'clock air hitting me in the face.

When I get to the bus, Matt's leaning against it, drumming his palms against the side of his pants. He looks great. His hair's a little damp but that expensive coat he got for himself makes his skin look warm and rosy. He looks completely at ease.

"Hey!" I stop about six paces from him.

He stops drumming and looks at me for a beat before breaking into a hint of a smile. "Nice outfit."

I look down at myself, still clad in wedding duds. "I dressed up for you."

"You look good." He pushes off from the bus and walks to me. "I'm getting ready to go here." He hooks his thumb back toward the bus.

"At least you're traveling in style."

"Yeah." Then he's close enough for me to hug him,

which I do. I bury my face in his neck and hear him say, "So you dug the show?"

I beam at his corny phrasing. "Yes, I 'dug' it."

"Good enough."

We look at each other for a moment, then are broken up by the arrival of a bevy of folks, business people and band members and Livvie and Alicia.

"Hey, Lic," Matt says when he sees her. "Oh, guys! I want to introduce you to the girl behind the music." And he introduces me to the drummer and the piano player and the bass player.

The piano player, whose name is Gus, clasps my hand and says, "Thanks for my job."

Alicia laughs at this, and then we all descend into silence. Livvie earns her paycheck by herding everyone onto the bus, leaving Matt and me to say goodbye in private.

"So, I'll call?"

"Okay."

"And I'll be nice with the 'Name That Tune.'"

"That'd be good."

"Echo, you forgive me?"

"Yeah. I forgive you. You forgive me?"

"Yeah." He holds my hand.

"Next time we break up, let's keep it a private affair."

Matt kisses the top of my hair, and touches my cheek. "No next time, Echo."

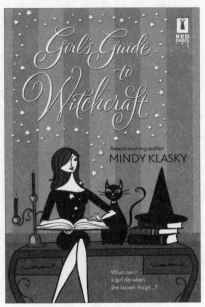

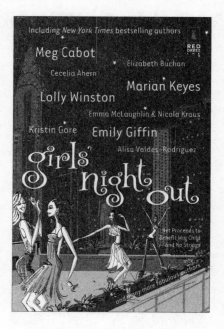

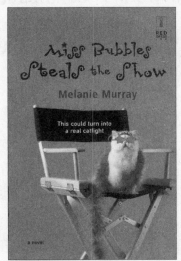

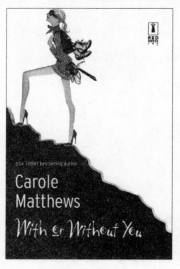